## Praise for the
### Kendra Ballantyne, Pet-Sitter Mysteries

## Fine-Feathered Death

"Exciting . . . Linda O. Johnston is a creative storyteller who not only writes a fascinating mystery but also creates a deep character study."
—*Books 'n' Bytes*

"A fast-paced who-done-it . . . Kendra is a fun character, and her supporting friends and assorted critters make an enjoyable read."
—*Fresh Fiction*

## Nothing to Fear but Ferrets

"Linda O. Johnston has a definite talent for infusing humor in just the right places . . . Pet lovers and amateur-sleuth fans will find this series deserving of an award as well as a place on the bestseller lists."
—*Midwest Book Review*

## Sit, Stay, Slay

"Very funny and exciting . . . worthy of an award nomination . . . The romance in this novel adds spice to a very clever crime thriller."
—*The Best Reviews*

"A brilliantly entertaining new puppy caper, a doggie-filled who-done-it . . . Johnston's novel is a real pedigree!"
—Dorothy Cannell

"Pet-sitter sleuth Kendra Ballantyne is up to her snake-draped neck in peril in Linda O. Johnston's hilarious debut mystery, *Sit, Stay, Slay*. Witty, wry, and highly entertaining."
—Carolyn Hart

*Berkley Prime Crime Books by Linda O. Johnston*

SIT, STAY, SLAY
NOTHING TO FEAR BUT FERRETS
FINE-FEATHERED DEATH
MEOW IS FOR MURDER
THE FRIGHT OF THE IGUANA

# The Fright of the Iguana

## Linda O. Johnston

BERKLEY PRIME CRIME, NEW YORK

**THE BERKLEY PUBLISHING GROUP**
**Published by the Penguin Group**
**Penguin Group (USA) Inc.**
**375 Hudson Street, New York, New York 10014, USA**
Penguin Group (Canada), 90 Eglinton Avenue East, Suite 700, Toronto, Ontario M4P 2Y3, Canada
(a division of Pearson Penguin Canada Inc.)
Penguin Books Ltd., 80 Strand, London WC2R 0RL, England
Penguin Group Ireland, 25 St. Stephen's Green, Dublin 2, Ireland (a division of Penguin Books Ltd.)
Penguin Group (Australia), 250 Camberwell Road, Camberwell, Victoria 3124, Australia
(a division of Pearson Australia Group Pty. Ltd.)
Penguin Books India Pvt. Ltd., 11 Community Centre, Panchsheel Park, New Delhi—110 017, India
Penguin Group (NZ), 67 Apollo Drive, Rosedale, North Shore 0745, Auckland, New Zealand
(a division of Pearson New Zealand Ltd.)
Penguin Books (South Africa) (Pty.) Ltd., 24 Sturdee Avenue, Rosebank, Johannesburg 2196,
South Africa

Penguin Books Ltd., Registered Offices: 80 Strand, London WC2R 0RL, England

THE FRIGHT OF THE IGUANA

A Berkley Prime Crime Book / published by arrangement with the author

PRINTING HISTORY
Berkley Prime Crime mass-market edition / October 2007

Copyright © 2007 by Linda O. Johnston.
Cover art by Monika Roe.
Cover design by Rita Frangie.
Interior text design by Stacy Irwin.

ISBN: 978-0-425-21802-0

BERKLEY® PRIME CRIME
Berkley Prime Crime Books are published by The Berkley Publishing Group,
a division of Penguin Group (USA) Inc.,
375 Hudson Street, New York, New York 10014.
The name BERKLEY PRIME CRIME and the BERKLEY PRIME CRIME design are trademarks belonging to Penguin Group (USA) Inc.

PRINTED IN THE UNITED STATES OF AMERICA

10  9  8  7  6  5  4  3  2  1

Linda wants to thank her dad, Steve Osgood, for the way he always promotes Kendra's books to his friends and acquaintances. Plus, she wants to thank Bruce Baker—a truly wonderful, caring, and giving man. Bruce is a pioneer in augmentative communication systems—using computer-generated symbols to help human beings communicate when they're unable to speak. For all we know, his company, Semantic Compaction Systems, may even be the first to figure out a way to translate Barklish into English and back again.

Oh, yes, and of course Linda has to get in her mention of her husband, Fred—another pretty good guy.

And Kendra? Well, she's too busy being a murder magnet to take the time to thank all her friends and far-off relations.

—*Kendra Ballantyne/Linda O. Johnston*

# Chapter One

MY CLIENTS CAN be incorrigible teases. The pet ones, not the law ones.

Which was why I wasn't freaked at first when I entered the home of Edmund and Hillary Dorgan—yes, *that* Edmund Dorgan and his delightful wife—and wasn't immediately met by their sweet, crumply, beige, and beautiful Shar-pei.

"Zibble," I called to the invisible dog, hearing my voice echo not only in the arched and open entry, but also along vast and plentiful hallways on this floor and above. "Come out, come out, wherever you are!"

The good thing was that this was a gorgeous, huge, Tudor revival–style mansion hidden in the hills overlooking Sherman Oaks.

The bad thing was that this was a gorgeous, huge . . . well, you get it. There were dozens, maybe hundreds, of places a persnickety middle-size pooch could hide.

And right now, Zibble wasn't zipping to my side.

Why did I want him to? I'm Kendra Ballantyne, pet-sitter extraordinaire, and I was there to care for the pup in the Dorgans' absence.

I'm also a litigating attorney extra-extraordinaire. Yes,

thanks to a temporary loss of my law license a while back, I do both, though seldom at the same time. Now, it was early A.M.—seven o'clock to be exact—and I had a meeting at my law office, Yurick & Associates, in forty-five minutes. That gave me about a quarter of an hour here before I had to hie my still-slender, thank heavens, bod down the hill to our Encino offices, on Ventura Boulevard. And hie was the operative word. If I hit any traffic, I was toast.

"Come on, Zibble," I called again. No response. "Okay, then, I'll feed Saurus first, and you'll just have to wait your turn to walk and have breakfast. Cross your legs."

Saurus was the other pet of the house. Rather, the estate. The young green and brown iguana dwelled in a custom-made cage outside, where he could soak in the sun—when there was any, this early in April—climb on thick, plentiful branches, hide in his artificial cave, or poop in his small swimming pool. He'd been named, Edmund had informed me, because of his resemblance to a mini-dinosaur. Not especially unusual for an iguana, of course. I'd recently taken on a couple as sometime-clients, although Saurus was my only current iguana charge.

I hustled along the shining parquet floor toward the rear of the house, beneath beautifully polished exposed rafters and beyond the wide wooden stairway with matching oak railings that led upstairs. I passed through the superbly equipped, sparkling clean kitchen into which I could have fit the entirety of my current apartment abode and out the rear door into the exquisitely landscaped backyard.

Question: Why didn't Edmund Dorgan, one of Hollywood's highest profile, highest sought, multi-millionaire film producers, and his family, not have an entire house staff holding down the fort and caring for their pets?

Answer: Usually, they did. However, Edmund was not only rich and famous, but he was also generous. He'd taken the whole human lot of his household on holiday with him for a month to the south of France. Oh, the staff would work there, too, in the villa he had rented. But they would also get time off to cavort and gambol. And even gamble in not-faraway Monte Carlo.

I'd wondered for a while whether I could moonlight as a

sous-maid for some short period of time, just long enough to rate a spot on that oh-so-alluring safari. But what would all my dual kinds of clients do then? Let alone my own adorable pet—my sweet, loving, and smart tricolor Cavalier King Charles spaniel Lexie.

We had options, of course. I just happened to have met a whole new slew of comrades in my pet-sitter profession, and—

I'd finished my brisk walk along the meandering backyard path and stopped short at the cage's location. The cage was still there, but I didn't see the iguana.

"Come on out of your cave, Saurus," I called. Did I smell bad today? Was that why these specific clients were shunning me—assuming iguanas actually gave a damn about odor? The three dogs and two cats I'd visited earlier had all been happy to see me, especially when I'd walked and fed them, as I'd intended to do with Zibble. Saurus's care was considerably different.

When he didn't immediately shamble into sight, I bent down to peer into the area of his cage that had been constructed as an iguana hideaway. I saw neither nose nor tail near the exit. In fact, I saw nothing inside resembling a reptile.

Only emptiness.

"Saurus!" I shouted. Of course the cave was shrouded in shadows, but still, shouldn't there be a sign of occupancy like a larger shape taking up space?

I carefully unlatched the cage door and maneuvered myself so I could reach inside the cave. Saurus had been handled and socialized since Edmund had acquired him, or so the producer had told me. That meant he was unlikely to attack my hand, as some iguanas were reputed to do.

But not only didn't Saurus bite or slap me with his tail; he didn't exist inside the empty space where my hand groped fruitlessly.

Frightened, I snatched back my fingers and re-latched the cage door—what, was I worried the lizard would sneak back in?

Where was he? And where was Zibble?

I quickly circled the cage, hoping beyond hope that I had

somehow overlooked the three-foot-long iguana. Or that the Shar-pei would prance up with the other pet gently in his jaws.

Only then did I notice the piece of paper pinned to the wooden frame beneath a pane of glass.

"What the—" I began, reaching for the sheet. I stopped short.

On the paper was a computer-generated note, contrived to resemble a clichéd story from the past. The words and letters look pasted unevenly on the page from magazines and newspapers, most in unmatched fonts.

No matter that the aesthetics stank. It was the contents that really unnerved me:

i have the dog and iguana.
Be prepared to pay for them
when you hear from me the
next time or you will never
see them again. and don't call
the cops.

SO WHAT IF pet-napping wasn't exactly murder?

It took the LAPD almost an hour to arrive. And then, the officers who appeared weren't my old adversary—er, buddy—Homicide Detective Ned Noralles.

Yes, I'd called the cops—Noralles, at least, since I knew him. I couldn't twiddle my thumbs until the next ransom note arrived. I'd other avenues, too, of course, and I intended to exhaust them all, ASAP, the better to get my charges home safe, sound, and soon.

I'd requested discretion from Noralles, after explaining the situation briefly, including that I was forbidden from calling in law enforcement. He'd promised to help. But before I began shrieking after answering the Dorgan door, I realized that he hadn't actually promised to *come*.

The two cops I'd buzzed through the security gate and now admitted into the house were also detectives, but not any I'd met over the multiple murder investigations I had been involved in over the last many months.

Did I happen to mention that I'm a murder magnet? That's a whole other story. One I didn't intend to get into now.

Nor did I want to think of another note I'd received some weeks ago—stuck in my car window while I was investigating a murder. It had threatened Lexie, but all had been resolved without harming a hair on her cute canine head—thank heavens.

I checked their badges before admitting these cops. One, a tall, bony female, was Detective Mabel Madero. The other, an even taller, heavier male, was Detective Domenic Flagsmith.

"Where's Detective Noralles?" I asked as I ushered them into the vaulted, beamed entryway.

"On another case." Detective Madero stared at me down a long nose, as if asking how I dared to ask for as august a personage as a homicide detective at something as paltry as a petnapping. Or maybe I simply read all that into her sneer.

"But I wasn't supposed to call the police at all," I said. "Can I trust you to keep this quiet?"

"First, let's see whether a crime was committed," said Detective Flagsmith. "Then we'll see if anyone else needs to know." His tone was neutral, and so was the look in his silvery blue eyes through his black-rimmed glasses.

"I explained to Ned," I started to retort, then iced my simmering temper. "Okay. Come with me." I motioned for them to follow me through the first floor toward the door to the backyard. "First, I'll show you the note. Hopefully, it'll convince you to keep your investigation low key—like, conducted so no one besides us knows there even *is* an investigation. The next thing you need to know is that two pets belong in this house. One's Zibble, the Shar-pei."

"That's a dog?" muttered Mabel the grouch.

"Yeah," replied her partner. "Funny-looking things."

"Adorable," I contradicted crossly as we walked. "So ugly they're cute. And cuddly. And Zibble's much too wonderful for this to happen to him. Or to Saurus, for that matter. He's the other missing pet—an amazing iguana. The way he watches you, almost smiling with that long reptile mouth, looking full of ancient dinosaur wisdom—"

Well, maybe I was carrying this a bit far. Dinosaur wisdom? Way too whimsical. I'd always heard that the size of dinosaur brains was much too puny for their mighty, massive bodies.

I finished, "Anyway, neither animal deserved to be snatched."

Flagsmith regarded me with coplike seen-it-all tolerance. "Ms. Ballantyne, isn't it? You're the pet-sitter, not the owner?" We'd stopped at the kitchen door, and he eyed me from head to toe. He wasn't coming on to me, but I knew what he saw: A rather ordinary face, with shoulder-length, neatly styled but dowdy, un-highlighted, brown hair. All okay for a person who parlayed her time into taking care of others' animals.

But below my neck, I wore a nice beige Jacquard jacket over a white blouse and deeper brown cotton skirt. Lawyerly wear, sure, but sorta overdone for a pet-sitter.

I was now late for my meeting. I'd called my boss and law partner Borden Yurick while waiting for the cops to come, and he was gracious enough to be cosseting my clients.

As I led the detectives through the kitchen, I briefly briefed them on my dual, compatible yet conflicting careers. Not that it really was any of their business.

"That's right," I acknowledged. "I'm an attorney, too. But I was here as the pet-sitter, and I really like my animal charges. Just ask Ned Noralles." I preceded them through the gorgeous garden to Saurus's empty nest.

I pointed out the ransom note immediately.

"You didn't stick this here?" asked the utterly irritable female detective.

"Not hardly," I huffed.

"Did you touch anything?" inquired her much nicer male counterpart.

I described how I'd hunted for Saurus and dug fruitlessly into his cave, in case he had somehow hidden there. "Otherwise, I don't think so," I said. "By the way, did Ned Noralles tell you whose home this is?"

"He just gave us the address," said Detective Madero, still scowling down her nose.

"Does the name Edmund Dorgan ring any bells?"

Eyes widened on both detectives.

"My ears are definitely ringing," said Detective Flagsmith.

"Let's call in a crime scene team fast," added his female associate.

"A small, discreet crime scene team," I insisted.

Why the heck hadn't I listened to instructions and kept the cops out of this?


STUCK IN AN area of the house that was out of the way, I decided to phone Ned again. What had he been thinking, calling in these apparently inept detectives? They hadn't even done their homework and determined whose home this was. Ned could have at least let them in on that—unless that was his supposed concession to discretion.

But before I called him, the good-looking African American detective, who'd considered me a thorn in his suit-clad side over the last few months and too many murder investigations, arrived after all. He caught up with me in the Dorgan living room.

"I thought I made it clear that I wasn't supposed to bring the cops at all, Ned," I started out by storming at him. "And you sent those—"

"Hello to you, too, Kendra," he interrupted in a drippingly droll tone. "I wasn't sure I could get here this fast, so I followed department protocol. And then I dropped what I was doing so I could make sure things here were handled right."

"Oh," I said, the wind whipped right out of my angry sails. "Thanks. I guess."

"You're welcome. I know you enjoy being a sidewalk superintendent at murder scenes, but at a pet-napping? Is that exciting enough for you?"

"Too exciting for a sometime pet-sitter like me," I replied. "Unlike you, I'm not a detective at all, let alone on homicide detail."

I'd been instructed to sit on one of the lovely antique sofas for my interrogation, then ordered to stay here until dismissed, out of the way of the crime scene investigation.

The ambiance of the Dorgan living room was appropriate to the Tudor-revival style of the house—or so I figured, although I suspected the flamboyant carving on the velvet-upholstered sofas and seats, as well as on the exquisite coffee tables and end tables, suggested some era other than Tudor. But what did I know? And the frames on the original paintings on the walls—primarily English countryside kinds of landscapes, and portraits of proud-looking people—were equally ornate. Probably all priceless. And there I sat as ordered, attempting not to disrupt an iota of anything around me.

Not so with Ned. "Nice place," he noted unnecessarily, wandering around the room. "I always figured Edmund Dorgan had good taste. His movies sure are prime productions. Lots of action." He studied some Shar-pei figurines on an étagère along one wall. And then he sat on the red velvet chair facing me, causing his dark suit jacket to gape enough for me to glimpse his shoulder holster. "I know you gave your statement, Kendra, but is there anything else you want to tell me?"

"Yes," I said sharply. "Why didn't you convey to your compatriots whose home this is? And I don't think they understand the whole problem. Like the command to keep the cops out. And bad enough that a poor, loving dog's been stolen, but the poor iguana, Saurus—his health could be in danger."

At least Ned had the decency to desist his eye roll after an initial round. But he didn't answer my question—which was essentially rhetorical anyway. Instead, he inserted one of his own. "And why is that?"

I explained that the young reptile needed to reside in an enclosure resembling the one he had here. Like Pythagorus the ball python, a pet-sitting client who'd been a huge help when I'd been accused of a couple of murders, iguanas were cold-blooded and required a suitable habitat that permitted them to partake of heat or coolness as they chose.

"Whoever stole him might not be aware of that," I finished flatly. "Please make sure the cops assigned to the case know to get him back both fast and quietly. Otherwise, he could die."

"I'll do what I can. But you have to realize—"

"These kidnapping victims aren't people," I said. "I know. But they mean a lot to the Dorgans. If you don't find them soon enough to ensure their well-being, I suspect Edmund has some friends in high places who can make things miserable for you."

For me, too. I'd already taken the forbidden step of asking for official help. And I was clearly first in line to take the heat for this horrible situation.

I had to find those pets, pronto. And that meant—

"So how's our mutual friend Hubbard?" Ned asked. Who knew I'd share a common train of thought with a homicide cop?

"I'll know soon," I said sweetly. "I figured having a great P.I. on the case can't help but get it solved sooner."

Jeff Hubbard was a super investigator. He'd been a cop with Ned many years back. They'd not gotten along—so much so that they'd engaged in fisticuffs with one another. That led to Jeff's resignation, and the onset of one wonderful P.I. career.

He was also my lover. Or had been, until a few weeks ago.

This situation would solve one of my current dilemmas. I needed an excuse to call him and see how things stood between us. Even though our current separation was my choice more than his.

But I hadn't counted on having to call him in on a case.

"Yeah, like we really need a private guy, let alone Hubbard," said Ned.

"Can I go now, Detective?"

"I guess so. You notified the owners yet?"

That was another dilemma to deal with. Should I call them in the south of France and scare them with this situation they could do nothing about long distance?

Well, hell, I was a lawyer. I knew it was better to disclose a problem up front. At least that way, whoever was hurt couldn't add deceit and fraud to any possible lawsuit . . .

Ugh! I now carried pet-sitters' liability insurance, but hated the idea of having to make a claim. And money was no substitute at all for prized pets. I didn't want to become a defendant in a case where the Dorgans sued me for the little I now had for negligence in caring for their dearest possessions.

So, I'd tell the Dorgans. By e-mail. That way, I wouldn't have to hear them rightfully scream at me.

"Not yet," I finally answered Ned. "But I'm going to, *tout de suite.*" At his quizzical expression, I said, "They're in France. That means 'immediately.' "

Which was an exaggeration. *Bientôt* would have been a better response. *Soon.*

Soon as I got to my office. Soon as I finished up with my meeting. Soon as I had an opportunity to talk to Jeff about how to start hunting for a stolen Shar-pei and his pal, an iguana. And by then, it might be so late in the south of France that no Dorgan would check e-mail until tomorrow, our time.

At least Ned got me my dismissal from the scene for the morning, as long as I remained ready to answer further questions when needed.

And he did promise to keep the investigation as confidential as possible—which I figured meant not at all, damn it.

I was far from relieved when I hopped into my aging BMW and began my drive to my office. I needed to talk to someone about how awful I felt. I ran down my roster of possibilities. My best friend in the world, Darryl Nestler, owner of the Doggy Indulgence Day Resort, came to mind first. He would absolutely and unquestionably empathize with me. And I'd see him later when I picked up Lexie. I could even lean on his skinny shoulders.

But better, for now, would be someone whose understanding evolved from an increasing professional relationship.

I pressed the number into my cell phone for a new close friend, Tracy Owens, president of the Pet-Sitters Club of SoCal, of which I was now an active member and an officer.

"Tracy, you won't believe what happened." I nearly cried as I described the terrible pet-napping situation that had just occurred on my watch, while directing my car along busy Ventura Boulevard.

When I finished, instead of the immediate sympathy I'd expected, there was a pause.

And then Tracy said, "Oh, Kendra—you, too?"

# Chapter Two

I COULDN'T GET much info from Tracy. Not then, since she was on a pet-sitting assignment of her own and was walking a handful of hounds. We made a date to discuss it at lunch.

All I knew, when I hung up, was that my situation was the third similar snatching of sat pets in L.A. that she knew about—including one of her own. A plague of pet-nappings? Other pet-sitting professionals as full of angst over AWOL charges as I was over poor Zibble and Saurus?

Still steering my Beamer, I quickly called Rachel Preesinger, my tenant and, more important at the moment, my pet-sitting assistant at my official company, Critter TLC, LLC.

"Rachel, listen up." I had already phoned her about what had happened to me, but she needed to know of the other pet-nappings afoot in L.A. "I'll talk to you more about it later," I said, "but the special precautions I told you about before? Double them. No, triple."

"Quadruple?"

"How's quintuple?"

"Got it." I heard a laugh in her young voice—she wasn't yet out of her teens—but I felt certain she'd gotten the message after I explained why I was so additionally stressed.

My worry didn't exactly encourage me to keep my mind on my driving as I sped down Ventura Boulevard toward my law office. I nevertheless made it safe and comparatively sound.

The Yurick firm is located in a former restaurant building. The hostess stand is currently the domain of our effervescent receptionist, Mignon. She looked up as I strode in and greeted me in her usual chirping tone. "Good morning, Kendra. Borden said you had some trouble this morning."

"Sure did," I acknowledged, but didn't choose to shout about it at that second. "Tell you later. Is the meeting still going on?" I peered to my right, through the glass of a closed door. The conference room resembled the bar it once was, with the addition of the compulsory large table in the center. Three people sat around it, and all seemed to be smiling. Fortunately.

"Yes." Mignon added a punctuating nod so her cheerful auburn curls bobbed about her perky, beaming face.

I hurried to join the group. After apologizing profusely, I learned that my lack of attendance had been accounted for by my wonderful laid-back boss and senior partner, Borden Yurick.

"Good timing, Kendra," he said in his high-pitched, ever jovial voice, as suavely as if we'd planned all along for me to miss most of the meeting. As always, my new firm's senior partner had chosen a colorful Hawaiian shirt for this session: deep blue, decorated with bright white flowers. "We've already gone over the allegations in the complaint served on Jasper and Angelica, and I'll fill you in later. We were about to discuss strategy—your area more than mine. And this case is right up your alley." He turned toward the clients. "She's a real pet lover. Right, Kendra?" His gaze aimed back at me.

"Absolutely," I acknowledged with a broad smile at the senior citizen couple sitting across the table from Borden and, now, me. Jasper and Angelica McGregor both appeared to be in their seventies, even a little older than Borden. "Tell me a little about the case." I wondered what it had to do with pets.

Borden had brought me in as a partner at Yurick & Associates because he had lots of legal business to attend to. Much arose from clients who chose him over the other partners at the high-powered firm where I, too, used to work—before the temporary loss of my law license based on unfounded allegations of ethics violations caused me to become a pet-sitter to assure Lexie and me of nutrition and habitation.

Most lawyers at Borden's firm—in fact all, except for me—were senior-citizen attorneys unwillingly retired from their former law practices. The majority of our clients, too, were of the aging persuasion, which meant that many of our cases concerned elder law matters.

But Borden decreed that everyone was to enjoy our practice. Consequently, I could keep pet-sitting, which abbreviated some of my available law-devoted hours. Plus, I was permitted to bring in my own pet-related clients of limited lucrativeness.

Pet-related clients. Missing best friends . . .

No! Right now, there was nothing I could do to locate my missing charges. Not even talk to Jeff. I'd left him an urgent cell phone message and talked to the people in his office, but he was temporarily unavailable, giving a local lecture on security systems to a group of interested entrepreneurs.

I had to concentrate on this meeting.

Jasper McGregor was chattering on about the complaint served on the indignant elderly couple yesterday. "I couldn't believe it." He jutted out a long and skinny chin far enough that the wattle beneath began to ripple. "Tallulah is my second cousin. We were very close before, like brother and sister. And when she said she was dying—well, I felt like I was losing my last real family member—blood, you know?" He looked apologetically at his solemn wife, who nodded. Jasper had a cadaverous face above an equally drawn body, on which his brown and white striped shirt hung from bony shoulders.

Kind of like folds of iguana skin . . .

"Get to the point, Jasper," Angelica said in an exasperated tone. Before her husband could obey, she continued, "Long story short?" At my grateful nod, she nodded back. She hadn't the wattle her husband had, not with her rounder face and body, but the dipping of her head forced a couple of extra chins to appear.

Rather like the folded face of a cute Shar-pei. A *missing* Shar-pei . . .

*Back to reality, Kendra.*

"Tallulah gave Jasper a deathbed gift—hers, not his, only she didn't die either, which is a good thing," Angelica continued. "I like the woman, too, but right now I could strangle her. Figuratively, of course. When it turned out the chemo worked and she would live after all, she wanted Whiskey back. But Whiskey's ours. We love Whiskey. Whiskey loves *us*. We couldn't give Whiskey back."

They couldn't return a bottle—even a case—of hard liquor? And they were having a love affair with the stuff?

Before I could inquire further, Jasper continued with a huge and happy smile, "We traveled cross-country with him. Showed him a few times—he's a show dog, you know? Fell in love with doing dog shows, all thanks to Whiskey. And Tallulah, of course. Whiskey won twice, best in class of all the weimaraners, and we toasted Tallulah both times with champagne."

Aha! Whiskey was a weimaraner. Even so . . . "While Tallulah was on her deathbed?" I asked, thinking that sounded as ghoulish as all get-out.

"I don't do well at funerals," Angelica said, fanning herself with plump fingers.

"And she was a whole lot better when we returned," Jasper said. "We were so happy. We thought she'd be thrilled, too."

"Until she demanded Whiskey back. But we'd invested too much into that wonderful dog." Angelica shook her head. "Tallulah didn't put any conditions on her gift when she signed Whiskey's pedigree papers over to us. But now she's suing us."

"I hate this," Jasper said. "I'd do almost anything to keep peace in the family. There aren't many of us left, you know. But Whiskey's part of our immediate family now. We can't give him back."

"We understand," Borden slipped in smoothly. "And we're here to help." He looked expectantly at me, as if he anticipated I'd sweep a duplicate Whiskey out from under the table and hand her over to them.

Fat chance.

But I did have some ideas. I was a great proponent of ADR, which meant Alternate Dispute Resolution.

Of course in my complementary career, it also meant Animal Dispute Resolution, and I was an absolute expert in that.

But right now I needed to end this session so I could get off to my anticipated lunch with Tracy. "Let's set up a meeting with Tallulah and her attorney," I said. "Maybe we can negotiate a win-win solution, even if you don't give Whiskey back."

"We've talked to her a lot," Jasper said dubiously.

"Sometimes things work better with lawyers involved and legal fees adding up," I said honestly, which earned a small warning scowl from Borden, followed by a smile.

"Nothing like trying to stick it to the lawyers instead of each other to get to a settlement," he said.

They left it to me to call Tallulah's counsel and set up a mutual meeting.

And then, at long last, it was time for lunch.


SINCE TRACY'S PET-SITTING realm was in L.A.'s west side and mine was in the San Fernando Valley, we decided to meet in neutral territory in between, at a deli in a small shopping center near the highest part of Beverly Glen.

"You look half-naked somehow," I said to my new friend as we joined up at the doorway, eye-to-eye since we were of similar height—five-five. Her eyes were light brown, and they immediately seemed startled until I added, "No Phoebe?" That was her adorable puggle, who she seemed to take everywhere.

"I could say the same," she retorted. "Where's Lexie?"

"Having a blast at Darryl's day resort," I said with a sigh, missing my pup, as always, when she wasn't with me.

"Phoebe's with Allen," she said. "He has the day off and they're bonding." Allen was Tracy's significant other, an insurance salesman or something of that ilk. Not exactly my type, but he seemed stable and was certainly devoted.

We chose a table outside, overlooking the not-so-glamorous parking lot. But this was an enviable April day in L.A.—no showers. No fooling—the sun was even out, so why hide inside?

"You're looking good," I soon told my over-the-hill counterpart as we sat across from one another, munching on bagel chips as we awaited our meals. She wore a forest green sweat suit with stripes along the legs and sleeves. She had appeared slightly chunky to me when we'd first met at a Pet-Sitters Club of SoCal meeting a month or two ago, but I'd figured out that was simply because of the jack o'lantern contours of her round and friendly face. Now, though, the contours of her cheeks seemed to have shrunken. "Have you lost weight?"

"I wish—although I haven't eaten much for the last couple of days, thanks to the stress."

Perfect lead-in to what I needed to discuss. "Because of your pet-napping?" I'd left my suit jacket in the car, which allowed me to gorge while in slightly less lawyerly pale blouse and dark skirt. I still felt a smidgen overdressed. Even though the other patrons here came from upscale nearby neighborhoods and tended to dress the part, at this time of day their garb leaned toward casual ultrachic.

"Yes," Tracy said with a sigh, leaning back without even half a bagel chip in her hand. Her close-set eyes shut as if in pain. "It just happened yesterday. I posted a notice on the members-only part of the PSCSC website and asked everyone to keep the information to themselves, but I should have realized that not all members would see it there. I thought about sending it out on our e-mail loop. But when it happened, I hoped it was all a mistake, that I'd find Augie myself, or my client would know where he was. But when I contacted her, she was angry, even more upset than me. I was frantic. I still am."

"Oh, Tracy, I'm so sorry. Tell me all about it." *And why didn't you call me right away?* But I stayed silent. The poor thing was already riddled with guilt. And I couldn't blame her—completely—for my own sorrowful situation.

She began talking solemnly and sadly, crying over her iced tea. Her missing pet client was a little wire-haired dachshund. And, yes, there had been a note similar to mine.

"Have you heard again from the kidnapper? Learned what he or she wants as ransom?"

"Not yet. Oh, Kendra, I feel so awful."

"Yeah, tell me about it. Who's our fellow victim?"

"Wanda," Tracy said with a gulping sigh as she sipped some soda and stopped crying.

"Wanda? I'm surprised she didn't get in touch with me."
*Either.* Wanda and I had bonded right away, since she, too, had
a Cavalier—Basil, a red and white one, the color combination
known as Blenheim.

"She wanted to, but our ransom notes said not to tell anyone."

"Mine only mentioned cops," I informed her. "But you
posted info about yours on the website anyway?"

"Members only," she reminded me, "so I figured that, if I
told everyone not to let it get any further, the thief wouldn't
find out."

That assumed no one in the club was involved—or might
inadvertently know the napper and whisper their new knowledge to exactly the wrong person. But I didn't mention that.
"In any event, no matter what the notes said, you knew about
Wanda."

"Only when she called me, after she saw my web post."

"Well, once the cats—or, in your situations, dogs—were
out of the bag, you could have called all the members. Certainly everyone on the board." Like me. I'd have appreciated a
heads-up. And as soon as lunch was over, I'd check on all my
other pet-sitting clients. Warn their owners. Not that I anticipated it would happen to me again, but who knew? "Who all is
aware of this now?" I asked when Tracy didn't respond to my
comment.

"As many members as possible. As soon as I heard from
you and realized this had happened three times, I called a
bunch of people and told them to call others and let them
know."

Good thing our food was served right then, since I was getting a mite miffed. Why not spread the word right away—and
possibly save me a pet-napping?

Tracy had ordered a pastrami sandwich that looked to die
for—and probably did add to unhealthy fats in anybody who
dared to ingest it. Tracy's included, assuming she ate it after
her proclaimed reduced appetite. But, boy, did it look good.

And me? I'd ordered a salad. A very nice-looking one. And
tasty. Chinese chicken—yes, at a deli. But it sure didn't compare with pastrami on rye.

It also didn't ease my irritation. I took a forkful of lettuce and chow mein noodles doused in soy dressing and watched Tracy bite into her sandwich. She caught me looking at her and reddened as she chewed. I was certain her embarrassment had little to do with her choice of food.

Sure enough, when she swallowed she said, "Kendra, I'm so sorry I didn't tell you right away, no matter what the ransom note said. I mean, you're a lawyer. You could have given me advice on what to do."

"I couldn't represent the club on this. But right now, as a board member, I suggest we call a special meeting."

"Great idea. You know we're all so glad you agreed to be secretary." She was obviously buttering me up now to try to soothe over this matter that had burned my buns. Of course there'd been lots of arm-twisting to try to get me to take over as vice president when the last one left. We'd compromised on secretary.

"Sure thing," I said. "I'd suggest you call the meeting ASAP. That way, you can make sure everyone knows what's going on, even if we tell the group to keep it low key, not let anyone else in on it or risk further harm to the stolen pets. I'm the third victim in just a few days. Who's to say there won't be more? Everyone needs to be warned."

"You're right, Kendra," Tracy conceded with a deep sigh. "I'll send out a bigger and better post on the loop. Warn everyone to take special care of all their pet clients because of what's been going on. Get everyone together tomorrow evening. Is that soon enough?"

"No, but it'll have to do."

So what did I do then? Undoubtedly something I shouldn't. But I could hardly sit and twiddle my thumbs while the cops were the only ones trying to find my missing clients.

I had to return to the office, sure. But I did it by way of the Dorgan home.

Rather, the Dorgan street. I knew the crime scene folks would be displeased if I did anything to disturb the site where my charges had been, so I instead walked the winding road and knocked on doors.

And met some irritated, some interested, and some peeved

neighbors. They'd been through all this with the cops. And no one, at least none who happened to be home that afternoon, had seen anything helpful.

I nevertheless passed my business cards around and begged those with whom I spoke to let me know if they thought of anything helpful. Perhaps even before they informed the authorities—or at least I so implied. I didn't want to be accused of actually obstructing an investigation, even if that was kinda what I was up to.

I felt scared for the personable Shar-pei, and indignant and unnerved over the disappearance of the iguana.

And I wasn't at all certain that the cops would put the manpower into this case necessary to discover the whereabouts of the missing pets. Even when their last name was Dorgan.

One way or another, I had to find them.

Fast.

# *Chapter Three*

WHEN I GOT back on the road, on a continued frantic foray to visit all my remaining pet clients and assure myself of their safety, I finally received the phone call I'd been both awaiting and dreading.

My cell phone sang its usual song of Bon Jovi's "It's My Life." The caller ID said it was Jeff. I answered with anticipation, ignoring my swirling nerves.

"I was glad to get your message, Kendra," he said in his deepest and sexiest all-masculine voice. It sent shivers of excitement slinking down my spine.

I shrugged them right off again. Reconciliation hadn't been the reason for my call. Er, well, not the *whole* reason . . .

I was sailing along Riverside Drive in my Beamer and decided that drowning in that voice could cause me to slide into someone. I pulled over into the nearest strip mall parking lot.

"I need your services, Jeff," I told him hurriedly. Then, hearing how that could sound if the guy was sex-starved—as he should be by now—I added, "Professional services. Private investigator services. I have a big problem, and I'm not the only one." I quickly told him about the kidnapped pets—all of them pooches except for Saurus, the iguana. "The cops are involved, but that's not good enough." I quickly went through the ransom note dichotomy and dilemma. "I want to make sure the pets are found and returned safely. The Pet-Sitters Club of SoCal is meeting tomorrow night to talk about it. Can you come?"

"Sure thing."

"But please start your hunt for the missing pets right away, will you?"

"For you, anything."

My heart soared, then dove into the pool of my mixed emotions. Without inflection, I intoned, "You'll need to get into the house to look around. I know you'll love to hear this, but Ned Noralles can get you the okay to check it out. I think his crime scene folks are finished."

"Ned? Was someone killed?"

"Only my sense of pet security."

"Okay. I'll get started. But I want to hear all the details about this pet-napping from you tonight. Over dinner."

"Well . . ."

The thing was, the major hurdle keeping Jeff and me apart had been eliminated weeks ago. I'd helped to clear his ex-wife of a murder accusation. In exchange, Amanda Hubbard had sworn never to darken Jeff's doorstep again. And Jeff had seemed mighty pleased. Had acted ready to settle down for good. Had renewed his invitation for Lexie and me to move into his home with his dear Akita, Odin, and him.

And how had I responded?

With confusion. After all the aggravation caused by Amanda, I'd considered a life without Jeff in it.

Had even started seeing someone else along with him: a really nice veterinarian named Dr. Tom Venson. Tom and I had a date planned for that weekend, in fact.

And I hadn't had a date with Jeff in over a month, partly because of his normal and extensive travel schedule. I watched Odin for him when he was gone, while Lexie and I stayed at his home, but I'd moved out, like the coward I was, as soon as Jeff was due back. That was the reverse of earlier, happier days between us, when I'd simply stayed around and spent many delightful nights with Jeff when he was in town.

Reconciliation? Hah! No way was I ready for that.

"I'll bring in Thai food," he coaxed. Our traditional favorite. Between us, it acted as an aphrodisiac.

It sounded damned enticing.

*Jeff* sounded damned enticing.

But if I agreed, I'd probably wind up in bed with him.

Well, hell, I hadn't had sex for weeks. Until I figured out this situation with two guys in my life, I'd intended not to complicate things further by jumping into bed with both.

Maybe serial monogamy was a mistake. Only, it didn't seem fair to compare them both that way, too.

Did it? Well . . .

"All right," I said. "Lexie and I will be by for dinner and discussion. As long as you understand that's all."

"Sure," he said, and we said goodbye.

But not before I'd told myself, *As long as* you *understand that's all, too.*


I DROPPED IN to see two more perfectly happy pups—Alexander, the pit bull, and Cicely, the Shih-tzu—and a couple of persnickety but otherwise healthy cats, Abra and Cadabra. All were fine.

All were there. And none even had the temerity to tease me by hiding upon my arrival, thank heavens.

I jotted down my visits in my official pet-sitters' log, which was obviously going to fill up a lot faster now that I had to drop in on my charges more often to see to their safety.

I also called my assistant Rachel to ensure that the pets she sat for were also where they belonged and that she, too, noted their well-being in writing. "Everyone's fine, Kendra," she assured me. "And I'll check on them often, like I promised. I just got done walking Widget, and I'm worn out!"

"No wonder, with that wild terrier." I thanked her, and felt a whole lot happier for me than for her when she said she'd no auditions scheduled this week to sweep her from her sitting obligations at a moment's notice. Like many youths in L.A., my pet-sitting employee was a wannabe actress who filled in time and took in work while waiting for her elusive, maybe unattainable, big break. She'd had a tiny part in a feature film that required her on location briefly a few weeks back. She had no idea when the movie would be released but was still excited—and hoped it presaged oodles of future roles.

In any event, except for the disaster at the Dorgans', all fortunately seemed well with Critter TLC, LLC, and its sitters and clients.

I made more calls, too, including to Detective Ned Noralles, to see if there were any leads about the location of Zibble and Saurus. There weren't. But he had heard from Jeff and given the go-ahead for my favorite P.I. to poke around the crime scene.

With nothing more I could do at that moment to find them, I spent another couple of hours as a practicing attorney, sent the e-mail I'd been dreading to the Dorgans, then headed off to pick up my own pet.

The oft-cleaned Doggy Indulgence Day Resort smelled of antibacterial cleaners overlaying accidents. Its spacious main room was laid out with several play zones for pets. As soon as she spotted me standing in the crowd by the sign-out desk, Lexie, my small, mostly black and white spaniel, lifted her little red eyebrows and tore toward me along the pine-look linoleum floor from her favorite canine play area, the one with all the people furniture in it. I knelt down and picked her up, nuzzling her furry snout as she laved my chin and neck with her soft, rough tongue. "Good to see you, too, Lexie," I said with a laugh.

"You okay, Kendra?" asked a familiar male voice from beside me. I looked up at the long and lanky form of the biggest indulger at Doggy Indulgence, its owner and my dearest two-legged friend, Darryl Nestler. At his feet was a pack of the pups in his charge. His human assistants were busy playing with canine customers and helping their owners sign them out for the day.

In one of my earlier calls, I'd informed Darryl of my stolen pet torment. "Sure, I'm okay," I replied. "More or less."

He peered through wire-rimmed glasses down at my apparently transparent face. "Looks like less to me. You want a drink of something strong?"

"Really?" I was familiar with the facility's kitchen. Darryl kept fixing me up with potential clients of both the pet-sitting and law persuasions, and our initial meetings were often held in that particular office away from home. I'd never noticed anything resembling alcohol there—a good thing, considering some of the screwball employees Darryl sometimes hired here.

"Sure. I've bought a bunch of those fitness waters with some really strong lemon flavor. You'll pucker right up."

"Lexie would like that." I finally pulled that particular pup away from my now-wet chin and neck. "But I'd better go. I've already visited my pet clients twice today and want to do it again."

"Any indication where the missing dog and iguana got to?" he asked, sympathy oozing from his already sweet face.

"Not yet," I said. "But I've got both Ned Noralles and Jeff Hubbard on the case. There's got to be a break soon."

BUT WHEN LEXIE and I reached Jeff's a couple of hours later—after my last call on my pet clients for the night plus a visit home to change from lawyerly clothes into casual—he'd learned nothing I didn't already know.

It took a while for him to inform me of that. He greeted me at the door of his pseudo-Mexican hacienda in the wilds of Sherman Oaks, his sweet Akita, Odin, by his side. The two dogs exchanged happy sniffs. Concurrently, both Lexie's long-haired white and black tail and Odin's short-haired beige tail, curled up over his back, wagged amicably.

And Jeff and I? Well, the hunky and tall P.I., with a hard body that didn't quit, held that very same hard body against mine and planted one heck of a kiss soundly on my lips, followed by some pretty sexy tongue action.

That was a whole lot more than amicable.

And made me consider tearing off his blue shirt and tight, sexy jeans. Better yet, turning my tail and running. But I did neither. I needed his P.I. expertise too much.

First things first. We walked Lexie and Odin along the flat streets of Jeff's neighborhood, allowing them to do what came naturally in the twilight of near seven thirty P.M.

Then we entered Jeff's house again, nuked our favorite take-out Thai dishes that he'd brought in—pad Thai and mee krob—and sat at the round, wood table in his small but functional kitchen.

I looked into his beautiful blue eyes, lowered my lids in my own attempt at sensuality, and said, "What do you have for me, Jeff?" I grinned at the smoldering stare that resulted, complete with his licking more than the taste of Thai off his lips, trying to ignore the melting of my own turned-on body. "About the missing pets," I added.

Which iced that ogle immediately.

"Nothing yet," he said in a tone so casual that I knew he was trying to torment me as much as I'd done to him. "I talked to Ned, got what little I could from him, and started my own investigation. I figured the police would have taken anything potentially useful from the crime scene, but I did a walk-through anyway. Nothing. I've got Althea"—that was his computer geek—"looking around online for anything helpful. And I've started canvassing the street, figuring some neighbor was bound to see someone who happened to have both a Sharpei and a three-foot-long iguana with him, but so far I haven't a clue."

"No neighbor let anything loose with me, either," I said. "Are you still joining me at the Pet-Sitters Club of SoCal meeting tomorrow night to see if you can learn more about the other pet-nappings?"

"Are you going to stay here tonight?"

I still had half a plateful of Thai before me, but I stood and glared. "Is that an attempt at extortion?"

His grin was so charming, boyish—and damnably sexy—in that great, angular face that I nearly melted and prepared to promise him anything. "Sure," he replied. "I'm not proud. I'll try anything." But then his expression grew so serious that every muscle in my terrifically tense body tightened even more. "Kendra, you know I love you. I want you to stay tonight. I want you to move in. You know that, too. I thought everything was resolved when Amanda finally promised to stay away. She's kept that promise, by the way, in case you're wondering."

I kinda had been—maybe more because if she hadn't, I would have a better excuse for keeping Jeff at arm's length this way.

And I couldn't exactly use my old standard excuse, that I was rotten at selecting men suitable for a relationship, any longer. Jeff really was a pretty good guy. Even if he had allowed his ex to insinuate herself back into his life. She'd had reason: A stalker had terrorized her, and she had turned to her onetime best protector and P.I., Jeff, for security advice and anti-stalker assistance.

The stalker was dead now. He'd been the one Amanda was accused of killing, and I'd uncovered the actual culprit. And she was apparently fulfilling her end of her bargain with me and avoiding her ex.

"I'm glad she's not bothering you anymore," I said simply to Jeff while looking down at the floor and feeding Lexie and Odin some of my unflavored white rice.

"But you're not responding to the rest of what I said?" He sounded disappointed. He sounded hurt. And I felt like a flirtatious flake for doing this to him.

But at this moment, I wasn't certain how I felt about him. Those few months fighting with and fixing things for Amanda took a whole lot out of me. And made me question the possibilities of a relationship with this hunk across the table.

Still, he deserved a response. I opened my mush-filled mouth—and I don't mean the Thai delights—and prepared to give him one. Not that I'd any idea what to say.

But he beat me to it. "Forget it," he said. "For now. But, Kendra, I'm giving you an ultimatum. And don't glare those daggers, 'cause they'll bounce right off me now. I need to know you're with me, ready to see how things go with us, or I'll move on. Soon. So you need to make up your mind."

WHO, ME? HAVE trouble making up my mind? I always considered myself one of the most decisive people I knew.

But that mind of mine remained ambivalent and angst-ridden about Jeff a little later as I drove my Beamer through the security gate onto the property I own, and spotted my tenant and employee, Rachel Preesinger, playing with Begorra—better known as Beggar—the Irish setter owned by her dad, Russ, and her.

Good. Something else important to focus my frazzled brain on. Rachel and I needed to discuss the pet-napping even more than we had in our few frantic phone calls.

The patch of grass where Rachel and Beggar romped was surrounded by the lush, tropical garden of my well-loved front yard. Illumination surrounded them from lights from the big, beautiful pseudochateau behind them, and from smaller lights lining the walkway up to it.

I pulled the Beamer into its outdoor spot alongside the garage. The apartment I shared with Lexie was right upstairs.

So why did Lexie and I occupy the garage apartment and rent out the chateau to people who once were strangers? Because I'd bought the place when my career was on the rise at a major L.A. law firm. When my soaring career had taken its nosedive, I'd had to rent out the main house or lose it along with my job. Now that my law license was restored, my career was on a different flight path, one less lucrative but in most ways more fulfilling than before. The property remained mine, but the rent from Rachel's dad, Russ, made sure I could make mortgage payments.

As soon as I opened the car door, Lexie bounded out and raced a lap around the yard with Beggar—a small, mostly black and white bundle of fur keeping pace with a larger, elegant red comrade in caninism. I joined Rachel on the footpath, where she opened her arms and surrounded me with a hug.

Though Rachel was just about to leave her teens behind, I suspected that when she turned twenty in a few months, she'd still look like a kid. She was small and waiflike and full of such youthful exuberance that I figured she'd even seem like a child at my age—sixteen years her senior.

"Oh, Kendra, it's such a shame! Is there any word about where Zibble and Saurus are?" She pulled back and studied me with huge, sad brown eyes.

"No," I said sorrowfully.

"Have you looked online to see if the kidnapper might have dropped them at a shelter?"

"No, but why would the snatcher do that? There hasn't been a ransom demand, but after the note that was left I have to assume whoever did it is after money."

"Probably," she said, "but it never hurts to try."

I didn't disagree, so after we rounded up the pups, I followed the small brunette with the shaggy hair, and even shaggier cropped top over tight jeans, inside my chateau and around the downstairs. I had once used the room with the astoundingly vast fireplace as a den. Now, it was an office with a really admirable computer setup right in the center, occupying a corner of a massive oak desk.

I sat beside her at the big desk in a similar black chair to the one she occupied. Her computer was snoozing, so she woke it.

I watched as she Googled, Yahooed, Asked, and used a couple of search engines I'd never heard of. She started a new favorites list that included a bunch of national pet search sites, as well as local shelters. Then, she visited each one and looked around for a newly arrived Shar-pei and iguana.

Nothing at all resembled my missing charges.

"It's been less than a day." She pivoted her behind in her chair so she faced me.

"That I know about," I inserted. "Whoever snatched them could have taken them as early as seven or eight last night, right after I last looked in on them."

"Even so, at most it's been twenty-four hours. I'll keep looking online, and so should you. I'll e-mail you the list."

"Great," I said. "Er . . . could I use your computer so I don't have to boot up mine? There's something I have to do."

"What's that?"

"Check my e-mail to find out whether the Dorgans have responded to the message I sent them earlier. I also had to let the detectives on the case know how to find them, so I'd imagine they've heard from the authorities, too."

Sure enough, they'd seen it and sounded as upset as I'd anticipated. At least one, Edmund or Hillary, would cut short their planned vacation and head home.

How could I ever face them?

I discussed continued sitting strategy with Rachel and how to best ensure the security of our clients. I'd have to talk about that with Jeff, too, when I saw him again tomorrow evening.

I didn't sleep much that night. The pet-napping weighed heavily on my soul. Jeff's ultimatum weighed heavily on my heart.

Would I have any possibility of lightening up the next day?

Not with so many things on my mind—and the meeting of the Pet-Sitters Club of SoCal, and its definitely dreaded discussion of similar pet-snatchings, to look forward to.

# Chapter Four

I WENT THROUGH all the right motions the next day. Visited pet clients and spent oodles of time with them, hugging the hounds and complimenting the cats. I considered bringing the lot of them to Darryl's along with Lexie, but that would only mean they'd get super supervision during the day. I'd still have to tote them all home that night, since Darryl didn't take in boarders—hence, his pushing me into pet-sitting. And if their owners had wanted days at a doggy resort, they would have said so. Plus, some were felines, not canines. No other iguanas just then, though. Or pythons or potbellied pigs.

I double-checked and rechecked the security systems my current charges' owners had installed. Then I checked them again. Only then did I head for the office.

I shouldn't worry so much, I told myself as I drove the Beamer carefully toward Encino. What was the likelihood that the pet-napper would nap again at one of my charges' homes?

I informed one of my law partners, Elaine Aames, of the pet-thefts. I doubted the culprit would break in and steal Gigi, the blue and gold macaw Elaine inherited from a former part-ner who'd been murdered right here a few months back. And, yes, I'd helped to unmask the killer. Now, Elaine brought Gigi into the office nearly daily.

My lawyering day passed quickly, partly because Borden had called an administrative meeting of firm attorneys. We didn't accomplish much, but it sure took up a lot of time. That left me scurrying to complete the actually worthwhile stuff I needed to achieve in the afternoon.

I called the detectives on the pet pilfering case yet again. Compared with my reception by the two who'd initially shown up at the scene yesterday, Ned Noralles almost sounded glad to hear from me. And my ears scorched something fierce after suffering his irritated assurances about continuing progress—with no real results so far.

Then, it was on to retrieve my eager Lexie from Doggy Indulgence, expend more than adequate time and intensity on my pet clients yet again, and pick up Rachel at our sort of shared homestead. We had decided last night that she needed an official intro to the pet-sitters' organization. Never mind that she'd been the one to tell me about it in the first place, after she'd seen a snippet about it in a local throwaway newspaper. Now, she needed to hear what was said about the pet-stealings so she could guard against them while on duty for Critter TLC, LLC.

Rachel's dad, Russ, was home, so after I said hi we left Beggar there with a clear conscience. Lexie? Well, she accompanied me often to club convenings, so she came along this night, too. I hurried my Beamer over the hill known as the Santa Monica Mountains to the pet-sitters' conclave.

The meetings were held in West L.A., in the back of one of the area's poshest puppy boutiques. As soon as Rachel, Lexie, and I entered, we could hear the buzz from behind the rear room, punctuated by peppy barks from the sitters' own excited pups. Lexie leaped forward on her leash, but I held her back. "Patience," I told her. "Even if your friend Basil is there, ladies need to learn to play hard to get."

"Basil?" Rachel inquired.

"Another Cavalier, owned by one of the club members—named for the British actor Basil Rathbone who played Sherlock Holmes in early movies, since Cavaliers come from the U.K. I've considered matchmaking and letting Lexie have pups, but if I did that, I'd want to have good homes planned for them first."

"Really?" Rachel exclaimed in exuberance that outshone even her normal excitement.

"I'm leaning against it at the moment," I informed her as we headed into the room. "Even though the idea was the only reason Lexie remains unneutered. For now."

Meetings I'd attended previously had seemed crowded here with only about thirty attendees. This night, my initial assessment suggested that there were at least ten more shoe-horned inside. The conversational hum was a loud drone, and leashed dogs of different sizes stood on the floor and sniffed one another. One member often brought a macaw, but no bird was perched on a shoulder that night. Shelves covered with pet food and accoutrements lined the large storeroom's walls, surrounding the gabbing group.

In the middle of the multitude was the face—and body—I'd first sought: Jeff Hubbard. How could one hunk look so extraordinarily good in an ordinary white shirt and khaki slacks? Who knew? But all the female pet people were already panting over him.

He was speaking with Tracy Owens, whose beige short-haired puggle, Phoebe, was beside her, on a leash. Puggles are designer dogs, a combo of pugs and beagles, and Phoebe was an adorable representative of the new quasi breed.

Tracy was dressed in a short-sleeved T-shirt tucked into a denim skirt. Her significant other, Allen Smith, stood beside her. I'd met Allen at my very first board meeting as the sitters' half-unwilling secretary. He was a friendly sort but seemed a little shy. He wasn't much taller than she and I, who shared a height of five-five. Except for his long chin, his face seemed somewhat ordinary. Or maybe it just looked long as he opened his mouth while hanging on her every word.

With them was another of my favorite PSCSC members, Wanda Villareal, a petite person who favored filmy blouses. Today's gauzy top was brilliant green, trimmed in gold. She hugged Basil to her bust, the Blenheim-colored—red and white—Cavalier whom Lexie, Rachel, and I had been discussing.

Completing the conversational enclave—at least until I

interrupted—was Frieda Shoreman. Tall and elegant and bottle-blond, Frieda was a bit older than I. If Rachel remained unlucky at her alternate but eagerly anticipated career, she could become Frieda sometime in the future. Frieda was a Hollywood has-been who never was, or so I'd understood, in undertones from Tracy and Wanda. She'd gotten a few bit parts in films and TV, but her acting career had never taken off. Fortunately, her pet-sitting career had.

Jeff had already spotted me. Our eyes met, and I had the oddest sensation that his gaze was drawing me toward him. Against my will?

*What* will?

"Come on," I said to Rachel, and began wending my way through the crowd, watching Jeff watch me all the while.

Was I making up my mind about him this soon? But I had a date this weekend . . .

"Hi, Kendra, Lexie," Tracy greeted us. The others echoed the welcome, opening their circle so Rachel and I could join the arc.

"I gather you've introduced yourself," I said to Jeff.

"Sure did," he said.

Tracy nodded her apparently thrilled acknowledgment. "What a wonderful idea, Kendra," she said. "Hiring a private investigator to help us out."

I may have met her significant other before, but she'd never met mine. When he was one. *If* he was one.

"I'm just here tonight to listen," Jeff said, "although I'll probably have a lot of questions to ask the group, particularly those who've experienced the pet-nappings."

"I'm sure everyone will cooperate," Tracy said.

"Amen," agreed Wanda.

After a few moments of general gabbing—with Jeff and me not looking at one another but nevertheless edging inevitably closer—I said, "Wanda, I've heard Tracy's story. Why don't you tell us about your pet-napping incident?"

"Better yet, I'll call the meeting to order," Tracy said. "Those of us who've experienced it will describe what happened."

In about a minute, she'd directed everyone in the group to grab a folding chair from the rented rack along the wall and take a seat. In about three minutes more, everyone had complied. The former roar settled down into the near silence of anticipation.

Coincidentally—not!—Jeff and I ended up beside one another, still studiously avoiding each other's gaze. Or at least I was.

Tracy stood facing the group, puggle Phoebe at her side. No need of a podium or microphone in this sizeable but overcrowded storeroom. She started the meeting with a general welcome. "I'm glad to see such a great turnout," she said.

"You scared us all, Tracy," hollered club vice president Nya Barston, who had barged her seat into the front row. She was tall and thin and wore glasses, with dark hair shot with gray pulled tight against her head and fastened in back with a small red scrunchy. "Of course everyone's here. And that means we're cutting into our schedules of what's really important—taking care of our pet clients."

"You *should* be scared," Tracy replied, stooping to lift Phoebe into her arms. "Our club isn't very big, but three of us are victims of these pet-nappings. I know you all are busy with your businesses. I certainly am. Or was. I've felt compelled to cut down on the number of clients I have to be sure I can take even better care of the ones I keep. Plus, I've told the other owners I work for about what happened, and some are so freaked that they've stopped hiring me to walk their dogs. And some who'd been traveling even returned right away from out of town."

I hadn't told her yet that I expected a Dorgan home at any minute, but I certainly empathized with Tracy's plaint.

She described what had happened to her first. Her usually chubby face looked even more drawn than when I'd lunched with her yesterday, and tears puddled in her eyes as she talked about the disappearance of the wire-haired dachshund she'd been sitting for. His name was Augie, short for Achtung. I glanced around her audience and noted the aghast and sorrowful stares of the other pet-sitters.

"I just wish I'd been there with one of my bats when that horrible person came for Augie," Tracy said angrily. She'd described at earlier meetings how she carried a baseball bat to prod off strange dogs who occasionally menaced her charges on walks. Not that she'd ever strike one, she assured us.

I was next. Likewise, I brought Lexie to the front of the throng for moral support. I, too, grew teary as I explained the awful, unanticipated snatching of Zibble and Saurus.

Then it was Wanda's turn. Like Tracy, she'd had only one pet purloined—a golden-colored cockapoo named Cramer. "It was so horrible." She started sobbing, and Basil, who'd stayed on the floor at her side, leaped up and pawed at her in insistence on being lifted. She complied, and he immediately started lapping at her tears. Of course, when a person receives Cavalier kisses, it's impossible not to smile, which Wanda immediately did, even while crying.

I joined her, again inserting myself at the front of the room. So did Tracy. We offered empathy and solace to one another, while the rest of the club members talked in shock and anger among themselves.

"I'm afraid our club is being targeted," Tracy said, "but I can't imagine why."

"Even more important, can anyone guess *who*?" Jeff asked, joining us. "Have any of you received any warnings, no matter how trivial they seemed at first? Or any other kinds of clues? I'll get the membership list from your club secretary, Kendra, and contact all of you, plus anyone who's not here, but if you think of anything tonight, let me know. Plus, I'll pass cards around so you can contact me if anything comes to mind."

I'd never felt more grateful for Jeff. Er, *to* Jeff.

"Mr. Hubbard?" Lilia Ziegler, the club member who appeared to be the oldest, waved a wizened hand in the air.

"Jeff," he corrected. "Yes?"

"Do you really think this club is being targeted? I mean, if it is, I'll quit. Right now."

Before Jeff could offer an opinion, Nya Barston stood and strode to the front of the room, usurping our place facing the group. "Now, wait a minute, Lilia. And all of you. You know I think the world of our club president." She pivoted to look at Tracy, but her glare appeared anything but adoring. "But just because she's undergone a difficult time, that doesn't mean she should be scaring all of us. Same goes for Kendra and Wanda. There are pet-nappings all the time. Since there are so many, of course some of them would happen while professional pet-sitters are on the job. There's no reason to think it has anything at all to do with our club."

"But, Nya," Tracy protested, drawing to the side of the sniping VP, "it's surely too much of a coincidence to think it has nothing to do with our club."

"I—" I began, intending to agree.

Instead, Frieda Shoreman, who'd been in our initial circle before the meeting began, stood and said, "We don't really know how much of a pet-napping trend there is in L.A. Someone should research it. Not many local pet-sitting organizations like ours exist, but there are national ones with websites. Maybe someone there knows."

"Great idea," Tracy said, sounding relieved. "I hereby assign that to you, Frieda. See what you can find and let us know at the next regular meeting, okay?"

"Well . . . okay." Frieda might have propounded the possibility, but she didn't sound eager to do the follow-through.

"What if they're not all reported to the websites?" Nya obviously hadn't completed her tirade. "You'll draw erroneous conclusions doing that. Our club is doing just fine."

"We certainly hope so," responded Tracy, "but we should still look into this. If someone is targeting us—"

"Don't be foolish, Tracy," Nya hissed, only somewhat under her breath. "We're both founders of this organization. If you can't lead it, if you want only to scare members away, then step aside and let me take over as president."

"That has nothing to do with it." Tracy sounded outraged. "It's just—"

"It's just that there is a definite problem," Jeff interjected smoothly, planting his six-foot bod in the middle so they couldn't see one other. Both looked up into his face, and he generously divided his gorgeous smile between them. "Whether or not this club is a specific target, the result is the same. Now, here are some security measures I'd suggest."

He started a short speech about alarm systems and those where outside companies were called if a signal was tripped. "That only helps, of course, if your clients already subscribe. If they don't, there are still plenty of things you can do to try to avoid any problems." He discussed enlisting the eyes of prying and helpful neighbors, teaming up to look in on each others' charges, and more, all excellent ideas.

"Wow," said Rachel, now beside me since I'd resumed my seat. So, eventually, did both Tracy and Nya. Wanda had left the front of the room as soon as the disagreement erupted. She sat beside Frieda Shoreman, whispering softly but with obvious emotion.

"Which of the many things that went on are you 'wowing' about?" I inquired softly.

"Everything. Whoever thought there'd be intrigue and politics in a group this small? Someone should start a TV drama about a pet-sitters' organization. Or maybe a movie."

I couldn't help smiling at the young entertainment industry wannabe. And then Jeff concluded his remarks and Tracy, still president notwithstanding Nya's bitter interjection, adjourned the meeting.

WHICH LED TO Jeff and me standing beside my Beamer a few minutes later. It was parked along a side street off Santa Monica Boulevard.

Rachel was still inside acquainting herself with the contents of the store to which the meeting room was attached. The shop owner had spoken her usual spiel about products before the group disbanded, and other members, too, had wandered in to shop.

"Thanks so much for coming, Jeff," I said. "You did a wonderful job."

"I didn't get much input from your group tonight," he said, "but I'll be following up. You'll get me the membership list?" I nodded, and he went on, "Does the club have a budget to hire me, or am I doing this as a favor?"

I looked up into his brilliant blue eyes as they sparkled under the streetlight. "How does 'favor' sound?"

"I figured. Well, I'll take it out in trade."

I expected him to step even closer, take me into his arms. So did Lexie, I guess, since she sat on the street, her leash slack, and looked up at us as though humoring the mushy humans.

Only, he didn't. Instead, Jeff bent down and met my lips with his in a brush more brotherly than loverly.

"I'll be in touch, Kendra. Good night." And then he turned his back and strode down the street, leaving me standing there staring—and as horny as hell.

What, had I figured on fighting him off that night? I wasn't willing to sleep with him again . . . yet.

"Conniving son of a bitch," I whispered aloud. I figured I knew his game. He'd back off until I begged.

No way would that happen.

I went inside to retrieve Rachel, then she, Lexie, and I headed home. Fortunately, before I crept into a cold shower, I checked my phone messages.

Tom Venson had called. I'd of course told the really sweet vet whom I'd been dating about my pet-napping trouble, and he knew of the club meeting this evening. "I didn't want to call your cell phone and disturb you," his message said, "but phone me any time you get home."

Which I did. It was a call I enjoyed to the utmost, without all the angst and innuendoes I seemed to get with Jeff. We confirmed our date for that Saturday night.

*Then* I took that cold shower.

I SLEPT SURPRISINGLY well. But my mind was on Jeff and his suggested pet-sitting precautions as I started on my rounds the next morning, Lexie at my side at first. I'd drop her at Darryl's later.

I visited two of my doggy clients first, and was on the way to the third when my cell phone sang "It's My Life."

I checked the caller ID. Tracy Owens. Did she want to re-hash last night's pet-sitters' emotional get-together?

"Hi, Tracy," I began, but barely got it out before Tracy broke in.

And *emotional* didn't begin to describe her over-the-phone demeanor. Hysteria, perhaps?

"Kendra? It's so horrible! I don't believe it! And they think, they think—"

"Tracy, please," I interrupted, attempting to sound calm but

feeling my insides swirl. "Take a deep breath and tell me what's
going on."

A pause. I believed I heard a gulp of air for cooling calm-
ness. And then Tracy said, "It's Nya. I don't even know what
she was doing at one of my client's. *My* client's." Was all this
an outgrowth of outrage? I was about to chastise her when she
continued, "But she's there. Dead. And they think I did it."

# Chapter Five

I COULDN'T BELIEVE it.

Correction: Murder magnet that I was, *sure* I could.

I might not have been best buddies with Nya Barston, but she'd absolutely been a vibrant person. An alive person, with opinions of her own. A sitter who probably cared a lot for her pet charges. She'd definitely cared for the Pet-Sitters Club of SoCal, enough that she couldn't believe anyone could be expressly targeting members of such a great group.

Whether or not she was right, she was dead. And Tracy had discovered her that way.

"I . . . I'm so sorry, Tracy," I said softly into my cell phone. "And I understand what you're going through."

"I know you do, Kendra," she wailed. "Can you help me?"

How could I answer—especially without knowing whether there was good reason for suspicions to be leveled against her? I responded honestly, if obliquely. "I'll be there soon as I can."

I hung up and turned the Beamer in a different direction: the address where Tracy had come across poor Nya's corpse. It was in the area known as the Miracle Mile, which meant I headed south along Highland beyond Hollywood.

And then I made another call. "Guess what, Ned," I said into the phone in as upbeat a tone as I could manage after finally reaching my favorite LAPD detective.

Favorite? Sure—favorite to fight with. And to prove wrong. At least when he made accusations of murder against my friends and acquaintances—and most especially against me.

"Let's see," he said. "You realized you'd only misplaced those animals and you've found them again."

"No," I said with a sigh. "It's even more serious than pet-stealing."

"Don't tell me you're interfering in another murder investigation." His tone was suddenly sharp and snide.

"Okay, I won't," I responded miserably. "Tell you, that is. And I'm not exactly interfering . . . at least not yet."

A muffled groan resounded from the other end of the phone. "I'm sure you will be, Kendra. At least tell me it isn't in my jurisdiction."

"Okay, it's not in your jurisdiction, assuming you're still in North Hollywood." I told him the location.

"Thank God," he intoned into my ear.

"I'll find out soon who the detective in charge is," I said. "Can you let me in on whether he or she is as nice as you?" I heard his intake of breath, as if I'd belted him but good by that compliment. Would he buy it? It was meant in sincerity, more or less. I'd come to respect Ned, at least in some ways. Knew how to deal with him, kinda. Otherwise, I wouldn't have called him at all after the Dorgan pet-napping. If I got involved in Tracy's situation, I'd be starting again from scratch with a new homicide detective. That had happened before, but that time Ned had elected to assist in the investigation. I couldn't count on him doing that again . . . could I? "And I'd really appreciate anything you can learn and pass along to help me."

"Help you what?" The guy had an expressive voice, as I'd learned from long experience. Now, he sounded utterly exasperated. "Let me do both you and my counterpart investigating this case a favor. Kendra, stay out of this one."

"I'd love to," I said sincerely. I slammed on my brakes as a light turned red. I had passed Hollywood and Sunset Boulevards and was nearing Wilshire, which would lead me into a more residential area. Then a few jogs, and I'd be at the murder scene where Tracy awaited my assistance.

"Then why are you sticking your nose in?" Ned grumbled.

I explained who the victim was, and that I'd been in her company only a night earlier.

"So you're interested because a fellow pet-sitter is the victim?"

"And because another fellow pet-sitter may be a suspect." As I filled him in on the little I'd been told by Tracy, the light turned green again and I continued driving.

"And you don't think that, maybe this time, there's good reason for someone to suspect your friend? I mean, I know you don't think much of my abilities as a homicide detective, but I get it right a good ninety percent of the time when you aren't involved. Maybe whoever's handling this has an even better batting average."

I wasn't to know how prophetic that analogy was until I reached the murder scene. And I knew that many crimes, even homicides, were never solved. Ned's proclaimed batting average must mean convictions when he had solid evidence against a purported perpetrator. Even so, that was as impressive as he'd intended. Assuming I believed it.

Meantime, I again asked Ned for his assistance if needed, and then hung up, assuming my inquiry was in vain. Cops didn't leap in to aid nosy citizens.

Especially a cop with attitude who'd probably cheer if this particular nosy citizen happened, this one time, to be wrong.


OF COURSE I really didn't know anything yet about this murder. For all I knew, Tracy could have done it. Nya and she hadn't exactly been on the best of terms last night.

But a bitching session over pet-napping statistics wasn't exactly a convincing motivation for murder.

A pet-napping was. That thought hit me so suddenly and horribly that I nearly swerved the Beamer. Nya had been awfully vocal in her opinion that PSCSC wasn't a target, but what if her vociferousness was a cover for her own culpability? What if Tracy had found her in the process of stealing a pet and, in fury, had killed her? That surely would explain Nya's presence at a client being served by Tracy.

But could I really believe that Nya was the unknown pet-napper? That seemed a stretch. So did the idea that Tracy would kill her, rather than call the cops.

Tracy was still in hysterics when I finally reached her, right outside a white stucco hacienda with red-tiled roof. The house was swathed in yellow tape along with cops and crime scene investigators. Clad in jeans and a green T-shirt, Tracy was puggle-less for the moment, but not Allen-less. I gathered from her guyfriend that she had left her own pooch at home while pet-sitting that day.

I gathered, too, from Allen that he had come the instant his beloved called, to stay at her side and soothe her and attempt to stave off the big, bad detective who'd been harassing her.

"I . . . I can't believe he thinks I did it," Tracy moaned, lifting her head from Allen's chest where she had been sobbing. Her round face was red and blotchy, and I could see a smudge on Allen's otherwise white shirt—wet from her tears and spotted with makeup that no longer enhanced her eyes.

"That's really a shame." I stuck sympathy into my voice, although she was clearly not in custody. At least not yet. "But why? Just because this home belongs to one of your clients?" *And because, just maybe, you did do it?*

"No!" Tracy wailed, almost as if she had tuned into my musings.

A suit strode out of the house toward us. The detective in charge? He looked like he'd been at this business for light-years—an older cop with a world-weary frown on an otherwise expressionless face.

Allen glared and moved Tracy so he remained between the suit and her, affirming my assumption that this was the official distressing her. The detective glanced sideways toward a uniformed cop accompanying him, maybe a third his age.

"Mr. Smith, please come with me," the uniform said. "You have to stay out of the way for now."

"No way," Allen said, his voice somewhat squeaky. He might aspire to soar like an eagle protecting Tracy, but he quailed while confronting authority. His long chin even quivered.

"Yes," the suit contradicted unequivocally. "I need to ask Ms. Owens some more questions."

I interceded with a brilliant smile. Might as well start from a position of strength. "Hi. I'm Kendra Ballantyne, and I'm an attorney." I held out my hand.

The man reached for it with apparent repugnance, although he did the polite thing and shook it. "I'm Detective Lunn. Are you representing Ms. Owens?"

"Heavens, no," I gushed. "I'm a civil litigator. I don't practice criminal law. But I gather this is a crime scene. Ms. Owens indicated that a friend of hers has been injured."

"It's a homicide, Ms. Ballantyne. And if you don't represent Ms. Owens—"

"Oh, I know enough to make a few basic inquiries. Has she been read her rights?"

"She's not in custody."

"She's also not answering any more questions without counsel of her own, right, Tracy?"

She looked at me blearily with bloodshot eyes, but she was conscious enough about what was going on to agree.

Detective Lunn glared as if I had assaulted him. In a way, I supposed I had. I'd at least assaulted his nice and previously unopposed ability to question an obviously scared and unsophisticated witness—and possible suspect. "Go ahead and hire a lawyer, Ms. Owens. It's your right." He turned and trotted back into the house.

Tracy looked around, apparently searching for her support, since she appeared ready to sink to the ground. I wasn't exactly sure where the uniform had led Allen, so I said, "Come here." I motioned toward the sidewalk. The street was lined with closely parked cars, so there wasn't anyplace to easily plant our butts while conversing, but I noticed a couple of lawn chairs in a neighbor's front yard. Sure, we'd be trespassing, but I doubted we'd be sued for it under the circumstances. Even if we were, I had a close relationship with a really good civil litigator.

I led Tracy there, and she sat down and sighed. "Oh, Kendra, this whole thing is one miserable nightmare."

"I'm sure." My tone resounded with empathy. Been there,

done that, and had the criminal lawyer's not-so-cheap receipts to show for it. But at least I'd fingered the true culprit in my case before I could be arrested. "I know it isn't easy to re-live what you went through, but tell me how you found Nya."

She shuddered, then started into a description of how this had been her third pet-sitting stop this morning. "What with all the pet-nappings, I was especially careful to check around outside and make sure it didn't look like the place had been tampered with. Everything looked fine, so I pushed in the code to shut off the security system and used the key to go in. The dog of the house, a really great sheltie mix, bounded right to me. At first, I thought everything was fine. But then Lassie—that's the dog—started acting funny. Running down the hall and barking. I followed. That's when I smelled something terrible. I should have called 911 right away, but I had to look . . ."

She stopped speaking, and an expression of horror made her already round features go rounder yet.

"Where was Nya?" I inquired as gently as I could.

"In the k-kitchen," she wailed. "Soon as I saw her, I knew. That's when I called 911."

I swallowed uneasily, but I had to ask, "Can you describe what she looked like?"

"Horrible." Tracy cried some more before she could continue. "She was on the floor. There was blood, and she was all curled up . . . horrible," she repeated.

"I know this is hard," I said, and it was. For both of us, even though it was worse for the percipient witness. But if I was going to help Tracy, I had to know absolutely everything.

And, yes, I'd come to the conclusion already that she hadn't committed the crime. How? Nothing that would sway a jury's opinion. I just knew, from the way she acted. And because she was a friend.

Could I be barking up an absolutely wrong tree? Well, woof. Of course I could. But why had Nya been there in the first place?

In any event, I continued, "Could you tell how she had died?"

"Y-yes. Or at least I think so. You know I always bring a baseball bat along with me when I pet-sit."

Oh, shit. I suddenly saw where this was going. "So a bat like one of yours—"

"Was on the floor beside Nya. And it was covered in b-blood."

ALMOST IMMEDIATELY AFTER that revelation, Allen Smith reappeared from down the street. His nerdish face was set in an angry scowl. "The cop told me to go away and come back later," he'd said. "Well, it's later now." He planted himself behind Tracy's chair and squeezed her shoulders.

"I've already advised Tracy to hire a criminal attorney," I told him. She blinked, but appeared so bleary that I was uncertain whether what I was saying sunk in. "I can recommend a good one, if you'd like."

He liked, so I provided him with info about my good friend Esther Ickes. She was the legal whiz who'd helped me through the bankruptcy fomented by my alleged ethics violation and banishment from my prior law firm, as well as providing the criminal representation I'd needed when I also became a murder suspect.

"I'll let her know that Tracy might call," I told them both.

Figuring I was leaving Tracy in supportive hands, I headed back down the street toward my Beamer, after taking one last look toward the bustling crime scene.

I couldn't help picturing thin, bespectacled Nya Barston lying on the floor, beaten into a bloody pulp with a baseball bat . . .

I shuddered. As soon as I was centered in the Beamer's driver's seat, I called Darryl.

Time to hear a friendly voice to help me deal with my own distress about what had happened, and to help propel that God-awful image out of my mind.

I'd left Lexie in Darryl's inestimable care early that morning. Without having any idea what horror had already occurred, but with the previous day's meeting on my mind, I'd discussed some of my associates at the Pet-Sitters Club of SoCal with Darryl. He'd known a whole bunch of them already.

"Hi, Kendra," he said. "To what do I owe this call? I just saw you an hour or so ago. If you're checking on Lexie, she's having a riot of a romp right now with a dog twice her size—a mixed breed who's as crazy as she is."

"Glad she's having fun," I said with a smile. It turned into a frown fast. "But what I'm calling about is for you to refresh my recollection. Did you know Nya Barston?"

"*Did* I know? Uh-oh, Kendra, not another one."

"Yep, it's murder magnet time yet again," I confirmed with a chilled sigh.

"Shoot. Well, I'm really swamped right now, but I'll get whatever info I can together for you. We can talk about it this evening, when you pick up Lexie. Meantime . . . are you okay?"

"More or less. At least I didn't see the—er, Nya. But Tracy Owens is apparently a suspect, and she's really a mess."

"I'll bet. Well, if you need a hug, I can always make time for that, even on a day as busy as this one."

"Thanks, Darryl."

Did I need an immediate hug? It certainly wouldn't hurt.

But what I needed even more was advice, most likely of the professional type.

And there was one place where I could get both.

With an ambivalent, yet eager, sigh, I signed off with Darryl and called Jeff.

# Chapter Six

GOOD NEWS: JEFF gave me carte blanche to call his office and instruct Althea, his computer geek, to research anything or anyone I wanted on her amazing, and not always kosher, diversity of databases.

Better news: I was on his office's side of the hill, so I could easily head there on my way home and talk to my buddy Althea face-to-face.

And if I also happened to see Jeff's hunky face while on his turf, well, so much the better.

I headed the Beamer along Wilshire Boulevard toward Westwood, which was, unsurprisingly, west of where I was.

On the way, my cell phone sang its—no, *my*—anthem, "It's My Life." I didn't recognize the number, but it was in the 213 area code, which once covered all of L.A. but was now one of dozens, and its range covered only downtown.

Downtown? And then I knew. I almost didn't answer. But the caller and I had a history of sorts, and I knew she would keep on phoning till she reached me. She had to be in her office, since my phone would have ID'd her cell right away.

"Hello?" I said, vainly attempting neutrality in my tone. Instead, it sounded as out of sorts as I felt.

"Hi, Kendra. This is Corina Carey."

"Corina, what a surprise. And exactly how is my favorite nosy reporter today?"

"I'd be doing a hell of a lot better if my favorite lawyer-pet-sitter combo had called me first thing this morning, when you learned about the murder of a fellow dog-watcher."

I forced a gasp to escape my mouth. "A pet-sitter? Murdered?" Though I sounded somewhat glib, the reminder gave my insides a heck of a jolt—not that I'd forgotten the murder, even for an instant. I stopped at a traffic light and watched the other oblivious drivers glide by. Bet none of them had someone they knew bludgeoned to death with a baseball bat last night.

But this was L.A. Who knew?

"Don't pretend you didn't know, Ballantyne. She's a member of that club you belong to, and I just got through talking to a cop, who informed me off the record that you were at the scene almost immediately."

"And this was . . . ?" The light changed, so I stepped lightly on the accelerator and continued my way toward Westwood.

"That's off the record, too." My lips nearly moved in sync to Corina's answer. Who had it been? Who could it have been, but that Detective Lunn? Ned Noralles? One of the uniforms?

Who really cared?

"Kendra, I'm waiting."

"For what?"

"I want a statement from you. Better yet, let's set up an interview. I want to know everything you do."

"Which right now amounts to little more than zilch, Corina." Of course the pet-nappings hadn't made the news, although that could be of as much public interest as the murder. Maybe more.

Did I want that info out in the world? Yes, if it would help other people from having their pets swiped.

But not if it would wind up in my own charges, Zibble and Saurus, being slain because I'd done what I was told not to do, and informed the police.

Although my note hadn't mentioned the media . . .

I needed to think this through. And I didn't have to answer

immediately. I didn't know if the murder and the thefts had anything to do with one another. Corina had been of assistance before in my plan for solving a murder, but that didn't mean she couldn't mess up this investigation. *These* investigations, if I counted the pet-nappings—which I indubitably did.

"Tell you what, Corina." I stopped at yet another light. I was in a commercial area, where pedestrians paraded by. Did any of them happen to have had an acquaintance . . . *stop thinking of bludgeoning bats, Kendra,* I ordered myself. Instead, I continued my comment to the reporter impatiently sighing on the other side of the phone. "I may have another interesting story for you, but have to talk to some people first. Don't call me. I'll call you—when I know if I've anything to say. Have a nice day."

I hung up before she could sputter—much.

IN WESTWOOD, I found a parking space and walked a block to the four-story building in which Jeff's office was on the third. As always, the elevator took its own pokey time getting me there. But soon, I was in the suite that reminded me of a wagon wheel, the hub of which was the usually empty reception area. Around it were the investigators' offices.

"Hello," I called after opening the door and strolling in. Interestingly for a place labeled as HUBBARD SECURITY, LLC, on the sign outside, the offices weren't exactly secure.

Except that, I felt certain, my presence was being recorded on some completely camouflaged camera, hidden perhaps inside the low, white ceiling, in the round, recessed lights, or among the plastic stacking shelves on the reception desk, or—

"Hi, Kendra," said a male voice from the doorway to one of the offices. My heart zinged, then flopped. Wrong male voice. It belonged to Buzz Dulear, Jeff's expert in security systems, a tall fellow with a buzz cut that didn't disguise that his hairline was receding.

"Hi, Buzz. Is Jeff here?"

"Not at the moment. Did he know you were coming?"

Hoping I succeeded at hiding the disappointment that surged through my sorrowful self, I said, "Nope, although I got his okay to talk to Althea, and—"

"Kendra! How wonderful to see you." That same Althea lunged from the nearest office and leaped close enough to envelope me in a hearty hug.

I gave as good as I got. "Same goes," I told her, stepped back, and shot her a grin big as the one she aimed at me.

Before I'd met her in person instead of simply over the phone, Jeff had always proudly described his prize computer geek as a grandmother. Which she was. But heck, I hoped that, if I ever walked in a grandma's shoes, I'd look half as good. She had five grown kids, I didn't know how many grandkids, and she was only in her midfifties. But she looked almost as good as any pop star—slim and with curves to make any woman envy green, which would match Althea's sparkling eyes. She dressed youthfully, too, in tight jeans and a brilliant pink cropped top that complemented her sassy midlength blond hair.

On top of all that, she worked closely with the guy who'd made my hormones hum most over the last several months.

Envy? Heck, if I were the jealous type, I might hate the woman in front of me. Instead, I adored her.

And needed her extremely competent assistance.

"Jeff told me you'd be calling," she said now. "But I'm happy you're here. Come in and tell me what I can do for you."

I entered her compact office that overflowed with computer gear. "Guess what," I started to say as I sat in a small but sturdy chair facing her desk.

"You're involved in another murder investigation," she said, swiftly stealing my not-so-loud thunder.

"Jeff told you already."

"He sure did. And here I'd hoped that this time I'd only be researching things relating to pet-nappings for you. He passed along the list of sitters' club members that you gave to him."

"Well, I'm still a murder magnet," I said with a sigh. "I knew the victim, and the main suspect so far is a friend—the president of that pet-sitters' society."

"Okay, tell me what you need on the murder stuff. I don't have much yet on pet-nappings but Jeff has me working on it, like checking other thefts in neighborhoods where the recent snatching occurred." She sat behind her desk and poised her hands, short nails polished in shiny red, right over her computer keyboard.

I quickly explained that I wanted everything available on the victim, Nya Barston, and anyone who showed up as being close to her—husband or significant other, if any. Also on my friend, the apparently favored suspect, Tracy Owens. "The murder took place on a block south of Beverly, not far from the Wilshire Country Club." I gave her the address. "I don't know the owners' names, but they own a dog who fortunately wasn't stolen—Lassie, a Shetland sheepdog mix."

"I can easily learn whose home it is," Althea assured me. "Are they out of town?"

"So I gathered from Tracy. She was their pet-sitter and had no idea why Nya was even there." Althea didn't need to know that, but bouncing facts off this friendly and intelligent computer expert could only help me determine what other info I might need her to dig for.

"I doubt I'll find that online," Althea said, looking at me with a small and irrepressible shrug, "but *no problemo* with the rest of the info. And I assume you need it in—" She looked down at the wide wristwatch on her slender arm. "Three seconds or less."

"Stress the less," I told her with a smile.

"I figured. So go away already and let me work."

"Sure thing. Oh, and when you see Jeff, tell him—"

"Tell him yourself," said a male voice from the direction of the office doorway. And this time, it wasn't Buzz Dulear's nice but not especially sexy tone that buzzed in my ears.

I stood slowly, not wanting to appear too eager. After all, I'd seen him only yesterday. It wasn't as if we'd had some huge, long absence between us making our hearts grow fonder.

Was my heart growing irritatingly fonder anyhow?

I faced Jeff, glad that, even though I'd dressed in office casual that day, since I hadn't any law client meetings scheduled, my outfit consisted of nice crisp olive green slacks and an even crisper floral silk blouse. They didn't exactly hug my bod and shove in his face what he was missing, now that we'd ceased having sex—but the suggestion was surely there.

"I didn't know you were coming to talk to Althea in person

about the research you needed," he said. His intense gaze that raked me up and down suggested that my duds were doing exactly as I'd hoped—inspiring him to look even deeper and use his sexy imagination to figure out what lay beneath.

"I didn't know I was, either," I admitted. "But I wasn't far away, so it was just as easy as calling."

"Good. You had lunch?"

I blinked and pulled my cell phone from my large purse that I'd by habit slung over my shoulder. Sure enough, it was nearly noon.

"Didn't even realize it was lunchtime," I told him. "But I haven't been to my law office yet, so—"

"Okay, we'll do it another time. I just got back from a meeting and need to sit down at my computer and make notes. I'll call you about getting together for dinner sometime soon. Okay, Kendra?"

He didn't even await my astonished and decisively chilly reply.

"Something wrong between you two?" Althea asked softly from behind me as I stayed staring at the empty doorway.

"There *is* no us two," I told her from between my teeth. "Remind me to tell you one of these days about the really delightful veterinarian I'm dating. Charming, sexy, sweet, and of course he loves animals."

"I think you just told me," Althea said wryly.

"Could be. Well, I'll give you a call later today and see if you've found anything yet to help me figure out why Nya Barston morphed last night from an outspoken pet-sitter person into a sorry, bat-beaten homicide victim, and whodunit. Or anything about the pet-nappings. Thanks, Althea."

I headed out as fast as my wobbly feet would carry me.

And exactly what was the reason I'd decided to come to Jeff's Westwood office in person?

Damned if I now knew.

# Chapter Seven

OKAY, ACCOMPLISHING ANYTHING lawyerly—at least officially so—seemed a total lost cause that day. No time. No state of mind that would suggest I could concentrate.

Consequently, I made an executive decision. As the managing member of Critter TLC, LLC, I was, after all, an executive of sorts. While walking along the busy commercial streets of Westwood toward my Beamer, I called the representatives of the other side of my multiple personality—er, career—and reached, as anticipated, our dear and dingbatty receptionist Mignon.

"I need to take a personal day," I told her. "I don't have any meetings or conference calls scheduled, do I?"

"Nope," she chirped. "And I assume that, by a personal day, you mean another murder day, right?"

"How would you know that?" I demanded with uninhibited irritation.

"It's on the news. I saw it on one of the local TV channels' websites."

Corina Carey, or her media vulture counterparts, had obviously been busy.

"I wasn't exactly clear what happened," Mignon continued, "but some pet-sitter was killed on a job, yes?"

"Pet-sitter, yes," I responded, "but on the job—no."

"Did you know her?"

"Yes," I said.

"Do the police think they know who did it, Kendra? And if so, do you agree, or are you going to solve another murder?"

"They may be considering a suspect," I said. "If it's who I believe it is, then, no, I don't agree. But will I solve it—"

"You *are* involved, I can tell. How exciting, Kendra! I'll tell Borden—"

"No. Please transfer me to him. I'll do it." Admittedly, I'd started out this call as a coward. But my initial idea of having Mignon cover for me because of a personal problem I chose not to disclose wouldn't cut it after all.

Fortunately, Borden understood, great guy that he was. "You really are a murder magnet, aren't you, Kendra?" I heard the cheeriness in his tone.

"Not by choice." At least not entirely. But these days, homicides hounded me. And not in a pet-sitter sense.

"Take today off. And as much extra time as you need—as long as you don't neglect any of your work here, of course."

"Of course. Thanks, Borden."

I appreciated his understanding, but also recognized its limits. I had to make good use of my law-free time today.

So where now, I wondered, as I got into my Beamer.

The thing was, I'd let the killing distract me from my own awful dilemma. Where were the animals who disappeared on my watch? I called Detective Flagsmith, but he hadn't anything new to report on the missing canine and reptile. "No more ransom notes?" I asked almost hopefully.

"Nope."

I thanked him—for nothing, though I kept that part to my unhappy self—and hung up. My e-mail from the Dorgans had indicated that Hillary would be home tomorrow, so I'd have to face her then.

With no update other than the fact I'd somehow allowed her friends to be stolen?

I decided to seek info from someone who was supposed to have some. Not specific to my pet-napping, though. Tracy had told Frieda Shoreman to research all recent pet-nappings around this area.

And just maybe she'd know something about Nya's demise, too.

Did I assume they were somehow related? Not necessarily, but I couldn't assume they weren't, either.

I called Frieda. Turned out she intended to dog-walk in the park on Huston Street in Sherman Oaks—part of my convenient neighborhood in the huge urban environment that was L.A.

She had heard, of course, of Nya's demise. "Isn't it awful?" she asked immediately.

"Sure is." *And can you pass along any information to lead to her killer?* I ached to blurt. Instead, I told her I'd been intending to take Lexie out for exercise and asked if we could join her. She sounded amenable, so I said, "Meet you there in an hour." That gave me time to get back over the hill, change my clothes, and visit Darryl to pick up the info he'd promised, along with my dog for walking.

WE SAT IN Darryl's messy office, he behind his cluttered desk and I in one of the chairs facing him. Lexie had greeted me effusively, but when she saw I wasn't ready to immediately spring her from this joint, she'd gone back to lie down on the people-type sofa in one sector of the main room.

"So what can you tell me about Nya Barston?" I asked my bespectacled friend. "Did you ever refer pet-sitting clients to her?"

He nodded. As always, he wore a Doggy Indulgence knit shirt, red today rather than the usual green. "I'd heard of her through some of my customers here, before I even met you. I knew she worked over the hill around Hollywood, and her references were good. I only met her in person a couple of times. She seemed a bit abrupt with people, but she obviously loved dogs."

"My impression, too," I agreed. "I don't suppose you know anything about her personal life."

"I didn't, but this morning I called a longtime customer who'd used her and commiserated over her loss. That customer knew her better than I ever did and said she had a boyfriend, by the name of . . ." He looked down at one of the dozen piles on his desk, dug through the top few inches, and pulled out a piece of paper. "Jerry Jefferton. I don't know how close they were, or where he lives, but I figure you or Jeff can find out."

"Sure will. Can you also give me that customer's name, and any others you know who've used Nya as a pet-sitter?"

"You think one of them killed her?" My dear friend appeared absolutely horrified.

"Right now, I've no idea who did it, but talking to her friends and acquaintances might help me figure it out."

"Make sure it isn't anyone I know and like," Darryl demanded grumpily, but he did take a few minutes to check on his deskside computer and compile a short list that he printed out. "Here's everyone I know about."

"Thanks, Darryl." I stood, as did he. "I don't suppose any of your customers or other friends know anything about the pet-nappings?"

"No, but they're a big topic of conversation, now that they've hit the news along with Nya's murder."

They had? I hadn't heard. Would that be a good thing, letting the world know of this latest rash of nasties, or might it only make things worse?

"Everyone's worried about leaving their pets home alone," Darryl continued, "which is good for my business during the day."

"I'll bet. Well, if you hear anything helpful—"

"I'll call you right away."


LEXIE AND I hurried west from Studio City and emerged from the Beamer at the pup- and people-filled dog park.

We soon met up with Frieda and Usher, the dog she was tending, a large mixed breed that appeared part rottweiler. Even so, Usher seemed a big softy.

Frieda was dressed in flowered leggings with her traditional flowing top, this one bright magenta. Her foot attire fit the occasion: pink athletic shoes, with pink-striped white socks.

We all slowly walked the path, letting the pups sniff the usual dog-park smells, puppy passersby, and one another. I had to look up at Frieda's graceful height to meet her amber eyes. They were enhanced by an array of makeup, overdone for a dog walk, but she was unquestionably an attractive lady.

I started with a question I figured she could answer, even if her response was negative. "Were you able to find anything about any other pet-nappings in the area?"

She shook her bleached blond locks. "No, though don't tell Tracy, but I haven't done much looking."

I wasn't thrilled that she hadn't even attempted her PSCSC project and looked for other local pet-nappings. It should only have required a Googling or review of past newspaper issues or recent TV news. These days, all that stuff is available easily on the Internet. Good thing I'd intended to do some searching anyway and not rely on her findings.

Not that it would necessarily assist in my own pet-absconding situation.

At least I was pleased that Frieda had brought up Tracy, giving me an intro to the other subject I wanted to discuss.

"Poor Tracy," I started. "You know, she thinks the cops believe she could have killed Nya." I stole a sideways glance to see if I could tell, by Frieda's expression, if she happened to share that point of view.

Instead, she looked shocked. "Tracy? Why, she's so gentle that she even traps rodents at the homes where she pet-sits and drives them way up to remote areas off Mulholland to let them out. She would never hurt a person, not even one she disliked."

Aha! "Oh, did she dislike Nya?" I asked quite calmly, as if speaking of whether the grayish April weather was about to turn sunny.

"Of course not. Tracy likes everyone. But you heard Nya and her go at each other at the meeting the other night. She could still have been angry that Nya didn't take her concern seriously, that our club was somehow being targeted for the pet-nappings."

We were speaking somewhat circularly. "But you haven't found anything to indicate that the problem is larger than PSCSC, have you?"

"No, but like I said, I haven't really looked."

Well, I'd look. And I'd ask Althea to check her even vaster resources for additional info, too.

But I might also be able to get one answer for Althea here. "Anyway, it seems strange that Nya happened to be at the home of one of Tracy's clients." Like, could she have been attempting to steal the unfortunate pet of the house? "I know the dog's name, but I don't think she ever told me who her clients were. Do you happen to know?"

We'd stopped because Usher was getting down to some serious business—a nice, big poop. Of course Frieda, being a pro at pet-sitting, came equipped with an adequate-size plastic bag. If she'd been unprepared, I could have handed her one of mine.

After she'd stooped to retrieve it, she cast it into a receptacle along the dog-ready trail. I reminded her then of the question still on the table—er, path—as we wandered off again, walking slower this time. That meant more dogs and walkers maneuvered around us, even as we stayed toward the right.

"Who owns Lassie and the house where Nya was found?" Frieda repeated. "The Ravels, or something like that. Tracy mentioned how upset they were when she called to tell them what happened. They were on location in San Francisco and were hurrying home."

San Francisco? Not a huge plane ride away. If they'd come home, found a stranger in their house without knowing she knew their pet-sitter, might someone have bludgeoned Nya to death without determining her reason for being there? Then, the guilty Ravel could have hopped another flight for SFO, or even driven there. If they played their stories right, no one would even know they'd been back to L.A.

Had I solved it?

No evidence, but sheer speculation. Awfully far-fetched speculation, too. And it didn't do squat to explain Nya's presence in the first place. But I'd toss the theory to Althea and have her check on whether anyone named Ravel flew in and out of one of L.A.'s airports yesterday, or rented a car, or bought gas with a credit card.

Yes, Althea had sources, even for stuff considered private.

I didn't voice these creative concepts to Frieda. Instead, I said simply, "Well, it's unlikely they could have harmed Nya, especially if they weren't home at the time." Since we were walking again, I stopped for a second, stooping to pick up

Lexie as my excuse. My pup wriggled to get down. She didn't understand when I used her as a diversion. I hung on and pretended she didn't squirm. "I don't suppose," I said to Frieda, "that you have any idea who killed Nya." I didn't get into the whole murder weapon scenario, and how whoever it was might be purposely framing Tracy.

"Not really," she responded.

*Un*really, then? Did she have a possibility in mind?

Turned out she was just mulling over club members who might have had an axe to grind with Nya: everyone. "If I had to pick the one with the biggest gripe, it would be Lilia Ziegler."

"Lilia?" I almost laughed out loud. She was the oldest member of the club, and I couldn't imagine someone as sweet-tempered as she arguing with anyone.

Frieda appeared to resent my incredulity. She stopped strolling, and so did the rest of our entourage. Hands on her enviably skinny hips, she glared. "You asked what I thought. I know that Lilia and Nya were feuding. Lilia apparently took over one of Nya's clients. I don't know how or why, but it definitely upset Nya, and she told everyone about how backstabbing Lilia was—which upset *her*."

Enough to kill her rival? But even if I could buy the motive, means was another far-fetched factor. Lilia wasn't extremely large, and she was on the senior citizen side of adulthood. Could she have wielded a baseball bat in such a lethal manner?

No need to point out that additional doubt to Frieda, who was clearly insulted that I had questioned her conclusion. I said instead, "That's really interesting. I think I'll see if Lilia wants to join me for a walk or cup of coffee one day soon. Just so I can get her perspective on what happened. By the way, do you know Nya's boyfriend, Jerry Jefferton?"

Frieda was still staring, head cocked as if she attempted to figure me out. "I've met Jerry but don't see him as a killer." She paused. "I've heard that you solve murders for a hobby. Are you going to figure this one out, too?"

"Unlikely," I said, wondering whether I lied.

I sure as heck was going to keep looking into it. After all, I genuinely liked Tracy, and I didn't think she did it.

And I seemed destined, these days, to assist those who are as unjustly accused of murder as I'd been.

A WHILE LATER, after ending our outing with Frieda, Lexie and I visited some pet-sitting clients to ensure their continued well-being. Hell, I knew I was still spending too much time on Nya's murder and not enough on my own responsibility of resolving the disappearance of Zibble and Saurus. Consequently, I made some follow-up phone calls as I drove, to the detectives on the Dorgan case and to a neighbor or two who'd been nice enough to exchange contact info.

Anything new? No.

And so we headed home. As I pushed the button inside the Beamer that opened our wrought-iron gate, I saw Rachel in the garage getting into her small blue car, Beggar beside her.

I drove quickly into my designated spot beside that structure, and Lexie and I got out, with my small pup cavorting eagerly on her leash toward her Irish setter friend.

"Off on pet-sitting rounds?" I asked my young employee.

She was dressed in a snug blue T-shirt and snugger beige denim jeans, excellent garb for dog and cat care. "Sure am. And guess what I did this afternoon. What we did, Beggar and I."

"Looked in on some of our charges, I hope."

"Besides that." A twinkle in those big brown eyes of hers suggested that, whatever she'd done, it was fun.

"Did you go to the beach?"

"No way. Something you'd approve of a whole lot more."

"What's better than the beach?"

Lexie and Beggar both began tugging on their leashes. I let my pup loose, and Rachel did the same. Both dogs bounded about the driveway.

"A really nice senior citizens' facility in Studio City. I'd read in one of the local throwaway papers that they were looking for people to bring in their pets, since petting dogs made some of the patients there feel more like home."

"Wow, Rachel, that's so nice of you," I said truthfully and enthusiastically. "That kind of place has to be depressing."

"Not really. The people were nice, and seemed so happy to

pet Beggar . . . I liked it so much I'm planning on doing it more, maybe a couple of times a week. Want to go along sometime?"

"Maybe." I wanted to equal her gusto but couldn't quite.

"Come on, Kendra. You'll love it."

"Okay, but give me a week or so before you schedule it. I've pet-napped clients to find, and a murder to solve, and—" And a love life, or lack thereof, to deal with, not that I'd say that to Rachel. In any event, I needed as many good excuses as I could convey to her if I chose not to participate in this good deed.

"Another murder?" Rachel's eyes widened even further in apparent awe.

"Yep." I told her the sketchy details.

"How amazing, Kendra. How do you keep getting involved with such things?"

"Wish I knew, Rachel. Wish I knew."

I SAID GOODBYE to Rachel and sent her off on her rounds. It was almost time for me to start on mine when my cell phone sang.

I grabbed it from the bottom of my big bag and glanced at the caller ID. And swallowed, unsure how to feel.

It was Jeff.

"Hi, Jeff," I answered pretty perkily considering my ambivalence.

"Hi, Kendra. Althea found some interesting stuff while doing your research."

"Really? That's wonderful. I hope. Is it good stuff?"

"Maybe. I've only glanced through it. I have it here at the office, and Althea had to go home early. She printed it all out, so I can't just e-mail it to you."

"Oh. Well, could I just pick it up later at your place?"

*Bad idea, Kendra. Real bad. Seeing Jeff again on his turf, where you've spent many sleepless, sex-filled nights? You barely got away last time. Where's your sense, kid?*

*Somewhere behind my horny little heart . . .*

"I have a better idea," Jeff said. "Meet me for dinner."

Already? He'd just said he would invite me to dinner *sometime*, whenever that might be, earlier that day. I'd taken that to mean he was backing off, and I wasn't certain how I felt about it.

I supposed this was sometime. Even so . . .

"Well . . ." I hesitated, searching fruitlessly for some kind of excuse not to go. I had to pet-sit. I had to—

"No dinner, no handing over of the data tonight. Do we have a date?"

What else could I do?

"Sure," I said with an enthusiasm I didn't feel.

Or did I?

# Chapter Eight

I HADN'T REMINDED Jeff that this remained the same day that he'd all but invited me to lunch, then slammed that door in my face. I should still be pissed over that.

I *was* still pissed over that.

And now I'd allowed him to manipulate me again. Talk about pissed. But what could I do? I wanted the Althea-generated info ASAP. And I apparently couldn't talk to her about it now, nor could I relay the bits of info I'd gathered from Frieda. I'd have to call her in the morning about the additional research I wanted to request of her.

And Jeff? Would I allow him to extort my nighttime presence in exchange for what was in his possession?

Was that even what he wanted?

We met at a really charming burger joint along Ventura Boulevard with a fenced-in outdoor eating area. Ergo, Lexie and Odin could accompany us. Jeff carried a manila envelope, which I assumed contained the information he had used to lure me here.

A jazz group entertained on the patio that evening, and the greatest contingent of diners was parents whose toddlers danced along. That made conversation difficult during musical sessions, which was copacetic with me.

I went for a zesty sausage sandwich, so I hadn't much food to pass along to Lexie since I didn't want her stomach suffering from spiciness. That left it to Jeff to treat both dogs since he ordered a giant burger. And treat them he did, handing over a good third of his dinner to the beggars beside him.

I simply watched. And ate, which kept my mouth busy instead of allowing it to hang open in lust while watching Jeff. Even if I was absolutely uncertain where our non-relationship was going, I had to admit to myself that he remained one awesome dude. I observed his lips and tongue as he savored the parts of the burger he saved for himself and imagined them on unmentionable parts of me. I attempted to ignore the twinkle in his sexy blue eyes as he looked me up and down, obviously aware of the effect he was having on me.

And me? Well, I gave as good as I got, even though I remained in my dog-walking garb that I'd changed into to meet Frieda: jeans and yellow PSCSC T-shirt. I looked at him flirtatiously frequently, glancing teasingly from beneath my mascaraed lashes and quickly returning my apparent attention to the delicious sandwich in my hands. And I took similarly sexy bites of that same sandwich as he did with his.

Eventually, the musicians took a rest, and so did my heated teasing. "Okay," I said, all business at last, "I'm here. We're together for dinner. Where are Althea's printouts that you promised if I played your games?" I reached out, expecting him to hand over the envelope that lay on the table near his plate.

"Got 'em in a folder I brought along from the office but left at home when I picked up Odin."

"Then what's that?" I demanded, reaching for the otherwise unexplained envelope.

"Something I brought to fool you into thinking I'd complied with our bargain."

"Come on, Hubbard!" I exclaimed, forming my fingers into fists that I considered hurtling into his hunky, craggy face. "What's your game now?" As if I didn't know.

His grin was sexy and somewhat contagious, although I restrained myself from smiling back. "Game? Me? I was just hoping to talk you into bringing Lexie and joining Odin and me at home tonight."

"Guess again," I said sourly, even as my insides started softening and swirling. I knew what he was asking, and my rebellious body was telling me how long it had been since we had made love: *too* long. Plus, I felt a hint of relief that he still wanted me, despite my ongoing ambivalence about him.

"Okay, Kendra, you win." His voice was a smooth, sexy leonine purr. "I'll hand it over. But you're still invited to come home with me."

The envelope was soon in my hands, and the stuff I pulled out was exactly what I'd set Althea on finding: info on victim Nya Barston and her apparent friends and family, plus stuff on the Ravels, owners of the home where Nya was snuffed out and its resident sheltie mix, Lassie, whom Tracy had been sitting there. I had intended to relay my newly acquired knowledge about Jerry Jefferton and the Ravels to Althea, but she had been ahead of me, as always, when it came to ferreting out info. And there was no indication that the Ravels had raced into town to kill Nya.

"Hey, this is all great," I said. "Thank Althea for me. Better yet, I'll call her tomorrow to thank her—and to ask her to do one more thing for me."

"What's that?"

"Run a check to see if there has been a rash of pet-nappings other than the three that occurred to members of the Pet-Sitters Club of SoCal."

"Your wish is my command," my dinner companion intoned. His smile grew even broader and sexier than before. "I've looked into that myself." From a pocket in his pants, he extracted a folded sheet of paper, which he uncreased with great pomp and handed to me. It showed the results of quests on several search engines about local pet thefts.

Only the three I knew about appeared on the list.

"This is all?" I asked.

Jeff nodded. "All those reported within the last couple of weeks. What I didn't print out was info I found on certain unmentionable websites that confirmed there weren't others of interest. There was one dog stolen along with a kid in a custody situation, and some other disappearances that appeared more to be dogs running away or cats becoming coyote food, but nothing that was clearly a pet-napping, complete with ransom note."

"By 'unmentionable websites,' can I assume you mean official in-house sites of authorities like police?"

"Assume what you want." But the slyness of his smile said I'd scored a bull's-eye.

"Thanks for checking, Jeff." I stood up enough to bend over and kiss him on the cheek. It was rough, as his light brown beard had started erupting in a sexy evening shadow. His scent was light—soapy and sexily male. He moved his head and turned my sisterly buss into something a lot hotter. Sexy.

And if you catch a certain theme here in my thoughts . . . well, so did I.

I needed to purge my mind of anything that could make me compromise my current vow of chastity when it came to Jeff. At least until I knew if we still had anything going. If I wanted to have anything going with him. If I wanted my not-quite-yet relationship with Tom Venson, whom I'd be seeing on Saturday, to replace whatever I'd had with Jeff.

I didn't want to try to digest, along with my spicy sandwich, the printed pages I'd pulled from the envelope. Not with Jeff there staring at me as if he wanted to eat *me*.

And not when I wasn't sure whether I wanted him to . . .

Which was when the energetic jazz orchestra started playing their next set.

"I'm finished here," I called across the table to Jeff. "I'm taking the rest of my sandwich home. You ready to leave?"

He nodded. We packed up our luscious leftovers and strolled out of the patio area onto the Encino sidewalk.

Twilight had finally arrived. The air was cool and calm, and even holding a substantial amount of takeout with the hard-won envelope and Lexie's leash, I felt I'd eaten too much.

"Care to stroll the Boulevard?" I asked Jeff, who similarly manipulated his bag and Odin's lead.

"It's a long walk home," he said, still sounding hopeful.

"Exactly," I said. "That's why I suggested strolling right here."

He aimed an assessing look at me, and I pretended to stare in the window of a nearby carpeting store. "Kendra," he finally said, "we really need to talk."

"Could be," I said, feeling as nervous as if he had pressed my back up against an unyielding wall. "But not tonight. I'm too tired."

And so we went our separate ways.

Mistake? Certain parts on and in my body sure thought so.

My mind? Well, it, too, didn't exactly give me peace about this decision. But even so, Lexie and I headed home, her to act her adorable, loving self, and me to brood.

AND BROOD I did. All night. *Alone* all night, except for my slightly snoring pup, tucked together into the full-size bed in the pint-size bedroom-and-office in our garage-top apartment. Lexie lay on top of the russet, rose, and gold print comforter, and I lay beneath it, surrounded by the coordinating sheets. Wide awake.

I felt sexually deprived, but could only blame myself and my stab at morals, until I knew what the heck I had, or didn't have, with Jeff.

Listening to far-off freeway noises, I also thought a lot about the pet-napping situation. Considered who else I could coerce into giving me more info. Ned Noralles?

I called him, but still no conclusions about where poor Zibble and Saurus had been taken. No admission, to me, at least, of any viable suspects.

I wondered if Tracy had shot to the top of that list, too, by virtue of her suspect status in Nya's murder.

I wondered even more whether there wasn't something additional I could do to find the missing animals. Especially since their co-owner, my client Hillary Dorgan, would be back home tomorrow from her formerly exciting European trip.

No more neighbors had called me. Most had wisely kept their contact info to themselves, but nearly all had been kind enough to accept my business cards when I'd made a frantic foray to interview any witnesses. Those cards not immediately filed in trash receptacles were now in the hands of people who would undoubtedly rather hand-carry their pets' excretions than to hire me as a pet-sitter. Or lawyer, for that matter. But maybe some would still contact me if they recalled something potentially helpful in solving the pet-napping.

Right now, I'd absolutely no clue about where Zibble and Saurus might be. Jeff's search was somewhat helpful in allowing me to continue to conclude that my pet-sitters' organization was the thief's special target, but I didn't know motive or, worse, ID of the deplorable perpetrator. Althea's research into the pet-nappings' neighborhoods thus far yielded no useful results.

I sighed, inhaling somewhat the soft smell of the detergent in which I had last washed the sheets.

Pet-nappings. A murder. Jeff.

What was I going to do about any one of the above, let alone all three?

CALL ME A masochist, a glutton for punishment, or a pet-sitter who wished more than anything that the theft of her charges hadn't happened—or, failing that, of at least convincing my human clients how much I cared. Whatever kind of fool I was, I'd e-mailed the Dorgans and offered to pick up Hillary at the airport. And cursed myself unequivocally when she accepted.

How could I face her?

How could I not?

I still wasn't about to hurry through my morning's pet-sitting rounds, since I was now undeniably paranoid about the well-being of my current charges.

I brought Lexie along to save the few minutes it would take to drop her at Darryl's. Plus, I enjoyed her company. But I wasn't about to leave her locked in my Beamer when I popped in to walk, feed, and play with the pets I cared for, so Lexie accompanied me on these enjoyable chores. I felt sure she liked them as much as I did—except at homes where the dominant dogs protected their turfs by growling and strutting their alpha canine stuff. There, I carried Lexie where necessary. That's one of many magnificent things about Cavaliers. They're armfuls, but are enjoyably portable.

We next headed for my law office, where Lexie also pranced inside. She was fussed over by Mignon as she greeted us, by Borden when he saw us in the kitchen pouring water and coffee for my pup and me, respectively, and by the day's contingent of present- and accounted-for elder-law attorneys and support staff.

Guess I should simply have said, "by everybody." Of course, I kept her out of the way of Gigi, the macaw.

In my office, the door closed for peace and quiet and accomplishing something, I finally finished setting up next Monday's settlement meeting between clients Jasper and Angelica McGregor, and their relative Tallulah and her attorney. We needed to discuss the formerly dying Tallulah's claim that, since she had survived, she wanted Whiskey the weimaraner returned. It was Thursday now. The litigants would have the weekend to mull over their respective positions and ponder a compromise to avoid allowing strangers to resolve this for them in court. Maybe.

With Lexie sometimes on the floor beneath my feet, but more often sitting on my lap, I performed masterful legal research for other clients for the rest of that morning, and even better and convincing brief creation for their cases.

And in the afternoon? Charley and Connie Sherman, some senior citizen clients of Borden's whom I'd been helping, came in to sign settlement documents.

I had Mignon show them to the conference room, so I could leave Lexie in my office. "Hi, Kendra." Charley held out his beefy hand for me to shake. "Are we all set?" Charley was a Pillsbury Doughboy sort of man, and he often dressed in puffy, faded jeans and red plaid shirts. His hicklike looks were deceptive. He was actually a well-regarded animal trainer for Hennessy Studios, although now he was semi-retired.

"I've got the settlement papers right here for you to sign," I told them.

"That's wonderful," Connie said with a smile. She was showing her age—early seventies—with a well-wrinkled face and slightly stooped shoulders, but her mind was absolutely intact. She'd retired as head actuary for a huge insurance outfit, but I gathered she kept active by managing the family investments.

Their legal issue? Connie and Charley had stayed in a

Santa Barbara establishment that had been advertised as a luxury resort. Instead, it made mere dumpiness look posh.

They'd sued, and they weren't alone. I'd discussed turning the matter into a class action with other attorneys, but we'd all decided it was in our clients' best interests not to drive the overzealous owners into bankruptcy. Their fraud had resulted more from enthusiasm for their new, but not yet refurbished resort than from intentional fraud . . . maybe. In any event, we all resorted to alternate dispute resolution consisting of a binding arbitration. The results meant refunding to our clients cents on the dollar, plus the satisfaction of knowing no one else would be snookered the same way again.

"Now, read the agreement carefully," I said. "I think it documents everything we discussed, but let me know if you have any questions."

They read it. They inquired about a couple of boilerplate points. And then they signed.

Charley sat his large form back in his chair. "So how've you been, Kendra?"

"I'd be better if a couple of my pet-sitting clients hadn't been stolen," I admitted. With his animal-involved career, I felt certain Charley would appreciate my anguish.

Which he did. "That's terrible. What happened?"

I told them about Zibble, the Shar-pei, and Saurus, the iguana, including the ransom note.

"I'm so sorry, Kendra," Connie said. "Anything we can do?"

"Not unless you're aware of other pet-nappings so I can identify a trend and the thief." I looked at Charley. "None of your animals has disappeared, have they?"

"Nope. But I've careful attendants at my ranch up north where I keep most of them. My only iguana—Impressario— well, no one would ever consider stealing him. Reaching into his habitat is dangerous to a person's health. I know how to work with him, but he loves to bite. Hard."

"Not Saurus," I said sadly. "Maybe if he bit, he'd still be home safe and sound."

"Well, you keep Charley in mind," Connie said as she rose.

"Sure," Charley concurred. "I work with all kinds of critters all the time. If I can do anything to help you catch the person who's pinched your clients, be sure to let me know."

"I'd love to visit your facility sometime, at least," I said sincerely, and Charley was gracious enough to agree.

When the Shermans had scooted out the door, I made notes about the meeting. And then? Well, I'm a confirmed listophile. Listoholic? Whichever, I'd already realized I had an awful lot of data rattling around in my confused brain, as well as the info Althea gathered. My handwritten notes were losing their usefulness.

With Lexie lying beneath my desk, I inputted everything onto a file in my office computer that I had established about the PSCSC pet-nappings, combining it with the nearly non-existent data concerning other pets in the area who'd disappeared under suspicious circumstances. I arranged it all in lists, then attempted to make sense out of any connections.

So far, all I had was speculation, and that didn't even lead me to pursue further directions . . . yet.

I added in Nya's murder, although I had no means of connecting this particular dot to any other on my preliminary pages. At least this might get my subconscious humming and hand me any inkling of association.

When I finished, I looked it over, along with the brief I'd drafted earlier that day. By then, it was well into the afternoon, and I had to head to the airport after Hillary Dorgan.

With her husband's wealth and connections, she could have had a stretch limo pick her up, along with her extensive luggage, without a second's thought. Instead, she got the nine-year-old Beamer, Lexie, and me. At least I'd had the scratch imposed onto the Beamer by a screwdriver during my last murder investigation repaired, so it now looked pretty spiffy once more.

As Hillary and I planned via e-mail, I hung out at the nearby cell phone parking lot, waiting for her call. And when she had her bags brought out by a skycap and was awaiting her ride, she did just that.

I picked her up a few minutes later, opening the door and hanging on to Lexie while the skycap loaded the luggage in my trunk. The tip was up to me.

I slid back into the driver's seat after depositing Lexie in the back and directing her, "Stay." Then, I turned to Hillary, who was belted into my passenger's seat.

She was an attractive woman in her late forties, with short, light hair and a perfect, unwrinkled beige travel suit to complement her perfect, unwrinkled face. She wasn't smiling.

"Mrs. Dorgan . . . Hillary . . . I want you to know how sorry I am about the situation with Zibble and Saurus. The police are working on it, of course, but I'm also—"

The airport policeman motioned me to move. It was illegal to stop at the curb longer than it took to load a passenger.

"Sorry." I stopped talking so I could safely pull out into traffic.

I realized that my passenger hadn't yet said one word to me except hello. Was she about to fire me? Too late for that.

To scream and holler and call me every name imaginable for being an unreliable pet-sitter? I doubted she could think of anything I hadn't already called myself.

I was wrong.

# Chapter Nine

"POOR KENDRA," HILLARY intoned, her words perfectly pitched yet too nasal to suggest she was a trained actor. "You were a patsy." She pulled open the mirror in my Beamer's passenger-side visor and carefully checked her makeup. Her scent was strong and pungent and undoubtedly expensive—and, fortunately, light.

I watched, bewildered, from the edge of my eye as I turned the car toward Sepulveda. I glanced into the rearview mirror to ensure Lexie seemed comfy in the backseat. She sat staring, tongue hanging out as if she laughed at what had been said.

"Do you know what that means?" Hillary continued. "It was a popular term before either of us was born." I guessed she was nearly fifteen years older than me, but her statement was still most likely correct. "It's used in a lot of old movies—good old black-and-white gangster ones, with Edward G. Robinson and all."

"I understand the word," I said, knowing that my confusion seeped from my tone. "It means someone who's a mark. A chump or scapegoat. The term's familiar . . . but I don't follow why you're applying it to me."

She pulled a lipstick from her Louis Vuitton handbag and applied it liberally, then made a kissing-sound moue with her mouth to ensure the bright crimson color spread equally. She didn't act like someone heartbroken over the possible loss of prized pets, but maybe Edmund wore the animal-lover's pants of this esteemed family. I'd mostly dealt with him when hired to help look after the fauna of the house. He'd been referred to me by another, happier client.

"It's like this, Kendra." Hillary turned back toward me. "Someone is always after Edmund and me in some bizarre way to try to get money. Usually, it's solicitation for some outré charity—helping to find a cure for a dread disease like plantar warts or whatever. Now and then it's threats against us, or even our kids. Obviously, some nasty sort learned that Edmund and I were going out of town and decided to take advantage by grabbing our poor pets while our security staff was so minimal."

"You had security staff around?" I asked incredulously. If so, no one had told me to watch for them. Worse, they hadn't been diligent enough to detain me, or even question my presence on the Dorgan property.

"Of course, and they knew you'd be around, too. We instructed them to let you alone to perform your services. Apparently they took that to mean they shouldn't stop anyone who appeared to be handling pets in our absence. That's a lesson they won't forget soon. They've cooperated with the police, at least. But Edmund is interviewing new security companies by e-mail, even as we speak."

"I see," I said, certain instead that I saw nothing at all sensible in this situation. Except the road. I was about to turn off La Tijera Boulevard onto the 405 Freeway heading north. "Does that mean you have security cameras on your property? Are there possibly pictures of whoever stole Zibble and Saurus?"

"Yes, and unfortunately no. The cameras are well hidden. And they apparently aren't plentiful enough. The police reviewed their footage with our disgraced security company and found nothing at all helpful. You're in a lot of them from the day in question, though, Kendra." She aimed an almost pleasant smile in my direction, as if in an unsuccessful attempt to soften any unintentional accusation.

I hoped suddenly that the 405 would be traffic-free so I could leave this lady's company as swiftly as possible. Client or not, victim of having her pets swiped or not, I had concluded I really didn't like her much

But wishing for a traffic-free San Diego Freeway, especially near evening rush hour, was like praying for three feet of snow in greater L.A. It resembled wishing for hell to freeze over, which some people would deem an apt analogy. We were practically at a standstill from the moment the Beamer's tires touched the freeway's surface.

I determined to make the best of the situation and extract any useful info I could. "I've no doubt that people as much in the public eye as Edmund and you run into all sorts of kooks, but in this case—well, this was the third pet-napping I'm aware of over the last couple of weeks, and there might be others I haven't heard of. You might not have been singled out as targets, but the thief knew you had someone watching your pets."

"Could be," Hillary said thoughtfully. "But how would that person know if they didn't have us under observation?"

I didn't want to publicize my concern that PSCSC sitters might be the specific targets, so I said simply, "Could be they're casing pet-sitters as much as their clients."

"Maybe . . ." She drew out the word, and I heard some kind of contemplation in the extension. "Someone targeting pet-sitters? Or at least using that as an excuse? Hmmm . . ."

"Did that give you an idea who it might be?" I asked with interest. Maybe I was missing something here.

"Not at all," she said with irrefutable finality, bursting whatever bubble of hope I'd begun to inflate.

Still, one more little thing I needed to learn. "Do you happen to know Nya Barston? She's also a pet-sitter."

"No, we've never used her. Did someone steal pets on her watch, too?"

"No, but . . . well, you wouldn't have heard of it since you were out of the country, but she was killed at the home of a client of one of my counterparts." I explained the tenuous connection with Tracy Owens and hastened to say I didn't believe my friend had anything to do with harming Nya.

"How interesting!" Hillary actually did sound so interested that I darted another glance at her. Her enhanced hazel eyes were so aglow inside the Beamer that I confirmed that the interior lights were off. She explained almost immediately. "I'm a screenwriter, you know, Kendra. That's how Edmund and I got together in the first place. This whole pet-sitter situation could make a rather exciting idea for a suspense film."

Really? I didn't think so, but what did I know?

Which was exactly Hillary's next thought. "You're not in the business, are you, Kendra? I mean, you're not thinking of using this yourself? And you're not doing research by having a friend snatch the pets? Or maybe that friend who was killed—"

"Now, wait a minute. Are you accusing me?" We were going slowly enough in the parking lot that was this friggin' freeway that I had time to aim an angry glance at my passenger.

"I'm not implying anything," she said equably, "but I'd hate to see us compete over the same idea. Since it concerns my pets, I'll use it." She seemed to dare me to deny it. "And I'll do a damned wonderful job. Get one of the world's biggest box office draws to star—not mentioning any names now, you understand. Get a major studio so excited that the execs pee their pants. Edmund will produce, of course. It'll make millions!"

Can anyone say "inflated ego"? Not that I said anything aloud, other than an admittedly weak, "Sounds wonderful." But I had to draw her back to the subject. "Wouldn't it go better with a happy ending? Like, the return of your own pets first?" As well as a solution to poor Nya's demise.

"Well, of course." She sounded as aghast as if I'd suggested she couldn't add one million plus two million. Or was that one hundred million plus two hundred? "And I'm willing, within reason, to pay the ransom and get dear little Zibble and even that odd-looking Saurus back." Obviously Zibble was her darling, while the iguana was more her spouse's sweetheart. And when she said "within reason," I was certain that her reason was a heck of a lot higher than mine would be. "But one thing we have to do here first, dear."

I was afraid to ask what that one thing was. And I was hardly her dear. Even so, I ventured, "What's that, Hillary?"

The frozen look she aimed at the side of my face suggested I had erred in the subservience department by failing to call her Mrs. Dorgan, and I realized I'd never before dared to address her by name. Oh, well. It wasn't like I expected I'd lose extensive pet-sitting fees by insulting her now. She wasn't likely to hire me again for those sorts of services—unless, perhaps, she needed a pet-sitting expert as a consultant to her film. And if she did, I felt sure she'd find someone other than me to feed her exactly what she wanted to hear.

I doubted she even knew—or cared—that I was also a lawyer, so the likelihood I was shoving lucrative potential legal fees out the Beamer's side windows was equally slim.

"We need publicity."

She hadn't even started on her screenplay and she wanted to publicize it? How bizarre! How . . . Hollywood!

"Well," I said extremely slowly, "That may be a good idea, since the film concept sounds really interesting, but . . ."

"Not the film," she inserted irritably. "We need it to get the pet-napper to show his hand. Send the next ransom note or whatever. We must get Zibble and Saurus back."

This was the first sensible thing this silly showbiz woman had suggested since I'd picked her up. "Great idea! Only . . . well, the idea of publicity might upset the pet-napper even more than the fact the authorities are now involved." I explained how the ransom note had said to keep the cops out. "Of course, in the other two cases the ransom notes said not to tell *anyone*."

"See," Hillary crowed triumphantly. "Whoever this insidious person is, he or she wants publicity now. Craves it. Who, in L.A., doesn't?"

Me, I considered shouting, but I didn't. Could Hillary be right? Damned if I knew, but any damage had already been done when I called in the cops. Why not give it a try? "Does your studio have any trusted media contacts?" I asked her.

"Oxymoron, my dear—trust and media in the same sentence. I have a couple of ideas, of course, but—"

A thought crossed my crazed mind. "If you don't know of anyone specific, I have an acquaintance who's been relatively straight with me in other crime-type situations—Corina Carey."

"I've seen her on TV. Do you suppose Ms. Carey would like an immediate media interview with Mrs. Edmund Dorgan?"

"Count on it," I said and groped behind the seat for my purse. I got a lick from Lexie before I found, and extracted, my cell phone.

Call me a glutton for media punishment, but since I had gotten Corina's assistance in a murder matter in the past, her cell number was programmed into my phone.

I'D BEEN CORRECT, of course. Corina was crazy about the idea of an interview over this odd pet-napping situation—especially since Edmund Dorgan's prized animals were the nappees. Her show, National NewsShakers, was a tabloid sort, although she also joined legitimate journalism with her free-lance articles for the likes of the *L.A. Times.* My proposing an interview with someone as illustrious as Hillary Dorgan justifiably got Corina jazzed, and she promised me scads of airtime.

She and her cameraman reached the Dorgan home within minutes of our arrival, almost as if she had been hovering nearby in hopes of the opportunity.

Leaving us in the landscaped backyard near the empty iguana habitat, Hillary excused herself to change clothes, which gave Corina and me a chance to discuss the situation—not exactly alone, since the camera guy set up his equipment while the formerly discreet or missing security staff suddenly hovered as if we were expected to pilfer the eucalyptus leaves or rose petals. Even Lexie seemed sedate, sitting at my feet as if she were one really well-behaved dog.

"Anything here about Nya Barston's murder?" Corina asked. She wore a bright burgundy pantsuit that set off the darkness of her pixie-styled short hair, as well as that attentive cameraman who now appeared to be her constant accessory to any outfit, though she'd filmed her own stories in the past. Her large brown eyes that suggested some trace of Asian ancestry regarded me with interest and near-fondness, since this time I not only hadn't run her off a story that concerned me, but actually contacted her.

"Not directly. I don't think Ms. Dorgan was even aware of it until I asked her."

Hillary reappeared shortly thereafter in a silky blue blouse and even more makeup. The interview went amazingly well—

maybe because Hillary's on-camera presence as she answered Corina's questions was all anyone in Hollywood could wish for. She was low key when needed, dramatic otherwise, and teary-eyed when begging for the return of her family's beloved pets.

I stayed out of the way, although I observed with keen interest. And when the interview was over, both interviewer and interviewee sought out my assessment.

"Looked good to me," I said.

"That damned thief has got to see this," Hillary snapped. "When will the interview air, Corina?"

"We'll give it a lot of airtime in the next day or so," Corina assured the film mogul's publicity-hound wife. "With any luck, that will mean the news at five—well, it's too late for that now. How about six and ten tonight, morning, noon, evening, and night tomorrow? Plus, most other stations are copycats. You'll hear from them, too."

"How wonderful!" Hillary sounded as if she might swoon from the excitement. She came swiftly to her senses under Corina's sharp stare. "The more publicity we get, the more someone is likely to recognize Zibble and Saurus and report any sightings to the authorities. As long as the pet-napper doesn't panic and harm them . . ."

"Unlikely," Corina assured her. "Not since you made it clear that price is no object in getting your beloved pets ransomed and back home."

"Almost no object," Hillary contradicted.

"Right," Corina said.

In any event, the interview was done. But whether it would actually help in the hunt to get the missing pets home again safe and sound . . . well, that I didn't know.

And I wasn't about to wait to find out.

# Chapter Ten

BUT FIRST, OF COURSE, Lexie and I had to take care of the pets still within our sitting purview. We took a long, leisurely visit at each home, petting and playing and feeding and cleaning up as needed, plus ensuring that all dogs and cats were as safe and secure as I could be sure of.

On the way from a house in Sherman Oaks to another in Studio City, I decided to contact the PSCSC top-dog-sitter—and possible chief suspect in Nya's murder.

"Hi, Tracy," I said as soon as she answered her cell phone. "I assume that, since you're on the other end of this call, you're still free."

"But not clear of suspicion," she said with an audible sigh. "And I saw your client Hillary Dorgan on TV, Kendra. How could you let her do that? The ransom note said not to tell anyone about the pet-napping, and now the whole world knows." Her voice had grown more hysterical, and I sought for a way to sooth her.

"My note just said not to call the police," I reminded her. "And Mrs. Dorgan wanted to go public. She thinks there's more of a chance someone who's seen her beloved pets will report them to the authorities."

"Maybe." Tracy sounded a whole lot dubious. She waited for an instant, then wailed, "I don't know how you dealt with those horrible detectives, but it was only yesterday that I found poor Nya, and they already seem to be taking over my life."

"Yeah, they do that," I said empathetically.

I turned left onto Moorpark, near the Studio City branch of the L.A. Library, and aimed my Beamer toward Coldwater Canyon. Lexie sat in her seat but stretched enough to stare out the window.

Impulsively, I asked Tracy, "Are you free for dinner tonight?" Lexie swiveled to stare at me. Yes, my pup knows the word "dinner," and many synonyms that signified she might be about to eat. "Maybe we can talk more about Nya and the whole pet-napping problem," I continued without encouraging Lexie's appetite, "to see if we can figure out any further connections."

Further? So far, I'd found zilch, except for the possible relationship with PSCSC. That still left a couple dozen club members, plus multiples of that number consisting of clients, their respective families, and their friends and acquaintances. And anyone else who happened to know about the organization and bear some kind of surreptitious grudge against it or any member.

With those six degrees of separation, multiplied by infinity, I supposed we could suspect nearly anyone residing in California. The United States. The world.

At least we could probably eliminate outer space. So far, I'd absolutely no indication of any alien connections.

"I'm exhausted," Tracy said. As was I. "I've already promised Allen that he could pamper me. He's been so sweet with all of this going on. If I were him, I'd probably dump me."

"Support's a good thing when you're a potential murder suspect—not to mention when you've had some of your clients stolen." I thought about how things had been with me. I had just met Jeff around the time my own pet-sitting owner-clients started turning up dead. I hadn't wanted to believe that my luck in finding men with genuine long-term relationship potential had improved, since I'd already proven to myself that I was a flop in that department.

Jeff hadn't been in town a lot, but he'd acted like my long-distance P.I. consultant. Had that been support? Sure. Plus, there'd been my dear friend Darryl.

But I hadn't had someone who was really there for me like Allen was for Tracy. Lucky lady—that is, if you could call someone lucky who was either a multiple victim of several miserable criminal situations, or possibly a pet-napper and friend-slayer.

"I understand," I said, assuming from Tracy's response that she simply wanted to curl up in bed with a good, if nerdish, man tonight and hang on for emotional support. "We'll do it another time."

"Oh, no, I'd love to join you for dinner tonight, if you don't mind Allen coming, too," she said swiftly. "I just meant I'd want to eat early, and no place too fancy that requires dressing up or staying out too late."

We soon agreed to meet at a local Marie Callender's restaurant. Nothing better than wholesome food followed by sinful sweets to take our minds off the miseries in our lives.

Maybe.

FIRST, I TOOK Lexie home. And finally segued into the sub-servient owner of her dreams by focusing every iota of my attention on her, walking her all alone on our winding Holly-wood Hills lane, then feeding her a nice, wholesome doggy dinner.

Of course, the poor pup had to pay for my obeisance. I left her staring sadly after me in our alarm-secured apartment a little while later when I went to meet Tracy.

As I started to climb into the Beamer, I saw the front gate open and Rachel's cute blue car enter the driveway. I hurried up to greet her and saw she had Beggar along.

"How are our clients?" I immediately asked.

"They're all great!" said my youthful and exuberant em-ployee. She wore her usual uniform of jeans, this time with a red T-shirt that read, "Universal City Walk Rocks." "And, yes, Kendra, before you ask, I did double-check all the security systems. And by the way, Dana Maroni, Stromboli's owner, is coming back early—tomorrow."

I liked Dana, her sweet shepherd mix, Stromboli, and her neighbor, Maribelle Openheim, whom I'd helped recently in a pet-related situation. Maribelle had dated a skirt-chasing friend of mine, Judge Baird Roehmann—Judge Roamin' Hands. I suddenly wondered if Baird had any new petting—er, pets, in his life, since for a while he had considered adopting Maribelle's dog, Mephistopheles, but all three had changed their minds.

"Anyway, Dana called to tell us her schedule and make sure everything was okay," Rachel rambled into my train of thought, "since she got your phone message about pet-nappings, and she'd seen something about Nya Barston's murder on TV. She sounded relieved to talk to me and I reassured her Stromboli is fine."

I'd left Rachel's number in phone messages to clients where I'd put her in charge of the pets. Made more sense for her to respond about how her responsibilities were faring.

"Sounds good. Anything else I should know about?"

"No, but you ought to bring Lexie with Beggar and me when we're visiting Methuselah Manor. It's wonderful to see all those old people pep up and play with Beggar. We have such fun, and—"

"Hold it a sec," I said, putting one hand up to stop her in her eager tracks. "Methuselah Manor?"

"It's really Medicure Manor, but most people there are so old that the staff uses this little nickname . . . it's from the Bible, and it refers to a guy who lived almost forever."

"I know that. Isn't it a little insulting to the inmates?"

"No, they love it! They all call it that, too, and tease each other about living as long as that funny biblical sort—hundreds of years."

"Right. I get it."

"So will you, Kendra? Come along, I mean. It's so great to see all those old people stop staring at the walls and pet a pup. Throw a ball or Frisbee for fetch. That kind of thing."

Was this the same self-centered child who'd first appeared here a few months ago on her dad, Russ's, doorstep, after running away from her mom, Russ's ex, in Arizona? Before I'd signed a lease with him directly, Russ was the subtenant of my big house when my former lessees left, and I hadn't initially approved his having anyone else live with him but Beggar. When I'd first met Rachel, who'd sneaked inside and settled in, I hadn't exactly been thrilled about her presence. She'd made it clear she wanted Russ, a location scout for a major movie studio, to make her a star. Why else would her dad have moved to Hollywood?

She'd gone on auditions and had a smattering of success, landing teensy roles including the one in which she'd recently been filmed. Mainly, she'd shone as an apprentice pet-sitter, and I'd hired her for as many hours as she could spare once I got my law license back and couldn't devote as much time to Critter TLC, LLC, as I had before.

She was excellent at it. I now liked the kid. I also liked the job she did. This charitable donation of time and energy only made me like her more.

"Sure," I said. "One of these days, when I have time, Lexie and I will come along. It may not be for a while, though."

"Yes, I know," she said. She *should* know. I'd already hit her with some of my excuses. "You've mentioned law stuff and the pet-nappings and murder to solve. Anything else?" She sounded suddenly cynical, and I hated that I'd burst her exuberant bubble.

"I'll think of something."

Rachel's sweet, gamin face looked shocked for an instant, but then she shot me a challenging smile. "Not if I can help it. I'll count on your joining us soon. I'll be doing this for a long time. It's too much fun to stop."

I HADN'T YET done a darned thing with the list of Nya's known pet-sitting clients that Darryl had given to me. List? There were only three occupiers of that honor.

Sitting on my comfy sectional sofa, Lexie leaning on me, I called the first phone number, but no one was home. I got luckier the second time. "Hello?" said a small female voice.

"Ms. Kane? This is Kendra Ballantyne. I'm a friend of Darryl Nestler's."

"Yes?"

"I understand you've hired Nya Barston for pet-sitting now and then, right?"

"Oh, yes, poor Nya. I heard on the news."

"Had you hired her recently?"

"A couple of months ago, when I went out of town on business. She was wonderful with my dog, Gravel. I'm going to miss her."

Didn't sound like she was a supremely likely candidate for Nya's killer.

"We all are," I agreed sadly.

"I don't know what I'll do next time. My company's thinking of sending me on a trip next month, too. I'll have to ask Darryl for another referral."

"Well, I didn't call to drum up business," I said, "just to help out and ensure Nya's customers are aware of what happened. But I'm a pet-sitter, and so are a lot of other good members of the organization Nya belonged to, the Pet-Sitters Club of SoCal." At her expression of interest, I passed along appropriate info for follow-up, then accepted her condolences for all of us.

My third call went similarly. I considered attempting to add to my list of Nya's clients to call on and question, but, if these two were any example, her customers had been happy with her services and devastated by her demise. At initial blush, at least, I wasn't about to solve her murder by using this angle.


DINNER WITH TRACY and Allen might as well have been a wake. Both were quiet, and when either spoke, it was to extol the virtues of the dead Nya or of Tracy's missing little wire-haired dachshund client, Augie. She'd left her own puggle, Phoebe, at home, as I'd done with Lexie. Pup presences might have livened up our meal, but since we ate inside the restaurant, canine company would not have been sanctioned.

The dining room was busy, and I stared enviously at more than one huge and tempting wedge of pie brought to tables nearby. Well, maybe if I ordered a plain, virtuous salad, I'd be able to justify a smidgen of sin later on. I found a description of suitable rabbit food—with too much lettuce to feed fussy vegetarian iguanas—then set the menu down.

Tracy's formerly pudgy cheeks appeared even more

sunken than the last time I'd seen her. Her pale brown eyes looked haunted, and her fingers fiddled constantly with her napkin. "Oh, Kendra, I don't know how I'll survive this. I hate it all. And I don't dare even mourn my friend Nya, since everyone will assume I'm doing it because I killed her."

"Now, now, dear," Allen said. Sitting beside her, he patted her shoulder clad in its white eyelet blouse. He looked like he'd just left the insurance office where he worked, or maybe he assumed our dinner required dressing up, since he wore a brown suit. His shirt was yellow, which made his pale complexion seem sallow. His long chin was drawn, and his close-set eyes seemed abysmally sad. "There's nothing to connect you to Nya's death, honey, except that she was at the house where you were pet-sitting. She was probably up to no good. Maybe she was even the pet-napper and planned to steal another of your clients."

"But someone killed her," Tracy wailed. "With a baseball bat sort of like mine. And the pet was still there."

"Which was a good thing," I asserted firmly. "We have no reason to suspect that Nya was involved with the thefts." Even though my thoughts had gone there, too. "Maybe she even stopped another possible pet-napping." Who knew? "I'll get more information about your clients, the Ravels. And if there's anything more you can tell me about Nya, or her significant other Jerry Jefferton, or her family, especially any in L.A., that would be great."

"Then you are on the case?" Tracy's teary eyes stared at me beseechingly. "I know you've solved murders before, Kendra. If you're investigating for me, then I'm sure I'll be cleared, since you'll find the real killer."

"I've been fortunate that way before, but there are no guarantees I'll figure it out this time," I cautioned.

"I know," she said with a sigh, and looked sadly toward Allen. "But we feel a whole lot better that you're trying, don't we, honey?"

"Of course." He, too, aimed a hopeful smile at me, which caused me to echo Tracy's sigh. I didn't like their reliance on me. But I also knew they couldn't depend on the overworked and uninclined-to-dig-deeper detectives to clear Tracy if they thought they'd glommed on to a credible suspect.

Which meant I was stuck trying.

A nice young server took our orders, and I used the interruption to change the subject—sort of. I decided not to mention my earlier calls to Nya's clients. "So how's business?" I asked Tracy when the server had left.

For the first time, she issued a genuine smile. "Not bad, even with all this going on. I love it. It helps me relieve the stress."

"But, honey," Allen said almost sternly despite his smile. "All that pet-sitting. That club. They're causing your stress in the first place."

"Could be." She looked lovingly toward him. "At least I know that, if I have to give it up, I have other options."

He beamed down at her, looking so loving that I felt a flip-flop of envy. For his devotion only. Allen was so not my type. I wasn't even sure he was Tracy's type, but as long as she thought so, that was what counted.

"You sure do, honey," he said and kissed her gently.

When she came up for air, Tracy was smiling even more.

I hoped there would be a happy ending for her.


OKAY, IF YOU want to know, I did eat a piece of pie. Lemon Cream Cheese. I left some crust, though. And I didn't weigh myself when I got home. I vowed not to weigh myself for a week, and then only if I walked my pet-sitting charges a lot more vigorously.

Lexie didn't scold me. She seemed glad to see me, and I soon got ready for bed.

I got two phone calls before I dropped off to sleep that night.

"Hi, Kendra," said the first caller in his kind, sweet male voice that charmed the animals in his care. His hands did, too—although I hadn't let them stroke me much . . . not yet, at least.

It was Tom Venson, the veterinarian I'd recently met who practiced in Tarzana, in a clinic on Reseda Boulevard.

"Sorry to call so late, but had an emergency this evening to attend to. Poor dog—a standard poodle—got hit by a car and had two broken legs."

I drew in my breath, picturing a fluffy poodle lying on the road in a pool of blood, legs flayed in different directions. "Will he be all right?" I whispered.

"With me as his vet? Of course!" But then Tom's voice grew more gravelly. "It took four hours of surgery, and we almost lost him a couple of times. But right now, things look good. Now, let's talk about something else. How have you been? Have you found the missing pets?"

I'd of course told Tom about the Zibble- and Saurus-napping. Not that I expected him to run into the missing Shar-pei and iguana in Tarzana, when they'd been snatched in Sherman Oaks, but I figured he could get word out to other veterinary professionals, in case my charges somehow showed up.

"Nothing yet," I responded with a sigh. "And nothing useful so far to help the police solve Nya Barston's murder, either."

"And I'm sure, with your background, that's a big disappointment, too. Well, I'll be all ears when we get together on Saturday for dinner. We're still on, aren't we?"

"Absolutely," I said. "I'm really looking forward to it." And I was. A date with Tom Venson was the diversion I needed to get my mind off all the other things bothering me.

One of whom called almost the second after we hung up.

"Hi, Kendra," said Jeff Hubbard in a deep, husky voice that sent shivers up my spine and suggested that he was already in bed—sadly, without me. "I just called to tell you that I've cleared my schedule and set aside tomorrow afternoon to devote to following up on the local pet-nappings. Care to discuss them with me at dinner?"

I immediately counted calendar days in my head. This was still Thursday—at least for another few minutes. My date with Tom Venson was scheduled for Saturday.

I had Friday night free.

But did I dare spend it facing Jeff, over a glass of wine and whatever else was placed between us?

I'd survived my last meal with him—which had only been

the evening before. But I'd been out to dinner almost every night this week. I needed some slow-down-and-eat-home time.

"Why don't you see if you come up with anything useful first," I told him in as businesslike a tone as I could belt out.

"Oh, I will," he promised. "Save the evening for me."

# Chapter Eleven

BEFORE GOING TO bed that night, I pulled a Rachel and reviewed all the animal rescue websites she'd shown me, for which she had subsequently e-mailed me the links. I searched for a found Shar-pei or iguana, a wire-haired dachshund who answered to Augie, and Cramer, the cockapoo stolen on Wanda's watch.

Nothing.

Oh, there were lots of pets who showed up on those sites, looking scrawny and sad and crying out silently for homes. I held Lexie snuggled on my lap the whole time and still couldn't keep my eyes from tearing up.

I felt fairly certain when I was through that none was Zibble. I wasn't so certain about Saurus, since I couldn't say for sure if I'd recognize him via a tiny photo. I knew, of course, that he was both green and beige, kinda like military camouflage—nothing unusual in that. I'd pet-sat for similar-looking iguanas. And since many web-listed reptiles had names beside their pictures, I assumed they had been dumped at shelters by former owners who'd provided some personal info while disposing of their defenseless iguanas. Which made me angry as well as sad. Why take on a pet, only to kick it out?

Lexie must have sensed my miserable mood, since she rested her chin on my arm and sighed softly. "My sentiments exactly," I said.

And Augie and Cramer? I hadn't met them in person, nor did I have their photos. If I was going to continue this sad search, I had to rectify that situation.

Tomorrow.


WHEN I NEXT woke up after a fitfully snoozed night, it was Friday A.M. Once again, I took my good old time visiting my pet-sitting clients with Lexie accompanying me. I almost couldn't bear to leave any alone, not when I couldn't come up with a clue as to who stole Saurus and Zibble. I was the last of the three local pet-sitters who'd had clients taken on her watch. What if I was now the target? What if all my charges were in danger?

Paranoia? Precisely. Especially since it wasn't I, this time, who'd found a dead body at a client's and been accused of murder. But the disquiet surging through my psyche was a relentless creature.

That meant I couldn't sit by and wait for someone else to slug me with a development, whether happy or worse.

I called Tracy on my cell phone, while sitting in the Beamer outside my final pet-sitting client of the morning. I'd dressed in a middle-of-the-multicareer-road outfit, light shirt and dark slacks that were a little dressy for pet-sitting and not quite dressy enough for lawyering. But, never fear, I was prepared with a tweed sport jacket in my trunk in case I needed to meet with a law client. I also kept a change of clothes there in case this outfit met its match in a pet with dirty paws or staining slobber.

"I'm in the pet-napping investigation biz this morning," I said to Tracy when she answered the phone. "Tell me all about Augie—where he lives, who his owners are, whatever you know."

She explained again that Augie was short for Achtung, and that the pup stolen on her watch was a wire-haired dachshund. "His owner is Libby Emerich. Augie and she live in a really pretty redbrick house in Hancock Park. Their money's from selling real estate—that's what Libby does, I mean."

"When is she due back in town?" I asked.

"She's already back. She was at a conference in San Clemente with other franchisees of the big-name broker she's with when Augie was stolen. She returned right away."

"Good. Tell me how to reach her." I jotted the info in a spiral binder I'd pulled from my large purse. I'd been using that notebook, similar to my pet-sitting log, to store my info and observations on the pet-stealing and Nya-killing situations until I had time to enter the data on my usual computer lists.

Before I called Libby Emerich, I contacted Wanda Villareal and asked similar questions about the pet-napped pup she had been watching. Cockapoo Cramer's owner was named Marla Gasgill, and they lived on the southern side of Mulholland between Laurel Canyon and Coldwater—not far from my edge of the pet-sitting universe. I obtained Marla's contact info, too.

And called both pet-nap victims, since Marla had also hurried home from wherever she'd been. Wanda hadn't given that tidbit of info, which was unlikely to be important anyway.

Libby was in her office negotiating a multi-megadollar real estate deal. But when it came to finding her beloved Augie, she promised to drop it all the instant I arrived.

Marla was a Sherman Oaks dentist. She, too, would make time to see me if the visit had any chance of getting Cramer home safe, sound, and fast.

I started with Libby, whose office was on Wilshire Boulevard, not far from her Hancock Park abode. It took up the entire first floor of a three-story office building that appeared newly remodeled. Unsurprisingly, there was a lot of money to be made selling Los Angeles residential real estate.

I'd of course called my law office and let them know I'd be late popping in—again. Thank heavens for Borden and his laid-back style of practicing law.

Libby was a tall, slender lady in a designer-look wraparound silky dress that clung to her every slight curve. Her hair was wraparound, too—ash blond, and sleeked into a tall upsweep around her head. The office I was shown into by an eager sales underling was as sleek as its owner, occupied by a bare-bones modern metal desk, a computer in a cabinet all its own, and photos all over the walls of homes that Libby must have helped to sell—all huge and obviously expensive.

Libby was on the phone as I walked in, Lexie leashed beside me. She looked at my pup, then me, and hurriedly hung up. "You must be Kendra," she said in a modulated yet excited voice. Her makeup was as flawless as any I'd seen in Hollywood, and her face was as lovely as any star's. It was a face I had seen before, on real estate sales posters on open house signs and bus benches. "Please sit down." She pointed toward an uncomfortably modern-looking chair with curves and angles like the other furniture, but when I complied and sat, its twists hit me in surprisingly comfy spots. Lexie leaped up onto my lap. "You're here to help me find Augie." Not quite to my surprise, this obviously poised lady burst into tears.

We chatted for a good half hour while she ignored her constantly buzzing phone. Augie was apparently the love of her life, who'd stuck by her side through a succession of lackluster lovers. She would do anything to recover her dear dog.

Lexie, ever the empathetic pup, got off my lap and begged to be lifted onto Libby's. The broker bent down and complied, snuggling my loving dog while we continued to converse.

"I haven't heard anything after the ransom note, if you can call it that," Libby said with extreme sadness equally reflected by the red moistness of her gray eyes and the unpoised dip of her head as she rubbed her cheek against Lexie. "It didn't ask for money or anything, and it didn't say how else I could get Augie back." Her formerly flawless makeup would undoubtedly have to be reapplied before she showed any more houses that day. Her complexion wasn't quite as wrinkle-free as it had formerly appeared, and its pallor also hadn't been there previously.

At my request, she showed me a photocopy of said ransom note. It resembled the one left at the Dorgans regarding Zibble and Saurus, but as Tracy had told me, this one said to tell no one at all, not just the cops.

"The police have the original," Libby told me, "although they apparently can't get fingerprints off it or any other helpful clue, not even what computer generated or printed it."

"Do you know of anyone who'd pet-nap Augie to harm you?"

"I've beat out some other brokers in sales lately," she said. "And I've dumped several men. I'll give you their information like I did with the police, but I don't see any of them resorting to stealing Augie, let alone serial pet-napping. That's what's happening, isn't it? Other people have had pets taken as well?"

I agreed this was so but took her proffered info anyway, jotting names into my notebook. I'd pass it along to Althea and Jeff, just in case. None of the names looked familiar. But you never knew when an iota of info might lead to something useful. I also obtained a photocopy of the photocopy of the ransom note.

I thanked the broker, got Lexie back as well as Libby's promise to let me know if she heard anything from the pet-napper—even if the cops told her to keep it quiet—and likewise promised to let her know if I learned anything potentially useful in getting her adored Augie home.

Next, Lexie and I headed back over the hill to Sherman Oaks. At Dr. Marla Gasgill's dental office, I wasn't lucky enough to be shown in first thing. Nor was I permitted, by her aghast staff, to bring Lexie inside—against state health codes or dental hypocritical oaths or some such.

"Please let Dr. Gasgill know I'll be outside on the street waiting for her," I said impatiently. Irritably. But Lexie was happy, since that gave us time for a walk.

We didn't go far before I saw a woman in a white lab coat hustle outside the office and start scanning the sidewalk. We hurried toward her. "Dr. Gasgill?" I inquired.

She was short, her black hair was curly, and she wore tortoiseshell-rimmed glasses behind which close-set blue eyes squinted. "You must be Ms. Ballantyne."

I nodded. "Kendra."

"Call me Marla. Do you have any word about Cramer?"

"I was going to ask you the same thing."

Her narrow shoulders slumped, making me wonder if her unbuttoned lab jacket, whose open front revealed an orange T-shirt and brown denim slacks, would slide right off.

She knew no more than Libby Emerich did about her missing dog. Ignoring what her staff had insisted on, she invited Lexie and me inside, where she took me into her smaller, more mundane office and also allowed me to review a copy of her ransom note. Again, I made notes on anyone she might consider, if not an enemy, then less than a friend, but no name meshed with any others I'd collected. I added another photocopy of a ransom note to my collection, and we likewise traded commitments to keep in touch regarding the pet-napping. Then, Lexie and I left.

I felt drained after this day of emotional meetings that amounted to apparently nothing helpful.

"Let's go to the office," I told my tired pup. "Maybe I can at least accomplish something there."

LEXIE AND I settled into my small but familiar law office, which I'd helped to make all mine some months ago, both in furnishings and degree of disorganization. Then I called Althea. "Thanks again for all the info you gave to Jeff for me," I began.

"That was two days ago," Althea interrupted, "and you've already thanked me. Who else do you want me to check out?"

"I'm pretty transparent, aren't I?" I said with a quasi-embarrassed laugh.

"Sure are. But my boss seems happy you're asking me all these questions. The guy really wants back in your good graces, Kendra." I heard the question in my buddy Althea's tone.

"I don't . . . I mean, he isn't . . . Oh, hell, Althea. I'm just so confused I don't know what the devil I'm doing around him."

Should I have admitted that? Probably not to someone who was clearly on Jeff's side. I waited for her sales pitch on how Jeff was totally reformed now that his ex-wife had exited his life. How he was miserable without me. How he really wanted me, and I was hurting him so much by my ambivalence. How—

"Well, you'd better figure it out soon, Kendra, or you'll lose him. Now, give me the new list of names and their relationship to the situation."

I swallowed whatever else I was going to say and complied with Althea's demand. I pulled my notebook from my large purse and dictated the pertinent names I'd collected from Libby and Marla. I thanked Althea yet again, including in advance for the info she was about to seek for me.

And when I hung up, I felt so confused I wanted to puke.

Was I going to meet Jeff for dinner that night, as he'd insisted?

More important, what would I do about him in the long run?

.  .  .

As it turned out, the decision about dinner was made for me without my having to make any determination.

Later that afternoon, while I worked on arguments about the weimaraner's custodianship for the meeting scheduled for after the weekend, my cell phone sang from somewhere inside my desk.

It brought Lexie, who'd been asleep on the Berber rug by my chair, to attention.

I yanked open the drawer and tugged out my big bag. I rummaged inside quickly till I came across my phone.

And blinked. I'd programmed the Dorgans' number into my address book, and that was who appeared to be calling.

"Hello?" I said quizzically, pretending no clue at all who was there.

Sure enough, it was Hillary.

"Kendra? I got another one."

I was immediately on board, sitting up straight and clutching the phone in two trembling hands. "Ransom note?"

"Yeah. It tells me how much and where, to get Zibble and Saurus back. I'm not to call the cops again, but it didn't mention you or anyone else. You want to come along tonight while I ransom my pets?"

"I'll be at your house in half an hour."

# Chapter Twelve

"THAT'S A LOT of cash to come up with in such a short time," I told Hillary a while later.

I had taken the entire half hour I'd promised, since I'd brought Lexie home and secured her inside before dashing to the Dorgans. Now, Hillary and I stood in her restaurant-size, amazingly equipped kitchen, counting twenty-dollar bills.

"ATMs work wonders," she said.

Sure, but that presupposed the cash was there to withdraw in the first place. Plus, "Aren't there limits on how much you can take out at a time?"

"Oh, we've gotten them to waive that. Every once in a while, we've needed cash quick to deal with a shoot, so we've gotten advance permission to take any amount we wish."

Even with a limitless bank account, who could they pay in cash and not get in trouble with Uncle Sam? Well, I might ponder the question, but the answer wasn't my problem.

It was nearly eight at night. Though Hillary wasn't dressed as chicly as she'd been for travel when I'd last seen her, she still managed to appear as though her embroidered denim blouse and matching jeans were designer wear. Her short, light brown hair hadn't a strand out of place, and her makeup might well have been newly plastered on. Apparently, it was de rigueur for fashionable women at the acme of the film industry to be at their lovely best while ransoming their pets.

We were packing the amount in question into a black nylon duffle bag. What amount? Fifty thousand dollars. Most people would have trouble paying that without blinking for their dearest human friend or relation. Hillary hadn't even questioned coming up with that amount for the family dog and iguana.

Zibble was a prime Shar-pei from a show dog family and was sometimes called upon to sire other Shar-pei pups, but he'd have to father a lot of expensive scions to reach a total worth of half the ransom. And I had no idea at all what Saurus could do to earn the other half.

How had the ransom note been delivered? Via the good ol' U.S. postal system. Hillary hadn't been at home when the mail arrived, so she had only just found the plain white envelope with the computer-generated address and ordinary stamp when she returned from a shopping expedition. She had watched enough TV to know to stick both note and envelope into small plastic bags once she realized what they were. The envelope was probably smeared already with fingerprints from everyone down the line in the post office, so the sender's prints would never be ID'd from it. The note itself, though? Well, it was worth a shot.

When we could call the police and pass it along.

So far, Hillary had obeyed the latest directive and called no one official, only me.

And I? Well, I hadn't much admired the lackluster detectives assigned to this pet-napping. I'd have considered calling Ned Noralles, even though we rubbed each other wrong in homicide investigations, but I chose to honor Hillary's wish to obey the command and keep the cops out.

But private cops? P.I.s were not expressly excluded. And so I had called Jeff.

We wouldn't do dinner tonight, but at least we might see each other. Later.

Right now, I intended to accompany Hillary to the ransom drop spot, a garbage Dumpster behind an abandoned restaurant on Victory Boulevard.

Victory? Areas of the avenue more resembled a boulevard of defeat, in relatively seedy neighborhoods, but the street tended to be busy. Wouldn't there be a danger of someone rooting in the trash there and absconding with the ransom before the pet-napper could retrieve it?

Hell, yes, but what else could Hillary do? The note said to leave, with the money, a cell phone number where the thief could text-message the whereabouts of the pets, after the money was in that slimy rat's possession. There wasn't any way for Hillary to communicate she'd left the package, as instructed. If it happened not to be waiting for the Zibble and Saurus snatcher, the poor pets might yet become toast.

Assuming they weren't already. Trust a thief's integrity? Not hardly.

"Ready, Kendra?" Hillary asked, zipping the duffle closed.

"As ready as I'll ever be. Want me to drive?"

"In the car you picked me up in at the airport?" Her aghast glare suggested she would rather walk, even though the location had to be five miles away. "No, I'll drive."

There was nothing wrong with my poor Beamer since its gouge had been repaired, except that it was growing old like the rest of us. However, I had to drool a bit and feel somewhat happy I wasn't driving when I saw Hillary's wheels: a gorgeous Porsche 911 Carrera, brilliant yellow.

As we drove out through the massive wrought-iron gate, I leaned back in the comfy leather seat and asked, "Are your security guys primed to leave us alone?"

"Yes," said the wealthy woman I'd never imagined would act as my chauffeur, even for an evening. "And that P.I. you said you were going to call in?"

"I called him when you were in the bathroom. He'll stake out the garbage dump and see who roots around there."

"He won't stop whoever it is, will he?" Hillary's voice rasped with emotion. "If he's seen, I'll never get Saurus and Zibble back."

"He'll take pictures using telephoto lenses, hopefully of both the snatcher and getaway car. Once the pets are safely home, he'll call the cops and give them copies of the photos so they can take over and apprehend the suspect."

"You sound like a cop."

"Heaven forbid," I said. "But I've been around them too much lately."

We arrived at the building—what was left of it—in about ten minutes. It had obviously been gutted by fire, maybe recently. Though there were streetlights around, and other businesses that were probably open and operational during the day, this block was basically black on both sides of the street.

We nevertheless exited the car, both walking slowly, gingerly, and nervously. This wasn't exactly a locale where two ladies wanted to be alone at night, even though it was not extremely late. At least we saw no one else around—like gang members intent on fencing stolen stuff or worse, or druggies ready to jump anyone available and steal money for their next fix. It was that kind of a lovely place.

There was a small alley behind, and we immediately picked out the Dumpster designated for the drop. Hillary had been carrying the bag, and I pulled up the bin's squealing metal top.

"Here goes," she said, and heaved the duffle inside.

I looked around, hoping to see Jeff, but if I'd seen him that would mean the pet-napper would, too, when he or she came to collect.

I only hoped there were sufficient lights and angles for Jeff to get good photos.

And then Hillary and I were gone.

So was the money, it turned out a while later.

That's what I learned around midnight when Jeff called.

Hillary and I sat in her spacious living room on a beautiful red velvet-upholstered sofa with carved back and arms that matched the two smaller seats facing it. On the parquet floor was a patterned area rug below an exquisite coffee table. The fireplace that took up one wall was surrounded by warm wood paneling and had a collection of artistic dishes arranged on the mantel. Then there were those old, original, and lovely paintings on the walls.

All gorgeous. All expensive. Of course.

So was the wine we sipped so nervously that I nearly dropped my cell phone when it began to sing. Thank heavens, it was Jeff. We'd been waiting for his call.

"Damnedest thing, Kendra." His tone suggested unabated rage. "I saw Hillary and you arrive and settled myself at the back of one of the buildings that was unoccupied at that hour."

"I won't ask how you got in," I said.

"Good thing. Anyhow, there I was, lying low and unobservable, taking post-drop photos without flashes, when a truck rumbled down the alley. I figured it had been sent to tow the trash bin and everything in it, so I took its picture including its license plate, photos of the driver in the cab, everything. But it didn't stop, just came through the alley and went on. The bin was still there, seemingly untouched."

"Seemingly?"

"Yeah. I waited for a while longer, and when no one else came, I carefully went outside and took a peek. There wasn't anything inside the Dumpster anymore. It hadn't held garbage before and it still didn't. No black bag, either."

"What? How—?" I began.

"Wish I knew," he interrupted. "I have Buzz Dulear checking on the company that owns the truck. He called but of course no one answers the phone at this hour. What do you want to bet they were just paid to take a drive tonight?"

"Not fifty thousand dollars," I said acerbically. "You gonna find it?"

"More important, have you heard anything about where the animals might be?"

I'd been holding my cell phone up between Hillary and me so she could hear Jeff, too. She lifted her own phone, which she'd been gripping in her left hand, and looked at it.

"Nothing," she said sadly.

"I'll call you as soon as we hear something," I assured Jeff, and hung up. And waited.

And waited.

My eyelids grew so heavy that they started to feel like the Dumpster's metal lid. After a while, I didn't even try to keep them open. I'd stay awake, of course, since I had to. Surely, the thief would contact Hillary, now that he had his money.

Sure . . .

I must have jumped three feet as a ding-dong sound reverberated through the room. Those weighty eyelids of mine suddenly lost their heft and popped open.

Hillary still sat on the sofa where I'd last seen her, her cell phone still in her hand. "It's vibrating, Kendra," she gasped groggily. "I think I have a text message."

Only then did I notice that the lights in the room now included a dim glow from outside the windows. Dawn? Had I actually slept, with everything that was going on?

"There *is* a text message," Hillary said, staring at her phone. "But damned if I know what it says."

"Let me try." I held out my hand and stared at the medley of letters:

"anmls at pcnc area seplvda bsn wildlife rsrv off woodley rt nw cm fst"

OKAY, SO THE note took a little translating, as many text messages do. My interpretation? "Animals at picnic area Sepulveda Basin Wildlife Reserve off Woodley right now. Come fast."

The result? Around twenty minutes after I'd understood what it said, I sped my Beamer along Woodley Avenue toward the turnoff for the Sepulveda Basin Wildlife Reserve. Hillary sat beside me as my passenger.

Why not let her chauffeur me some more in her prime Porsche? Because our intent was to retrieve two good-size pets. They would fit in the back of my Beamer. Not so in Hillary's gorgeous sports car.

Besides, though not a Porsche, my Beamer had power when it chose to. Like now. Fortunately, at this hour, I didn't see any cops.

I didn't see Jeff, either, though I'd called him immediately to inform him of what we'd heard. I wasn't sure where he'd spent the night, but his hazy voice had suggested I'd awakened him, too. He had promised to head there immediately, and since his home was closer than Hillary's I figured he might have gotten here faster.

"Do you know where the picnic area is?" Hillary asked me for the umpteenth time.

"No," I responded, still surprisingly patient, "but hopefully we'll figure that out when we get there." Or maybe my patience wasn't so amazing after all. I was a whole lot worried about whether we were off on a wild Shar-pei chase. Or iguana escapade. Sure, the thief had instructed us to wait for a text message, but even now, hours after the ransom was paid, there was no guarantee he or she would come through with the pets.

Or, if Zibble and Saurus happened to be there, that they'd be happy and healthy after several days in someone else's care. Or lack thereof.

Not too surprising, I was wearing the same clothes as yesterday. My light shirt and dark slacks were a little wrinkled but were fortunately of materials that weathered most wearing well. I'd left my tweed jacket in the Beamer's trunk. No need to look especially lawyerly to rescue a couple of pets.

Hillary might have objected, though, had I suggested to her that anything less than superb fashion was essential for our outing. Despite my urging that we leave immediately, she had taken a few minutes to don a white deep-dipping knit shirt decorated with rows of pseudojewels over brown slacks that suggested a gold cast in certain light. And of course the pants had a matching jacket, although she had carelessly cast it onto the Beamer's floor by her feet.

Fashionable, *sí*. Perky Hollywood producer's wife at this hour, no. She looked as exhausted as I felt, with dark circles under her eyes that she had made a gallant effort to disguise with lots of makeup.

And all this, surprisingly, had been accomplished in less than ten minutes.

We reached the road designated as the way to the Sepulveda Basin Wildlife Reserve and the Japanese Garden and made a right turn. Several driveways converged there, and the signage didn't exactly sing out which way to go. I nevertheless followed the lower road to the right, since it appeared to be the one we wanted. There were also signs to cricket fields—the game, I assumed, and not the bugs even though this was a wildlife area. Plus, the place was surrounded by golf courses. A pretty, parklike oasis, right in the middle of the San Fernando Valley? Absolutely. I'd even hiked here and birdwatched now and then, when I'd had a few spare hours.

But that had been a while back. I had no idea where the picnic area might be. Still, I soon located a likely spot. "There," I said excitedly, pointing to a place just beyond an empty parking lot. "That looks like picnic benches."

And it was. We parked next to a couple of port-a-potties at the edge of the paved parking and exited the Beamer. In front of us, in the dim light of the still-early day, was a small expanse of reddish concrete tables, all numbered and in rows, and unoccupied, as the parking lot had been. Guess it was too early for picnicking, although one reason we'd hurried here—in addition to the instruction to come fast—was the fear that early A.M. joggers and bikers might come upon the missing pets first and abscond with them.

So far, we'd only seen a few exercise freaks, and they'd run or power walked on tracks inside the fencing along the roadway as we'd approached. None were here—not yet, at least.

Here and there in the picnic area were flimsy metal grills for people who planned to barbecue. The ground was sandy, though surrounding areas contained lush green lawns. Above were huge firs, interspersed with palms that apparently hadn't been trimmed in ages, their trunks covered with browned, dipping fronds.

Beyond was a small kiddy playground, with swings and slides of colorful plastic.

But we weren't here to picnic or barbecue or play like kids.

Where were Zibble and Saurus?

"Zibble?" I called out. I didn't imagine Saurus would answer, but a Shar-pei just might.

I heard a bark from somewhere ahead.

"There!" Hillary shouted excitedly and pointed past the nearest tables to somewhere around the farthest.

I ran behind her, ducking through the concrete obstacle course of tables until we reached them.

Zibble was tied to a table. Saurus was inside a metal dog crate.

By the time we reached them, Zibble was leaping and whining in a canine frenzy of excitement. Hillary knelt, untied his leash, and held out her arms. Her Shar-pei leaped into them and showered her with slobbery kisses from his huge, sagging lips.

But Saurus. The iguana wasn't leaping or even moving, not that I could see.

This wasn't the kind of habitat that would allow a reptile to thrive.

Had he failed to survive?

Were we too late to save him?

Only then did I see another car cruising toward us from the opposite direction—a big black Cadillac Escalade.

Jeff's.

Had he nabbed the pet-napper?

# Chapter Thirteen

AND WHEN THE heck was I going to stop asking questions and do something useful?

I waved toward Jeff, then ducked down on the ground to check on Saurus. I opened the crate and reached inside, half expecting him to snap at me, as iguanas were wont to do.

He didn't move.

I felt his scaly skin. It was cold—but, then, he was a cold-blooded creature.

He seemed to be crouching on a bunch of rags. Was that an okay substrate—or surface—for him, even temporarily?

At least he wasn't listing sideways or, worse, lying on his side. And his eyes appeared to be open. Even the one on top—his third eye that was supposed to be a light sensor for iguana safety, although it didn't actually see.

But I was far from an expert.

And, thank heavens, I happened to know someone who was.

"Hold on, Hillary," I said. If we weren't on a first name basis by now, tough. I yanked my cell phone from the ubiquitous bag I'd unthinkingly slung over my shoulder and called Jeff. "Hi, don't bother stopping. The animals are here, but we need to get them to a vet right away. I don't suppose you saw some-one lurking to see who retrieved them, did you?"

"No, damn it," he said. He had stopped in the lot anyway and spoke to me as he approached. He slipped his phone closed as he reached us. Which turned out to be a good thing, since Hillary had her hands full with the eager Zibble and was of no assistance at all in lifting Saurus's makeshift enclosure.

"Hi," I said. "Please help." I gestured toward the cage.

"Is he alive?" Jeff asked dubiously.

"Yes, but he sure doesn't look healthy. Of course, I'm not certain I can tell the difference between a healthy iguana and one who's not well. That's why we're heading to the vet."

He grabbed one end of the crate and I latched onto the other. Together, with Hillary and Zibble bringing up the rear, we maneuvered around picnic tables and into the parking lot, where Jeff and I shoved the cage onto the Beamer's backseat.

"Can you tell me in ten words or less if you saw anything at all helpful this morning?" I asked. The hunky P.I. looked more exhausted than I had ever seen him. And that included after some wild, wanton, and exhausting nights of wonderful sex . . .

*Don't go there, Kendra*, I shouted silently to myself.

Especially since I was about to pay a visit to the other man in my life, who just happened to be the best veterinarian I'd ever met.

"Unfortunately, no. I figured you two would go after the animals, so I cruised around looking for anyone suspicious. A couple of cars parked, and people got out and started jogging. Others drove by, and I jotted down license numbers that I'll get Althea to run, although I can't say I noted a genuine sus-pect."

"That's more than ten words," Hillary complained from the front seat, where she had planted herself. Zibble was in the back on the far side from Saurus's cage. They were ready to go. And even in the growing daylight, I couldn't quite tell the iguana's condition.

Time for a visit to the vet. *Past* time, probably.

"Thanks for trying, Jeff," I said, and I hurried into the driv-er's seat to head out of the park and toward Tarzana.

DR. THOMAS VENSON'S veterinary clinic was along Reseda Boulevard. It was a squat gray building, drab for a place where death-defying acts like saving animals' lives were done.

The time was nearing seven o'clock, and I'd called Tom on his cell phone. He promised to be present when we arrived, and when I pulled the Beamer into the small parking lot behind the clinic I saw his car, a beige Ford Escape—less ostentatious than Jeff's Cadillac Escalade, but big enough to transport most of his patients of the nonhuman persuasion.

I knocked on the back door and it immediately opened, as if Tom had been standing there, waiting. "Hi, Kendra," he said, but his smile aimed over my shoulder as his brown eyes scanned the parking lot for where I'd left his new patients. He obviously gave a damn, a damned good quality in a vet.

"They're in my Beamer with their owner, Hillary," I told him. "The Shar-pei looks okay and can walk in on his own four paws, but I'm more concerned about the iguana. He's been out of his nice, safe reptile habitat for a few days, and—"

I'd started talking to Tom's back. And a nice back it was, clad in his usual white lab jacket.

He was of ordinary height for a guy, less than six feet. I'd noticed before how long and lean his legs were in the jeans he wore under his lab jacket. Now, he used them to stride quickly through the parking lot.

I let Hillary lead Zibble toward the building on his leash, and again took an end of the crate in which Saurus lolled. With Tom's assistance, I toted it out of the back of the Beamer.

"Let's put it down a second," he said. When we did, I watched him give Saurus a once-over. Tom was a nice-looking guy, not extraordinary, but I adored his attitude. He cared—about people, as well as his patients. He treated owners like the parents they were, understanding their emotionalism about their pets' medical problems. "Okay, let's get him inside." Tom's tone suggested concern. So did the way his dark eyebrows knit below the widow's peak of his equally deep brown hair.

I again took the front end of the cage and let him bring up the rear, which gave him the better view of the possibly suffering iguana. Hillary held open the clinic's back door while stopping Zibble from tripping us with his leash. They followed Tom, Saurus, and me inside.

"Let me get one of my assistants," Tom said. We lowered the crate, and he hurried down the hall.

"He looks worried." Hillary's immaculately made-up face reflected a matching emotion.

"Yeah," I agreed, "but Saurus is in good hands." Or he would be when out of the cage and in the care of Tom and his capable staff.

Which vet plus two assistants clad in blue lab jackets appeared at the end of the hall and rushed toward us. As if practiced in emergency drills, the aides, one male and one female, lifted the crate and hurried away with it hanging between them, its progress even and steady so as not to further disturb the occupant.

Tom shot me a short, distracted smile. "I'll examine him, then come and talk with you as soon as I can."

"What about Zibble?" Hillary asked anxiously.

Tom glanced at the watch on his wrist. "It's nearly seven. One of the other vets will arrive at any moment, and I'll leave word at the front that Zibble's to get the first exam. But judging by his behavior"—that same Shar-pei was tugging at his leash once more, apparently interested in a small storeroom to our side where shelves were lined with prescription pet food—"I'd guess he's okay. But of course we'll need to confirm that."

"Of course," Hillary echoed toward Tom's disappearing rear.

In seconds, the three of us including Zibble were left alone in the hallway. I'd been here before several times, the first thanks to a dispute between one of my clients and Tom Venson a few months ago. I'd helped them work it out well, fortunately. I'd eventually had more empathy with Tom than with my own client, although I'd of course represented her with utmost lawyerly care.

"Let's sit down," I suggested to Hillary and led Zibble and her into the waiting room. It was small, and I'd never before seen it so empty. That could be because the clinic wasn't officially open yet. Seats lined three sides, and the fourth contained doors to the outside and into the inner sanctum. Between them was an opening into a room where the reception staff generally sat. The color scheme consisted largely of restful blues, and the aroma was the clinic's usual antiseptic smell.

Hillary sat along the wall closest to the door. I joined her, but knelt on the floor next to Zibble. The middle-size, many-pleated pup nuzzled up to me. Actually, his wrinkles and folds were mostly around his face and front, rather than on the rest of his thin body that was covered in light brown short fur. When I petted his head, he gave me a doggy kiss with his dark tongue—strange in shade for most dogs, but characteristic of this breed and a few others.

"How are you, Zib?" I asked. He wagged the thin tail curled over his back. "Were you treated okay?" He didn't say otherwise. In fact, he didn't say anything at all, a situation I often found frustrating with my pet clients and even my own Lexie. I wished we had some mutual shared language. Right now, I'd have given a lot to have Zibble provide a detailed description of his pet-napping and the perpetrator.

An African American lady in a white lab coat that resembled Tom's entered from the door to the side of the reception desk. "Hi, I'm Dr. Savitt. Dr. Venson gave me a quick rundown on what happened, and I'd like to examine your dog."

She looked at me, probably since I still sat on the floor with Zibble. I quickly set the apparent misunderstanding to right. "I love this guy, but he belongs to Ms. Dorgan."

I nodded toward Hillary, who remained on a waiting room chair. She rose regally and sent a smile toward the lady vet. "Please make sure Zibble is all right, Doctor."

"You can come into the exam room," she said. She reached for Zibble's leash, and Hillary handed it over.

I started to follow, but Hillary shot me a stay-there stare. It was her prerogative as Zibble's mistress, but her pulling rank that way nevertheless rankled.

I took a seat. There I was, all alone in the waiting room, fretting about both returned animals.

"Can I help you?" asked a voice that at first seemed disembodied, till I realized someone at last occupied the reception desk over the half wall at the far side of the room.

I walked over. I'd seen the young lady here before. Her nametag said she was Edith, which sounded more appropriate for a much older person than this twenty-something clad in a blue lab jacket like the other assistants. Her eyes were hazel

and surrounded by long brown lashes that belied the natural-
ness of her softly pale hair. They regarded me expectantly.

"I'm a . . . friend of Dr. Venson's. I helped to bring in some
animals who'd been pet-napped to make sure they were okay,
and—"

Oops! Some officer of the court I was. And amateur P.I.
and concerned citizen and member of the Pet-Sitters Club of
SoCal. I'd neglected to notify the authorities that we had these
two stolen animals back in our care and custody.

"Anyhow," I concluded hurriedly, "please let me know
when Dr. Venson and Dr. Savitt know how Zibble and Saurus
are doing."

Without explaining which animal was who, I turned from
her and reached into the big bag I'd tossed over my shoulder
by habit as I'd exited the Beamer. Extracting my cell phone, I
called Detective Domenic Flagsmith. He answered immediately.

"Guess what!" I said with complete chipperness. "We have
the Dorgan animals back."

"Really?" Amazing how much dubiousness can roll
through a telephone connection.

"Yes. Ms. Dorgan paid the ransom, and—"

"What ransom?" I'd gotten the cop's attention with that.
"Where are you, Ms. Ballantyne?"

I sighed but provided the info he requested.

"Don't leave. We'll be there as soon as possible."

Which I figured, in cop-speak, meant sometime today.
Maybe.


BY THE TIME I got off the phone with Ned Noralles—yes, I
called him, too, to treat him to my side of this story—other
people and pets had begun storming the waiting room.

I considered handing out some of my pet-sitter business
cards but decided that would be too crass. Besides, I had all
the referrals Rachel and I could handle from Darryl and from
former and existing contented customers.

Which just might disappear now that I'd initiated a reputation for having beloved pets napped from under my nose . . .

"Kendra?" called a voice from the inner clinic doorway. Tom stood there grinning broadly, thank the powers that be. I took the smile to mean that Saurus was sufficiently okay to assume he'd survive this ordeal.

Even so, I hurried to Tom's side. "How's—"

"Saurus? He was dehydrated and probably hadn't been in a warm enough environment for the last couple of days, but I think he'll be okay."

"Wonderful! Can I see him? Have you checked Dr. Savitt about Zibble?"

"Yes, and yes. Zibble will be fine, too. You can see both of them."

He accompanied me along the hall first into a small room that appeared to be a surgery area, only some shelves lined the walls. On them were a variety of tanks, perhaps where ill fish and lizards and other nonmammal patients could reside while recuperating. On the first shelf, in a fairly large enclosure beneath a light of bright intensity, sat the beige and green iguana I'd come to know and like.

He was motionless, but when I looked inside he seemed to give me one of his inscrutable, long-mouthed smiles. He took a few steps along the glass and started to turn around.

Smiling all the while.

"He looks so much better already!" I exclaimed, then settled down. "Assuming I can tell the difference between an ill iguana and a well one."

Tom put an arm around my shoulder and squeezed. I liked the feeling. I also liked his encouragement when he said, "You've got good instincts when it comes to animals, Kendra. I've seen that a lot already."

"Thanks, Tom." I looked up at him and saw a kiss coming, judging by the way his deep brown eyes suddenly smoldered.

Hey, why not? I gave into the urge—and a good thing, too. We'd kissed briefly before, but this one was deep and hot and a hell of a lot of fun.

And I liked being tight against his body. He was more moderate in height than my most usual squeeze lately, and perhaps not as buff, but he was hard in the right places. *All* of them.

Eventually, I pulled back. I was certain my grin up at him was loony and logy.

"You're welcome," he whispered huskily, then added, "Are we still on for tonight?"

Tonight? I did a mental calculation, no easy feat considering the current muzziness of my mind. Oh, yes, it was finally Saturday. I still had pet-sitting clients to tend, and might even drop in at the law office, but it wasn't a regular legal workday.

And Tom and I had planned a date for this evening.

"Sure," I said. "I'll be delighted to go out with you tonight."

"Don't count on it, Kendra," boomed a voice from the door. I swiveled fast to see Ned Noralles glaring at me. "You might be in jail tonight for obstruction of justice."

# Chapter Fourteen

WHAT WAS WORSE than a homicide detective glaring daggers from a veterinary clinic doorway and making terrible threats? *Three* detectives, all obviously full of ire.

No, Ned hadn't arrived alone. Hovering behind him, and apparently itching to be allowed into the room to arrest me, were the two detectives first assigned to the Dorgan pet-napping: Mabel Madero and Domenic Flagsmith. Both appeared to have arrived after color-coordinating with Ned. Or maybe it was a requirement this week that all LAPD detectives wear dark suits with white shirts and blue ties. Even women, although the blue scarf around Mabel Madero's scrawny neck was a little fuller and lighter in shade than the male neckties.

"Who are you?" Tom asked. "And what are you doing here? This is a private area." He might not have known who these people were, but he clearly sensed the immediate animosity. He stepped in front of me, as if for my protection.

A *private* area? Because of our kiss, or because Saurus and other nonmammals were housed here and could be contaminated by cooties from irritable cops?

"I don't suppose you've solved the burglary from the Dorgan home, have you, Kendra?" Ned continued, his arms folded so tightly against his chest that I suspected he held them there to save himself from sailing around Tom and strangling me. "I mean, you do that so often with homicides. Do you have a suspect picked out, and have you obtained sufficient evidence to be used in court to convict him or her?"

I was uncertain whether the snort from over his shoulder came from the him or the her who glared from behind Ned.

"Kendra recovered the animal victims," Tom said from in front of me. "She brought them here so I could make sure they were all right. That's not obstruction of justice. That's saving lives."

Detective Madero elbowed her way past the obstruction of Ned. Didn't the woman ever eat? She looked so thin it was painful. And cops were supposed to be trained in self-defense stuff, weren't they? I didn't observe even a hint of what could be muscle beneath her somber black suit.

"How can we be certain she didn't steal them in the first place?" she demanded, her wrath so directed at Tom that I had an urge to step in front to protect *him*.

Instead, he held out a hand as a signal to me to stay still. Not that I had to obey, but I didn't move—for the moment. Meantime, Tom didn't budge an inch as he faced this woman and prevented her from drawing closer to me. Sweet man.

"It's awfully convenient that they were stolen when she was their caretaker," Madero continued, "and now she's returned them."

"Isn't it interesting," I said to no one in particular, "that cops who attempt to cover up their own ineptitude are prone to accuse others of crimes without a shred of evidence?"

Ned's arms uncrossed in time to block Mabel's charge toward me. Good thing. Otherwise, I might have been taken into custody for breach of California Penal Code, Section 0.00: telling an ill-tempered officer the insulting truth. After being roughed up a bit by that same skinny hen of a cop.

And who knew how the glass animal enclosures along the wall might fare in a female fistfight?

"Let's not make accusations . . . for now." This was the soft voice of reason from the third detective in the compact room, Domenic Flagsmith. He had struck me before, with his thick, black-rimmed glasses and calmer attitude, of being much more reasonable than his rash lady partner. Now, he bolstered that initial impression. Of course, this could just be an example of a habitual good cop–bad cop routine.

"Great idea," said Tom. "Can I get you all some soft drinks? Coffee—although I think there's enough energy in this room without adding more caffeine hype. There's also dog fitness water in the back room, if you'd rather have some of that."

"What I'd rather do," stormed Detective Madero softly, "is interrogate Ms. Ballantyne to find out exactly how she located the missing animals and whether there's any evidence left to indicate who stole them in the first place—assuming, of course, that it wasn't Ms. Ballantyne herself."

"We've been through that part already, Mabel," I said in an equally quiet tone that I hoped came across as firm without threatening an officer of the law . . . much. "I did not steal the pets. I did, however, help to get them back. Ask Saurus."

I pointed briefly toward the small habitat that now housed the retrieved iguana. Saurus gently gestured with his long and dinosaurlike tail, but clearly wasn't talking.

"You want evidence?" I continued, barely taking a breath. "Fine. The place to look is the picnic area at Sepulveda Basin, on the way into the wildlife viewing area. That was where the thief left the animals, and—"

"How did you know they'd be there?" Ned interrupted.

"Mrs. Dorgan received a ransom note, apparently in the mail. It said to leave a cell phone number to receive a text message about where the pets would be once the ransom was received. She paid the ransom, and sure enough, she received a text message some hours later directing her to that particular picnic area. The animals were already there. End of story." Almost. I didn't want to tell these detectives, particularly not Ned Noralles, that Jeff had been involved and had attempted to identify a suspect both at the ransom drop point and the pet drop point, since the intent of his assistance was foiled both times.

Which would cause Ned no end of pleasure, and, consequently, Jeff no end of embarrassment.

Besides the fact that I didn't want to bring up my P.I. sometime lover in front of the guy I'd just kissed so heatedly and would join for dinner that night.

What if Ned latched on to my mention of Jeff and began gabbing about my relationship with him, and how I'd helped clear not only him, but his ex-wife, too, from separate murder allegations?

"You lost both my card and Detective Flagsmith's so you couldn't call when you became aware of Mrs. Dorgan's receiving the ransom note." Detective Madero was speaking, and what she said wasn't a question but a snide placing of words in my unwilling mouth. She had maneuvered her skinny bod between Tom and me, and she clearly angled to get in my unenthusiastic face. "And you didn't think of calling Detective Noralles to get that information. I don't suppose you told Mrs. Dorgan what to do with the note to preserve any fingerprints that might be on it."

"Sure I did," I contradicted. "I've seen enough of this game to know how it's played."

"Someone who knows how this game is played would also know to let the authorities in on it from the first." There was a snap to her tone absent an instant earlier. But her next words were again coolness personified. "Okay, you couldn't contact us then, so you allowed Mrs. Dorgan to pay the ransom, and *she* didn't know how to contact us, either."

"Hate to disappoint you, Detective," I said, savoring every word, "but no one tells people of the Dorgans' wealth and power a whole lot of anything. They do pretty much as they please."

"But you, Ms. Ballantyne, are an officer of the court, are you not, as a *currently* practicing attorney?"

Oh, shit. Was my law license being threatened yet again? Could this be changed into a claim of a new breach of ethics?

Hell, no!

"I most certainly am," I said sweetly. "And that's exactly why I had to maintain client confidentiality." Okay, so I exaggerated a little. The Dorgans were my clients—pet-sitting type instead of law clients. "They wanted their pets back without intrusion by awkward and difficult law enforcement sorts who might scare the pet-napper away and prevent the return of their beloved animals. I wasn't about to contradict their wishes. But I'm more than happy to cooperate now and give you what limited info I can."

"Are you claiming that you represent them as their attorney?" I'd never seen someone both sneer and drool at the same time, but Detective Mabel Madero appeared to do both. She was clearly attempting to goad me into a misstatement that would allow her to arrest me for something. Maybe even the obstruction of justice that Ned had previously suggested.

"My relationship with them is confidential," I said, my tone chiming a whole lot more confidence than I felt. "In any event, Detective Madero, I would think the LAPD would give kudos instead of threats to someone who did their job and helped to retrieve stolen property of some of the area's most prominent citizens."

Surely, someone assisting in a situation like this should get pats on the back, not up the legs or other strategic areas where strip searches were conducted during an arrest . . . right?

I looked at Detective Flagsmith for support, but he regarded me sternly. No help there.

Ned Noralles? He looked more amused than authoritarian, and I didn't think he'd step in to assist me, either.

Tom Venson would. He stood off to the side, in front of the glass enclosure containing Saurus, his arms crossed as Ned's had been before. He scowled darkly in his white lab jacket, and I was certain he'd do something rash should the cops decide to take me into custody for . . . well, whatever it was that the nasty Detective Madero had on her mind.

I didn't want Tom in trouble, too. "Look," I said. "If I could have done things differently and still gotten Saurus and Zibble back, I would have. But if I'd stepped in and tried to involve the authorities—"

"I wouldn't have my dear pets back and ready to bring home," inserted a chilly voice from behind the bevy of irritating and irritable detectives.

The wave of detectives parted as Hillary Dorgan entered the room with Zibble still on his leash.

"Ms. Ballantyne did an admirable job of helping me. I suggest that the LAPD commend her, rather than attacking. I'm sure my husband will so inform the mayor—you know we see him socially, don't you?—who will undoubtedly let your chief know what a fine job you are doing in this matter, too."

The three detectives exchanged glances, and for the first time Mabel Madero appeared appalled.

"And now, Kendra," Hillary continued, "I would appreciate it if you would drive Zibble, Saurus, and me back home."

WHICH I DID. Pronto. As soon as Tom gave the go-ahead to depart with Saurus. Zibble, as we'd anticipated, was given pretty much a clean bill of health. As long as he ate, peed, and pooped okay over the next few days, and didn't show any other signs of a change in well-being or personality, there was no cause for further concern.

With Saurus, Hillary would need to take special care, keeping close watch on where he hung out in his habitat, whether he ate and drank sufficiently, and whether he, too, acted any differently from the way he normally did. Assuming one could observe any differences in such an inscrutable creature.

On the drive to the Dorgan home, Hillary expressed indignation over the way the cops had acted not only toward me, but also—and mostly—over her actions to retrieve her animals. "What was I supposed to do—contact the authorities and let them insinuate themselves so intrusively into the situation that the thief killed my pets while the cops scratched their butts over how to get them back?"

A colorful way to put it, one I liked a lot. "They have their procedures," I said mildly, "even if civilians don't find them the best way to achieve what everyone wants."

"That's for sure."

I certainly understood her ongoing rants, but I admit my relief to reach her home. I helped her move Saurus back into his habitat. As I left his presence, he seemed to watch me, perhaps thanking me in his own inimitable, incomprehensible manner.

Hillary was less subtle. "I really appreciate all you've done, Kendra," she told me. The check she handed me for my pet-sitting was way above my standard fee, and I attempted to return it in its entirety.

"I still feel terrible about all that happened, Hillary." Yes, by now, we were genuinely on a first-name basis—both of us. "You don't owe me anything."

"You helped me get Zibble and Saurus home safely," she contradicted and refused to shred the check.

I decided to keep a minimal amount and send the rest to a pet rescue organization, although I wasn't sure yet which one. I'd give it some thought and get advice from Darryl.

Or maybe I'd use it to further the senior citizen pet-visit program that Rachel had become involved with.

Guess I had some pondering to perform before making a decision.

Good thing it was still Saturday, but almost half the morning had passed. I felt terrible about leaving my pet-sitting charges alone for so long.

I determined to spend much longer with them than usual.

After, of course, taking care of my own prized puppy, Lexie, who remained home alone.

And so I didn't take the time to report in to Tracy or any other Pet-Sitters Club of SoCal members about my triumphant retrieval of my missing pet clients until way into the afternoon.

Tracy was, of course, the first I called. When she didn't respond on the first ring, I had a fleeting wonderment about whether she had been arrested for Nya's murder. Followed by a feeling of deepest guilt. Over the last many hours, I had barely spared a thought for my murdered compatriot or the friend whom the cops apparently thought had killed her.

Well, I'd remedy that as soon as—

"Hello, Kendra?" Caller ID is a wonderful thing, I thought as Tracy immediately knew who I was.

"Hi, Tracy," I said. "Guess what!"

"Oh, you already know? I meant to call you earlier about it, Kendra, but so many members of the club are already aware, and I've been getting one call after another."

"Really? I wonder how word got out so soon, and—"

"They're so scared," she interrupted. "Maybe you could give another talk about how to cope with it."

What the heck was she saying? Everyone who knew what had happened with the Dorgan pets should be celebrating, not scared or coping.

"I don't understand, Tracy," I said. "The Dorgan pets are back home, safe and sound. Isn't that what we're talking about?"

There was a moment of silence, then she said, "Apparently that's what you're talking about. And that's a good thing, Kendra. But what I'm talking about is the other two pets stolen on our members' watch yesterday and today."

# Chapter Fifteen

SHE'D CALLED A makeshift meeting for four that afternoon. Lexie and I had to hie ourselves over the mountain to get there on time.

And, yes, this time I'd done the right thing and informed the authorities in advance. Detectives Flagsmith and Madero said they'd be there, too. They didn't tell me till I asked, but they had also been called in on one of the new pet-nappings, since it occurred in their jurisdiction. They seemed suddenly to be the cops assigned to investigate what had become a serial crime.

I reached Rachel and asked her to meet me, but she was at the senior citizen center with Beggar again and couldn't break away in time. She apologized, but I excused her. What she was doing was important, too, and I could fill her in on any meeting details she needed to know.

Plus, she promised to stop in at all our current Critter TLC, LLC, clients on her way home to ensure nothing had changed since our respective visits this morning—and that all our dog and cat charges remained exactly where they were supposed to be. I put the keys and entry instructions for the pets I cared for safely behind the security of my own locked gates, but a place where Rachel could access them.

Lexie and I arrived at the meeting with minutes to spare. The back room of the West Hollywood pet boutique hummed so loudly that Lexie let out a bark when we entered the shop.

"Easy, pup," I admonished. "Let's not get excited . . . unless and until we have to."

At our last PSCSC meeting—had it only been four days earlier?—I'd been impressed by how many people were shoehorned into the small storage room, and now there appeared to be even more. The unfolded folding chairs arranged in neat rows remained largely unoccupied at the moment, and I wondered whether there would be a sufficient number to seat everyone.

Probably a fire hazard, but I wasn't about to call it in. Detectives Mabel Madero and Domenic Flagsmith were already there. That would be their bailiwick, if it actually was an issue.

The crowded room smelled of people perfumes, pet scent, and the food and stuff stored around the edges. Someday, if the club continued to grow this way, a new venue would need to be voted on. One that also allowed dogs and the couple of parrots that were also present.

Although, of course, if we stopped and solved the pet-nappings, there might be less interest in the organization afterward.

I saw Tracy in the midst of a crowd at the front of the room. Allen Smith stood beside her, holding Phoebe, the puggle. Gaunt now and pale, Tracy appeared distraught and distracted. To join her, I'd have to elbow my way past a bunch of people, pets, and chairs. Instead, I wriggled my way through the hot, heated crowd and their mostly canine companions toward Wanda.

Cavalier Basil in her arms, she stood speaking with Lilia Ziegler and a man I hadn't met. Instead of one of her usual gauzy tops, Wanda wore a black T-shirt, but it managed to convey her usual style with its gold swirly trim at the front decorated with faux jewel-like stones.

Older Lilia appeared even more animated than ever. Her brown hair shot with gray was pulled back from her face and clipped behind her head, stressing the laugh lines around her deep-set eyes. Her wrinkled hand waved, as it often did to punctuate her sentences, and she seemed to speak in excited paragraphs.

She caught my eye as I approached holding Lexie. "Kendra, what's going on? Tracy said you got the animals back that were taken on your watch, but two more of us—Frieda and I—had pets stolen. And Jerry, here, who's been trying so hard to deal with losing Nya, has been all but accused by the police of not only killing her, but doing the pet-napping, too. Just because they had some spats now and then. Well, all couples do, don't they?"

Jerry? This had to be Jerry Jefferton, Nya's significant and live-in other. I'd been wondering why the cops chose to harass Tracy as their main suspect over Nya's main squeeze. Now, looking at Jerry, I figured the cops hadn't arrested either because they hadn't yet decided on the best accusation prospect. Not that Jerry appeared to be a murderous maniac. But he was a big guy, one who could likely wield a fatal baseball bat with ease. He had shaved his head and was enough on the plump side to appear almost sumo-esque, although he wore a shirt and tie and looked more like a businessman than a wrestler. He seemed to study the feet of Wanda and Lilia, although that could be his grief, weighting his head too much to lift it to meet their eyes.

But a suspect in the pet-nappings, too? This was new to me. "Hi, Jerry, I'm Kendra." I didn't attempt to offer my hand for a shake since it was occupied with calming a wriggling Lexie, who wanted down. Not a great idea in this crowd. She'd get stepped on by a person or nipped at by another pup.

"Hi, Kendra. I've heard about you." Jerry raised his gaze to look at me with bloodshot brown eyes, and I suspected that whatever he'd heard about me wasn't flattering. "You solve murders. Do you know who killed my Nya?" His shoulders seemed to square, as if he anticipated the blow of my accusing him.

Well, I hoped it hadn't been Tracy who'd done it, but I didn't have reason—yet, at least—to suspect Jerry. "Not so far," I said. "And right now, I'm so preoccupied with these pet-nappings that whatever my reputation for getting involved with murders, I may not be too helpful in solving Nya's."

"Oh," he said softly, as if I had dealt him another blow. "I'd really like for justice to be done."

Which suggested strongly that he hadn't slain his lover.

Unless, of course he was lying to deflect suspicion from himself. But if not him, then Tracy . . . ?

Well, I hadn't leaped deeply enough into determining a list of alternate suspects to know who else might have had cause to off Nya. I'd need to do that. Soon.

But first . . .

Tracy had taken her place at the front of the crowd—with the two cops standing cross-armed behind her. "Can I have everyone's attention?" she pleaded rather than announced.

"People, listen up," yelled Frieda Shoreman. Standing beside the clearly exhausted Tracy, Frieda appeared tall and slim and stylishly clad, as usual. "This special meeting of the Pet-Sitters Club of SoCal is hereby called to order."

Her shout somehow got everyone's attention. Or maybe the group was simply waiting for someone to take charge. In any event, voices stilled, and people took their seats.

Me, too, with Lexie on my lap. Jerry Jefferton became my next-chair neighbor.

This meeting seemed similar to the one several days back, except that I was called up to the front first to describe my good news—getting Zibble and Saurus back.

I grinned as the group cheered when I finished. But I turned to the others who'd suffered similar pet-nappings. "Tracy, Wanda, did the people whose pets you were sitting for receive any additional ransom notes, like the Dorgans did?"

"No," Tracy said sadly, and Wanda seconded it. "And there's still no sign of where Augie or Cramer are now."

Which put a big damper on my eager excitement over the recovered Dorgan pets.

"And now, Frieda, Lilia," Tracy said, "would you please tell us about your pet-nappings?"

The descriptions were similar to what had happened previously—only Frieda's loss was late yesterday afternoon, and Lilia's not long after. Two dogs disappeared from one house, and a cat from another.

Before Hillary Dorgan paid the ransom for her pets.

But the notes were similar, with orders not to tell the cops, and so were the stories, though both sitters, alerted by what went on before, had increased their security.

To no avail.

Copycat pet-nappings—especially now that a cat had been napped, too? Or was it the same person?

I'd little doubt that our local club was targeted, although other pet-sitters could be experiencing similar nastiness. I'd ask Althea to amend and increase her online search.

In any event, if it was a single napper, he or she must already have had these three new pets in possession when the Dorgan ransom was swooped up. Where were they when Saurus and Zibble were dropped at Sepulveda Basin? How about the other, still-missing pets?

Did Nya's murder have anything to do with this difficult situation, or was it simply coincidental?

Hard for someone like me to buy—since I was a huge skeptic about coincidences.

Detective Flagsmith also got a turn to speak. He passed out cards and told anyone with any information to be sure to call Detective Madero or him. He asserted that the LAPD was extremely concerned about this rash of crimes and intended to stop it and haul in the perpetrator.

Sure. All they needed was to figure out the right identity. And I, for one, would do all I could to ensure that happened. With or without the cops' involvement.

The meeting ended soon afterward. I maneuvered my way up to the front of the room to see Tracy.

"This is getting way out of hand," I told her.

"Can't you do something, Kendra?" she pleaded in apparent panic. "You've solved mysteries before. Why not catch the person who's doing this? And whoever killed Nya, too, while you're at it. This is just all too much." Tears had started running down her roundish face, and she popped a hand over her mouth as a sob spilled out.

Nothing there I hadn't told myself lately. A whole lot too often.

Allen, one arm still holding Phoebe, put the other around Tracy and pulled her closer. He looked up at me, shaking his head. "I've told her over and over that she doesn't need to do this anymore. She could quit this club, pet-sitting, too. Tell her, Kendra, please. Things would be so much easier for her."

After stuff I'd gone through in my own past, I was an unlikely convert to quitting. Even when things had been hardest,

I'd somehow held on. I'd stopped practicing law for a while because I had to, not because I'd chosen to flee from the profession where I'd first been hurt. And then even pet-sitting had added additional pressures, like finding people-clients' dead bodies at homes where I was caring for hounds.

Had I been right? Well, I had been vindicated, and now I couldn't be happier that I'd held on. But advise someone else to do the same?

"Hang in there, Tracy," I said softly, watching over her slumped shoulder as the detectives worked the dispersing crowd, asking questions and seeming full of answers they didn't yet have. I almost felt sorry for them—but I felt sorrier for the friend in front of me. "Make whatever decision seems right to you, but don't continue to do everything unless you want to."

"See," said Allen, sounding a slight bit triumphant for someone who'd barely ever uttered an opinion before, at least in front of me. I nevertheless admired, even envied, the way he seemed to protect and care for Tracy.

"I'll think about it, Kendra," Tracy promised on a sniffle, as if I'd advised her to chuck it all.

If she wanted to take it that way, so be it.

"One thing I wanted to ask you," I said. "You, too, Lilia and Frieda." They hovered nearby comparing notes on the latest pet-nappings. "I don't know if it'll help, but hopefully it won't hurt. I have an acquaintance who's a kind of investigative reporter. At least she's nosy, and she puts things in front of the public."

"She's that Corina Carey, the one who interviewed Hillary Dorgan, right?" Frieda said. "Did that help get her pets back?"

"It obviously didn't hurt," I responded. "I think that the more people who hear about these pet-nappings, the more likely it is there'll be tips phoned to the cops, if any pet victims are seen. I'll try to get her to report on these latest pet-nappings, too. Okay with you?"

"Sure," Frieda said, and Lilia agreed.

"I'm not sure," Tracy said.

"It'll give your club a bad name," Allen said, supporting her.

"It already has a bad name," I said.

I didn't ask the detectives their opinion as I said what I was sure would be a temporary farewell.

But I vowed inside to call Corina Carey on my way home.

FIRST, THOUGH, I extracted the latest version of my list dealing with the pet-nappings and added the three new ones: the two dogs, stolen from the Westwood area, named Pooky and Piranha—a dog? Why such a nasty, fishy name?

Then there was the cat from Laurel Canyon who was named Amanda. As I've said often, I don't believe in coincidences, and this certainly wasn't one, either. But Amanda was the name of Jeff's catty ex-wife, and she kept cats of her own.

Okay, so there was no reason for me to think the missing cat's owner had ever met the Amanda who'd intruded into my life. But how appropriate of this person to have appropriated Amanda Hubbard's first name.

About then, Lexie began barking and lunging around the Beamer. She'd spotted some non-PSCSC people walking a big black dog who looked equally ready to take on my pup.

"Time to go." I put down my list and turned the key in the ignition. We started toward home.

But I managed, when we stopped for a red light, to place a call to Corina Carey. I used her office number, since I figured I'd just leave her a teaser of a message for Monday. Meantime, I'd gather some more of the facts I wanted to foist on her to get her started on her next story about the pet-nappings.

I, however, was the one who was surprised, when she answered. "It's Saturday afternoon," I said after we'd both said hello. "Why are you in the office working?"

"Why did you call me here if you didn't expect to talk to me?" she countered.

I didn't want to explain my somewhat illogical reasoning. Instead, I said, "I've got something hot for you."

"You've solved the Nya Barston murder?" Excitement screamed through her otherwise calm voice.

"Other than that, what's the best story update you can think of from me?" I countered.

"The Dorgans have their animals back."

"Bingo! I can't give details since it's an ongoing investigation, but I'd love for you to give the serial pet-napping situation more airtime."

"There've been more?"

"There've been more," I confirmed.

"Hot damn," she said. "Let's talk about it. Do you suppose Hillary Dorgan would agree to be interviewed again?"

"I doubt it, now that her animals are back safe and sound."

"Darn. I mean that she won't talk, not that her animals are okay."

"I hoped that was what you intended," I said dryly.

Still being Corina, she didn't sound chastised in the least.

"Let's meet tomorrow, Kendra, okay? Eleven in the morning? Tell me where, and I'll be there."

# Chapter Sixteen

NOTWITHSTANDING RACHEL'S EXTRA rounds that afternoon, Lexie and I commenced our evening pet-sitting a couple of hours early because of my upcoming date with Tom Venson. Besides, after the meeting about additional animal snatchings, I needed to assure myself that all my current charges were still where they belonged.

Which, thank heavens, they were. An especially good thing, since over the course of the time I'd been a pet-sitter, I'd gotten to know most of this crew well. I'd hate to have any more animals snatched on my watch, but I knew I'd feel especially awful if something happened to Abra or Cadabra, Harold Reddingham's Siamese and tabby cats, or Alexander, a particularly friendly pit bull.

Plus, I'd heard from a longtime client Cal Orlando. He owned Lester, the Basset hound, whom I'd helped to clear of an accusation a while back of biting a neighbor without cause. Turned out the neighbor had instigated it himself, which I pointedly proved. Cal was heading out of town and wanted me to stop by for his key so I could care for Lester.

Which I did—while also, in an abundance of client caution, informing Cal of the rash of pet-nappings.

"I trust you, Kendra," Cal said.

So of course I took on Lester's care once more before Lexie and I dashed home so I could dress for my date.

Worrying about being tardy was why I didn't call Rachel. I thought about her, sure, but figured I could contact her while waiting for Tom to pick me up.

If anything went wrong during her rounds, I knew she'd call me.

Which was one reason I felt so shaken and startled when I took Lexie outside for a short walk after her dinner and found Rachel standing in the open-doored garage, Beggar's leash clutched in her hand, her pup pacing nervously beside her.

My employee was crying her pretty, big brown eyes out.

My heart immediately plummeted to beneath the high-heeled fashion sandals I'd donned for my date.

"What's wrong, Rachel?" I cried, while Lexie tugged on her lead trying to get close to console her—a role already assumed by her own adorable Irish setter. "Did you check on all our clients?" I waited while she stopped sobbing before she could respond, all the while considering what I'd do next to find any missing charges. I couldn't count on every client being able to pay the kind of ransom the Dorgans did. Even assuming they got a note demanding payment, since so many of the victims had heard nothing after the first notice that their pet was napped.

This couldn't be happening again. Not to me. Not to any poor pet, especially those being cared for by Critter TLC, LLC.

"It's so awful, Kendra," Rachel finally screeched. Beggar stopped sitting quietly on the floor and climbed so his paws clutched his mistress around the middle, as if he insisted on comforting her. It was an adorable gesture, and even Rachel noticed it.

"What is?" I insisted that my cracking voice remain calm.

"It's those horrible people at Methuselah Manor."

I instantly quashed the relief that soared through me. No missing pet-care client after all. I hadn't a thing to do with the senior citizen center where Rachel took Beggar to cheer up the inmates. But whatever had happened there had obviously shaken Rachel to the core. And I cared a lot about the kid.

"Let's go inside, and you can tell me about it," I said. She looked so shaky and sorrowful that I was concerned she would somehow hurt herself out here, stumbling in the garage or walking to the house.

"M-my dad's out of town this weekend, but he's due back on Monday. If he hears I'm accused of stealing things from those old farts, he'll hate me." Rachel's wail echoed in the garage and instigated an answering bark from Beggar. Rachel knelt and threw her arms around her dog as she cried once more.

"I assume you didn't steal whatever it was," I said. Even when Rachel was at her sneaky worst, when she'd first moved into my rented-out main house without informing her traveling father, I'd never had the sense she was a thief. No reason to assume so now, no matter what the accusations leveled against her.

I believed wholeheartedly in the basic precept of innocent until proven guilty. It sure had helped me through my own ugly circumstance of being a criminal suspect.

"Of course not!" Rachel stood and glared indignantly, probably a preferable emotion to depression. "Why would I? The people in charge of the home make sure the residents' families take home anything of value anyway, like good jewelry. Some of the stuff they say I took is costume, so why bother? And the rest—it's wristwatches, of all things. No one's interested in watches anymore, so why steal them?"

I glanced at her empty wrist, then at mine—where, sure enough, I wore a watch. Not an especially valuable one, but it managed to tell time, which was all I needed.

"Some people wear watches, Rachel," I reminded her, also recalling Tom Venson's checking his.

"Yeah, like those old people there," she acknowledged. "But hardly anyone my age does."

"Really?" That was news to me.

"What are cell phones for?" she asked rhetorically.

Oh, yeah. Why wear watches, where you had to set the time and could be off by minutes or more, when you could look at your phone and get the actual, accurate time disseminated by the cell phone company? Interesting observation—and it managed to make me, at merely thirty-five, feel like a darned dinosaur.

Rachel finally started strolling slowly out of the garage and along the path toward the main house, Beggar trotting sympathetically at her side. Lexie and I joined them.

"So what happens now?" I asked. Like, did they call the cops on you? Will there be a criminal investigation? But I decided to let her tell me what she knew.

"I don't know," she said dejectedly. She reached into her small bag and pulled out her key.

I tried not to be obvious as I glanced inside, in case I saw the glint of some costume jewelry or an errant wristwatch that had somehow jumped inside.

She caught me. "Do you think I did it?" she shouted. And then her shoulders slumped again. "If even you don't believe in me, why would they? Several of the old folks reported stuff missing right after I'd visited them."

We walked into the entryway. I wanted to stay longer to help her, but knew that Tom would arrive at any minute—according to my old-fashioned wristwatch.

"I believe you," I told my treasured tenant. If I didn't trust her, I'd never have hired her to help me pet-sit in homes of clients to whom I owed a duty of due care. "Let's talk about this more tomorrow, okay? I'm expecting someone here any minute."

"Jeff?" Rachel asked. "He's really a hottie."

I shook my head somewhat sheepishly. "Not this time. I have a date with Tom Venson."

"The vet? He's great, too. You're on a roll, Kendra." For the first time that evening, she smiled, albeit a bit soggily. "But how will you ever decide between them?"

"Good question," I said, just as I heard a car roll up to our closed wrought-iron gate.

I turned to see the beige Ford Escape owned by my date.

"Good luck," Rachel called in a too-sweet tone. "And have fun."

WE WENT TO a really nice wood-fire barbecue place in Sherman Oaks. One without an outdoor eating area, so it was a good thing that I'd left a peeved Lexie in our apartment.

What, a vet not inviting his date's pet along for dinner?

I couldn't help commenting about that as soon as we'd ordered our food. The restaurant decor suggested a TexMex milieu, with serapes and rodeo photos on the walls. Our tablecloth was checkered red and white, and the rolls we'd been served were mini-loaves of homemade bread.

"As much as I love animals," Tom responded with a smile, "it's nice now and then to be around people." He took in the rest of the restaurant with a gesture.

Unlike our dining place, Tom wasn't at all country barbecue. He had chosen a classy button shirt in deep charcoal with threads that glistened dressily in the light from the flickering candle on our table. His slacks were black, his belt conservative.

The dark duds went well with his even darker hair, and set off his widow's peak. He had a nice, if ordinary, nose, sincere brown eyes, and a few small wrinkles in the middle of his forehead. Because his hair was so dark, there was a hint of beard beneath his skin even though he'd shaved close enough not to scrape a date's skin during a kiss.

How did I know that? I'd experienced it again tonight—nothing extremely hot and heavy, but a nice greeting before we'd gotten on our way.

"You know," I said, "I've never asked"—and I'd never been to his home. In fact, his picking me up at mine tonight had been his first glimpse of my own humble abode and surrounding less humble property the bank and I owned—"but do you have any pets? Or do you just get a vicarious thrill out of handling the health of others' beloved babies?"

There was a whole lot I didn't know about Dr. Thomas Venson. Like his past history with women. Did he have an ex-wife lurking about somewhere, ready to leap back into his life if he and I developed any kind of relationship?

Boy, would that convince me even more that I could only choose the worst of men to get involved with.

"Yeah, I do," he said. "And I have to be careful not to adopt too many at a time, but when strays somehow appear at the clinic, they seem to wind up staying at my place. I've got three dogs and a cat right now, all neutered and healthy, although one of the dogs only has three legs. Fortunately, my house isn't far from the hospital. You'll have to visit sometime."

His eyes caught mine, and I sensed an invitation a lot more heated than simply meeting his animal family. My insides flamed.

Was that what I wanted?

Was I that through with Jeff? I wasn't about to sample sex with anyone else unless I'd finished with my former lover.

And I knew that Jeff could still press the right buttons to turn me on, even without touching me. Was that enough?

Was that truly all there was between us?

I sighed, grateful for the interruption as our server brought a big bowl of salad that she served onto our plates with a large wooden fork and spoon.

We chatted casually about all sorts of stuff, even through our ribs, corn, and slaw.

Damn, but I liked the guy.

"I've been waiting for you to tell me more about the stolen animals," he finally said, looking somber and concerned.

"Damned pet-napper," I replied. "At least the two animals pinched on my watch are back home, safe, sound, and healthy, partly thanks to you. But two other dogs were taken around the same time, and three more animals since—that I know about. So far, they all seem to be grabbed while one of my associates from the Pet-Sitters Club of SoCal is watching them. I've got someone checking to see if there are any others, of course."

"Your friend the P.I.?" His tone didn't suggest he had any idea how close my friend the P.I. and I were—or at least had been. Or maybe he didn't care.

Was it possible I was misreading proffered friendship from this really nice vet for something more personal?

Heck, knowing my own penchant for misunderstandings and selections of wholly inappropriate guys for relationships, what was more likely?

Which kinda hurt—suggesting I really was attracted to Tom Venson on a deeper level.

"Not him," I said so brightly that I outshone the candle on the table between us. "He has a wonderful researcher in his office, and she's looking into it for me. You haven't heard of other pet-nappings, have you?"

"No, but I have asked around about the missing animals I've heard about. Plus, I'm going to an educational session with other vets tomorrow afternoon, and I'll check there, too."

"Would you? That would be wonderful." Our eyes met and caught, as if we had been discussing something a whole lot sexier than stolen pets.

Tom smiled. I smiled back. And started simmering inside.

By then, we were through eating. Neither of us wanted any coffee or dessert, so we left the barbecue joint, our hands joined as we strolled to Tom's SUV.

He drove me home so fast that I could hardly believe it when we reached my place. Or maybe my mind was in such a stupidly sensual fog that I hadn't taken in the landmarks on the way.

But then, there we were.

"Would you like to come in for a while?" I hardly believed I'd invited him. It sounded like a suggestion of a whole lot more.

Was that what I wanted? Was I ready?

No surprise. He did want to come in.

We shared some wine. And we made out on my comfy sectional beige couch while Lexie nosed first my legs, then Tom's, causing us both to laugh.

Tom's hands began wandering afield on my perversely eager body, and that helped me establish an answer to one question I'd asked myself earlier.

No, I wasn't ready.

"It's too soon," I whispered against his neck. He smelled good close up like that—a little tangy, a lot male. And not at all like a man who spent much of his time tending unaromatic pups and kitties.

"I'd better be going, then," he said. "Can we get together again next weekend?"

"Sure," I said with a smile.

"I'll call you." He dropped down to give Lexie a farewell pat, and then he was gone.

Well, heck.

Seemed like I had two guys firmly ensconced in my life and psyche now.

And I wasn't at all certain I wanted even one.

# Chapter Seventeen

So DID I go to bed that night thinking about what I was missing, lying there alone save for Lexie. No Tom? No Jeff?

No. What I pondered as I waited for sleep to shut down my conscious mind was what I'd say to Corina Carey the next day. And what else I should be doing in an attempt to resolve all the matters that currently disrupted my life—like the pet-nappings and Nya Barston's murder.

I decided that the best move to encourage Corina to give this story more airtime was to make it more human interest. That meant getting people to talk about the doggy and kitty disappearances and how they'd affected their lives.

Rubbing it in the faces of the animals' owners didn't seem like a good move, but displaying the anguish of other pet-sitters might do the trick.

I made calls first thing the next morning—realizing I might have to delay my eleven o'clock meeting with Corina.

Tracy declined being interviewed on air. She was already too frazzled by all that had occurred to become a public spectacle about it. Besides, she didn't want the adverse publicity for the club that would result if the PSCSC president shouted out about it.

I pondered that point for a while. Perhaps the same issue would result if Frieda Shoreman, its de facto treasurer who kept the books without accepting the office, was interviewed about the pet-napping on her watch. And Wanda Villareal was considering the vice presidency now that Nya, who'd been the Veep, was gone.

That left Lilia Ziegler, who'd also had an animal napped while she sat for it. She wasn't an elected or acting officer, and surely someone as scrappy as she would make a good on-air interview subject.

I decided I'd talk to her first, just to be sure. Fortunately, she had some time that morning after her own pet-sitting rounds and invited me to her home.

I called Corina and said I'd need to reschedule, but I was hoping to have someone really great for her to talk with on her National NewsShakers show. Sure, Hillary Dorgan would be a hard act to follow, but I had just the right character in mind.

I hoped.

LILIA LIVED IN the hills overlooking the Cahuenga Pass. It was an area considered part of Hollywood, as was my farther west neighborhood, though neither quite sat on the side of the hill where people expected Hollywood to be.

More surprising was that Lilia's two-car garage sat flush with the street, but her white adobe cottage was way up the mountainside, reachable only by several long flights of steps.

Good thing, since this was Sunday, that I was dressed for pet-sitting, in a yellow T-shirt, khaki slacks, and athletic shoes. Heaven help me if I'd been wearing the heels I stuck my feet into for lawyering! I was winded when I got to the top. How did Lilia, who had to be in her seventies, handle this climb?

I asked her, huffing and puffing when she answered her double wooden door.

Her smile dug parenthetical divots on the sides of her mouth, adding to her already plentiful wrinkles. "I've owned this place since before you were born, Kendra. I'm used to it, and I'm not about to move. Were you assuming I was ready for some old folks' home?"

I considered poor Rachel's quandary with the senior citizens she tried to amuse, who'd apparently accused her of thievery. Could I imagine Lilia, in her slim jeans and red plaid ruffled shirt, sitting and twiddling her thumbs while a young woman attempted to entertain her by letting her hug an Irish setter?

No way.

This woman was still employed as a pet-sitter. If anything, she'd be the one to attempt to coax smiles out of the other old folks by bringing a big dog along.

"Not hardly," I told her. "But *I* may be, after this climb."

She laughed and led me inside, straight into a small living room with a fireplace along one wall and rows of filled bookshelves along the other.

"Have a seat." She pointed to a fluffy white corduroy-covered couch. It faced a small coffee table nearby, and a wide-screen TV on a stand near the opposite wall. "I'll give you the grand tour of the place once you've caught your breath."

A sweetish smell hung in the air, and I suspected Lilia used either incense or a plug-in air freshener. As I sat there, a large gray cat entered the room, flicked its tail disdainfully, and observed me as if determining whether I was worthy enough to be here.

"That's Fortuna," Lilia said. "I named her that because we're good luck for one another. I rescued her from a shelter, and she rescues me from talking to myself."

"Cute," I said. "And I gather that you pet-sit cats a lot, too." The pet stolen on her watch was the cat from Laurel Canyon named Amanda.

"Dogs, cats, birds, whatever." She waved one of her thin, wrinkly hands in the air as she was wont to do. "Now, tell me what you wanted to talk about. Something about a TV interview? Why would anyone want to talk to me?"

I explained that Corina Carey was the reporter who'd adored having Hillary Dorgan talk about her missing pets a few days back. "I want to keep the momentum going, keep on the public's mind that other animals are being stolen so they'll let the authorities know if they see anything strange."

"But why me?" she repeated. "I'm not married to anyone famous, and I'm certainly nobody myself."

I grinned at her. "Of all the folks in PSCSC, I think you have the most guts, Lilia. And presence. Put you in front of a camera talking about how awful you feel about the missing cat, and the audience at home will weep right along with you."

"You want me to cry?" Her small blue eyes widened in apparent astonishment, standing out in their sea of facial wrinkles.

"Only if you feel like it. But you certainly can get all emotional, can't you?"

"Sure can." She suddenly appeared small and sad and utterly helpless, with sagging shoulders and droopy head. "What do you think?" she asked. She looked up enough to meet my gaze. "I really do feel awful about losing Amanda like that, you know."

"I figured." Strange, hearing the name Amanda again. The cattiness fit. But I hated the idea that any pet could be stolen from her own home, even if I wasn't wild about her unknown sort of namesake.

"Well, go ahead, if you want, Kendra. Tell that Corina person I'll talk to her and give her a good story. Now, come on and I'll show you around."

She provided cheerful commentary as she pointed out pictures of herself in her younger days, with a couple of men who were husbands she had outlived. "Great guys, both of them," she said with a grin. "I think I wore them both out in bed." I must have looked as startled as I felt, for she cackled, then said, "I didn't think I'd embarrass someone your age, Kendra. Especially since rumor has it that you have two guys on the hook at the same time."

"Rumor's only partly right," I said irritably, then exclaimed about how nice her compact kitchen was, mostly to change the subject.

She took me out on the back patio and showed me the swimming pool. Behind was a small outbuilding—a place she could conceal missing pets if she'd napped one of her own charges to throw off any suspicion that she was the general thief.

Why had that crossed my mind? I'd no real reason to assume she was the napper, any more than I thought she'd killed Nya. Besides, she led me there and pushed open the door, obviously not attempting to hide anything.

A full set of gym equipment sat on the low-carpeted floor inside. "Love this stuff," Lilia said. "I still work out every day. That's one reason I don't have problems with the steps."

Hmmm. I'd shrugged off Frieda Shoreman's suggestion of Lilia as a murder suspect, since Nya was slugged with a baseball bat. I had figured that someone as senior as Lilia couldn't have bashed someone so much younger to smithereens that way.

But now . . . "You're amazing," I said admiringly. "I don't have the stamina to work out every day. That's one reason I'm delighted to pet-sit, since I at least do a lot of walking."

"Well, I'd suggest you get in the habit of doing more now, young lady, so it won't be a chore when you reach my age."

How to turn the topic to the additional questions that shot into my mind? "You ought to give a talk to that effect to PSCSC members," I said. "They'd all be interested. I've gotten sort of close to Tracy and Wanda, but less so with the others. I find Frieda's trying to take charge annoying sometimes. How about you? Do you have any special friends there? Any members you could do without?" Like Nya, but I kept that silently to myself.

But Lilia got the underlying message. "I like some better than others, sure, Kendra. And I didn't especially care for Nya. She kept suggesting I'm too old to pet-sit. And when one of her clients got tired of her not taking good care of their cats, she was furious when they hired me next time they went away. I defended myself, and we argued a lot over it. And before you ask—though I suspect you're too polite to say it outright—yes, I probably had enough strength in these skinny arms to do her in with a baseball bat." She raised those arms, whatever strength they might have hidden beneath the long sleeves of her plaid shirt. "But I didn't do it, and I'll even say so on television if the question arises in my interview."

I HAD SOME hesitation about calling Corina but felt somewhat committed. Especially since I was convinced that keeping the pet-nappings public might help stop them—and get the still-missing animals back to their grieving owners . . . and pet-sitters. And I didn't genuinely believe that Lilia was guilty of anything.

And so, call her I did. She immediately galvanized into action, and showed up at Lilia's soon thereafter.

Yes, I stayed for the interview. Even made a few astute observations on camera. Helped by locating Lilia's cat, Fortuna, and bringing the irritated kitty in to be part of the filming. I thought it went fine. And Lilia seemed the epitome of innocence.

When it was over, I thanked Lilia, Corina, and the cameraman, then headed for my law office. There, I did some digging into the file I needed to review for my meeting tomorrow and locked up the building. I visited my pet clients all over again and spent time taking care of each. Not to mention ensuring they still seemed secure.

I finally headed home, feeling a little lonesome since I'd left Lexie there. I hadn't wanted her adorable face broadcast over Corina's air, not with a pet-napper on the loose. Maybe so far the victims were all pet-sitting clients, certainly distressful enough, but who was to say that the thief wouldn't start picking on the sitters' pets themselves?

As soon as I pulled my Beamer through the front gate, I saw Russ Preesinger barreling down the path from the main house. Rachel's dad and my main tenant had been out of town, so I hadn't seen him lately. Since he was a Hollywood location scout, his being home was more unusual than his being on the road.

"Hi, Russ," I called after I'd parked at my spot in the shadow of the garage and exited my car.

"Have you heard what's going on with Rachel?" No greeting, simply an explosion. Russ was a fine-looking male specimen, of moderate height and a build that wouldn't quit. His hair was reddish, which gave credence to the old cliché that people picked pets who looked like them. He did, after all, own Beggar. The Irish setter had followed him from the house and seemed excited at the exercise of hustling down the walk.

Viewing Russ's scowl, I considered some hustling of my own . . . away from here. "You mean those claims at the senior citizen home? Yes, she told me—"

"Those miserable old so-and-sos had better watch who they're accusing. Otherwise—well, you're a lawyer. I'll hire you to sue the whole lot for defamation."

I was absolutely a litigator, but I avoided cases I felt sure were losers. Was this one of them?

I didn't believe Rachel would steal from anyone, let alone the senior citizens she'd been so excited to entertain with visits with her hound. But truth was always a defense to a defamation suit, and it was one Methuselah Manor and its inmates were bound to assert. Would a jury accept truth from the mouth of a cute but sassy kid—or assume a whole group of elders instead spouted all veracity?

"I'm not sure that's a case I want to take on, Russ," I told him, "but I'll definitely look into it, to see whether it would have any merit."

Talk about dark expressions. My tenant's face turned thunderously ominous in about an instant. "You're not suggesting she really could have done it, are you?"

"Of course not, but I need to find out the basis of accusations before I consider representing anyone in a lawsuit."

"Then do it." He clenched his fists as if he considered taking out his fury on me. Instead, he pivoted and hurried back toward the big chateau that constituted my property's main house.

I sighed. I'd found Russ attractive enough to consider dating him when my fledgling relationship with Jeff had first turned rocky—when his ex insinuated herself back into his life. I hadn't followed up, and now I was glad.

The guy had one hell of a temper.

Besides, I was having enough trouble managing two possible relationships. How might I have handled a third?

Horribly, no doubt. At least as badly as I dealt with two.

But I had promised the guy to look into the allegations against his daughter. As I headed up the steps toward my garage-top apartment, I considered how I'd conduct the research.

An interesting idea sprang to mind . . . but I wanted to mull it over prior to following it up.

LEXIE WAS NEARLY as excited to see me as I was to see her. She leaped all over me, and I laughed before taking her for a walk. I fed her, then settled myself in for a relaxing evening alone with my pampered pup. I stuck a frozen dinner into the microwave and sat on my comfy couch in my compact living room. I used the remote to turn on the TV and scan the channels.

Until I got to the one that ran Corina Carey's newscasts.

Okay, I've no thirst for fame but was curious how I'd come across, asking for people's help in watching for napped animals.

I finally found the story, right on the local station where I'd anticipated it would be. I didn't look half bad—although I told myself I should have my hair highlighted again, the way it used to be when I was a high-powered litigator, in the old days prior to pet-sitting. Most important, I think I made my point.

If I didn't, Lilia Ziegler sure did. Looking like the grand-motherly senior citizen she was, she tearfully told the camera about how she did pet-sitting to supplement her Social Security. Plus, she loved every animal she cared for.

And now, a cat had been cat-napped right from under her.

She showed photos. With my urging off camera, she let her own kitty Fortuna steal the scene. All this, evoked by Corina's careful questions.

"Then you think, Lilia," Corina eventually said, the microphone in front of her large mouth, "that everyone in our viewing audience could be at risk of losing their own beloved animals?"

"I certainly do. And believe me, Corina, when I say that my fellow pet-sitter Kendra Ballantyne has skills that the awful thief doesn't even know about. If the authorities don't stop the pet-napper, she will."

Great, I thought as the screen segued to an appropriate ad for dog food. She must have said that during one of my frequent jaunts to locate the oft-fleeing Fortuna. Lilia had made me sound like I'd find the pet-napper single-handed. That wouldn't exactly shove me into the cops' good graces. As if I was ever there.

And not only the police, but the pet-napper would have more reason to hate me now. Would he or she take it as a challenge? Try to snatch more of my charges?

Lexie?

For the first time, I considered kicking myself for suggesting that Corina Carey keep on this story. I hoped I hadn't made a major mistake.

# Chapter Eighteen

I WISHED I'D stayed home alone with Lexie the next day.

First, I'd some problems on pet-sitting rounds. None of my charges was missing, thank heavens. But my longtime client Alexander, the usually playful pit bull, had an upset tummy. Which necessitated a run to his vet—not, unfortunately, Tom Venson, but at least it was someone closer. And of course a call to his owner, who okayed medical treatment, including a special diet for a few days to counter the effects of the new food that such owner had left. It turned out to be the cause of the poor pup's stomach ailment—nothing I'd done, I was relieved to learn. That still necessitated some extra visits by me—and by Rachel, whom I called to back me up since I couldn't hang around there very long.

Most of all, it meant an extra hour's worth of cleaning stuff that had erupted from both ends of the ailing dog. I didn't even think of leaving that messy chore to my young employee . . . well, I didn't consider it long.

But all that nearly made me late for my law meeting. And absolutely left me out of sorts.

I'd suggested the settlement session to try to resolve the dispute between my clients, Jasper and Angelica McGregor, and Jasper's extremely hale and hearty second cousin Tallulah. I'd offered my office's bar-conference room. Everyone was there at eleven A.M., as scheduled.

And I yearned to be back on the road pet-sitting. Well . . . not exactly as I'd done *that* morning. Better yet, at Darryl's Doggy Indulgence Day Resort, where I'd left Lexie so my dear friend could keep both eyes, plus those of his active staff, on her—now that I was so freaked about the pet-nappings.

Instead, there I sat, Jasper and Angelica at my side. The two septuagenarians seemed dressed for serious discussion, Jasper in a natty suit with a white shirt and a plaid tie knotted beneath his wattle. Angelica wore a bright scarlet dress that emphasized the rosiness of her round cheeks.

Sitting behind them, quite calmly, was a weimaraner—a lanky dog with long legs, an almost taupe coat, and beautiful pale blue eyes. Those eyes seemed awfully anxious as he regarded the room, but he still sat absolutely obediently—near my clients, I noticed, not her former owner.

But, then, Jasper held the end of Whiskey's leash.

Across from them was Tallulah, tall and imposing and as old as they were. Her hair was a helmet of shining silver, her lips reddened enough to suggest she was out for blood. She wore a blue blouse with a collar held together with a long gold pin from which a locket dangled. Big diamonds glittered on her earlobes and ring fingers. Even her glasses sparkled, although I assumed the stones set into the plastic frames were paste.

"I'm here," Tallulah stated to start the meeting. "But the only thing you can do to make me end my lawsuit is to give me back my dog. These people got her under false pretenses."

"The only pretenses were yours," Jasper stormed. "You gave Whiskey to me because you said you were dying."

"I thought I was dying. Well, I fooled you, you old fool. I survived."

"You didn't say you were only lending Whiskey to us if you lived," Angelica said in a much more reasonable tone than her husband. "You even signed his papers."

"But you must have known I'd never have given him up if I had any idea I'd live."

At which point Whiskey whined. Tallulah appeared as anguished as if the sound had stabbed her. And Angelica rose, knelt, and threw her arms around the poor pup who obviously felt the friction in the room.

"That argument's a little circular," I interjected and looked at Tallulah's lawyer for acknowledgment or other input.

Yes, she'd brought her lawyer along, as I'd insisted. This was, after all, a meeting in the hopes of settling her lawsuit. And knowing that she was represented by counsel, I couldn't meet with her without that attorney present.

Gordon Yarber simply smiled. He was a short man with long, light hair, maybe a little younger than me, and his mission in life appeared to be to take things lightly. He offered no opinion. He said nothing at all.

He obviously would be no help at this session unless his attitude was a ploy to put me off guard. Maybe, at an appropriate moment, he'd interject some pithy input to somehow convince me his client's case had merit.

Maybe not.

"In any event," I said, drawing my disappointed gaze from opposing counsel, "I'm sure that Gordon has told you how high litigation costs can be. If we can find a way to settle this, it would be better for all three of you."

Tallulah changed her position slightly, crossing her arms tighter and shutting out my statement with her argumentative body language. I saw, rather than heard, her "harrumph."

"Now, as you know," I continued insistently, "Jasper and Angelica have traveled with Whiskey. Shown him, and done well with it. Incurred expenses."

"It's not the money," Jasper all but shouted at my side. "We fell in love with that dog."

"But they did think about you," I continued to Tallulah, attempting to ignore my fractious client. "They even toasted you each time Whiskey won."

"I'm sure," Tallulah snarled, heaving a furious glare at her second cousin.

"They didn't understand any supposed restrictions on your gift. In any event, we're talking about another living being here. Obviously compensation won't help. I've handled animal custody situations before." And been quite creative about it, I might add. Some were before I even got my law license back, so I *had* to be creative. I couldn't actually practice law then, or even appear to be. And I'd get creative here as well, if these people wouldn't work it out themselves. "We could do this like child custody is handled. How about joint custody, in which you each get a share of Whiskey's time?"

"Forget it," Tallulah barked. "I want my dog back."

"You can't have him," Jasper responded, standing at my side with his fists clenched. On his other side, Angelica, too, had stood and appeared menacing.

"Even if you win at trial, Tallulah, all you'll likely get is money," I said, staring at Gordon with exasperation. Wouldn't he say anything at all to further the intent of this session?

Apparently not. Maybe all he wanted was his legal fees at trial, no matter what the outcome.

"I've sued for Whiskey's return," Tallulah trumpeted triumphantly. "Gordon called it specific performance. Equitable relief. And I'll definitely be relieved to get my poor dog back." As if waiting for the opportunity, she hurled herself from her spot at the table toward Whiskey.

The dog stood and wagged his long, thin tail.

Jasper moved to put himself in his cousin's path.

I maneuvered myself between them to avoid bloodshed—I hoped—and found myself snagged on Tallulah's spiteful glare.

"But you signed documents transferring ownership," I said to her, attempting to sound reasonable. "I'm sure your attorney explained that."

I glanced at that still-silent counsel. Gordon simply smiled. Again.

At least Tallulah backed down—just a little. She stopped storming toward Whiskey and looked down at her ample wrist. Obviously she was a member of an older generation—as well she appeared—since she wore a watch. "Time's up. I promised to come for half an hour, and I did. We didn't settle anything. I didn't get my poor Whiskey back—although if we gave him a choice, I'll bet he'd come with me. Right, Whiskey?"

She edged sideways enough to give the dog a clear view of her. Whiskey whined again.

"Just let me give him one pat, please," Tallulah said to Jasper. "And then I'll go. For now."

I glanced at my client and gave a small nod, which he fortunately returned.

Watching large Tallulah engulf thin Whiskey in a hug was almost heartbreaking. But my clients had a good point.

How could this be resolved without a judge turning into Solomon and offering to split the dog in two?

I'd have to consider harder how I'd handle that.

But right then, Tallulah rose. Tears shone from her eyes. "I'm leaving. Come on Gordon."

He stood on that cue, and they both strode from the conference room.

Leaving me with my clients and Whiskey.

"I told you it wouldn't do any good, Kendra." Jasper shook his head sadly.

"It was worth a try," Angelica added. "But Tallulah is anything but reasonable. I'm afraid we're going to trial—but surely no judge would make us give up Whiskey, right?"

"I can't promise anything," I warned. "Paperwork or not, she was Whiskey's owner for most of the pup's life."

"We get it," said Jasper. "And like I said before, it hurts like hell to lose my last living blood relative—especially while she's still alive. But at least we have Whiskey."

"How does it look, Kendra?" Borden asked anxiously a while later, peering at me over his bifocals. His usual Hawaiian-style shirt seemed a bit muted—soft beige amidst small white flowers that matched his great shock of hair.

We sat in his office, the largest in the former restaurant. I loved his taste—the old antique desk, the oak paneling with shelves on one side containing rows of the obligatory law books. I sat on my favorite of his client chairs, with its ornate carved back and arms, and blue embroidered upholstery.

But right now, I felt uncomfortable. "I'm not sure we accomplished a lot," I admitted. "Too much emotion. Lots of hurt feelings, on top of the dispute about the dog."

"Any chance of settling without going to trial?"

"Not unless I come up with something Solomon-like," I said, reiterating my prior thought.

"I don't like the idea of dog-splitting any more than

baby-splitting," he said with a sigh. "You've got to come up with something less messy."

"I'm certainly going to try."

I RECEIVED A call from Rachel later in the day. "Could you please come check on Alexander?"

I immediately sat up straighter at my law desk and gripped my cell phone even tighter. "Does he seem to be feeling bad? Has he had any more . . . accidents?"

"There's nothing I've had to clean up. And he seems pretty perky. But he doesn't want to let me go home. Every time I try to get near the door without him on a leash, he blocks my way. And he's big enough that I haven't been able to push him aside."

"I'll be there right away," I told her.

"IMMEDIATELY" TURNED OUT to be an exaggeration, thanks to the slew of traffic heading east toward Alexander's.

While I was on my way, I got a call from an unknown number. "Kendra Ballantyne," I answered, glad my mouth had something to do besides curse other drivers filling the 101 Freeway.

"Kendra? This is Jerry Jefferton. I'm calling to thank you."

"Hi, Jerry. Thank me for what?" My mind curled over the last time I'd seen him—possibly the only time, at the PSCSC meeting where I'd met Nya's significant other, possibly an equal contender with Tracy for Nya's killer.

"For cluing the police into reality so they finally got that I didn't harm my sweet Nya," he said.

I did? "I'd say you're welcome, Jerry, only I didn't do anything." I pushed the turn signal lever as I slid the Beamer into a small opening in the left lane beside me. The maneuver distracted me from my conversation, so I had to think a second when Jerry responded.

"Really? Well, I figured you had a hand in their change of heart. Before, they didn't seem to believe anything I said, no matter how many times I said it. But they suddenly seemed to buy into my argument that I'd have been damned stupid to clean a bunch of baseball bats so thoroughly that not one yielded a fingerprint, then stick them inside an open shed on my property."

"I see," I said, and I did. Jerry *was* a prime suspect. As Nya's significant other, with whom he'd apparently argued in public, and who was likely to know his lady's whereabouts at least some of the time, he had motive and opportunity. He'd be even a better bet for jailbait if the cops could prove he had means, too. Bats similar to the one that had beaten Nya to death could provide that additional angle.

"I don't use baseball bats or anything else to ward off unfriendly animals when I'm walking dogs," Jerry continued. "I've taken over a lot of Nya's clients now, since some people are still out of town. It's kinda fun, and I used to go along with Nya sometimes for the ride so I know what to do."

"What's your regular job?" I inquired. My conversation wasn't distracting me from driving just then, since freeway traffic was almost at a standstill. I craned my neck, hoping to see that the next exit was nearby. I'd take it, whatever it was.

"I'm a landscape designer, and I supervise the guys who implement my plans. That leaves me flexibility to pet-sit, since my hours are my own."

More so than mine, I thought.

"Anyway," he went on, "that Detective Lunn started questioning me almost the moment after Tracy found Nya, and he got a warrant to look around my home and office. I'd have given him permission anyway, since I'd nothing to hide—only he found those damned bats there. I told him right off that if Nya didn't stick them there without my knowledge, then someone put them there to frame me, but he didn't buy it."

I would have, and not just because I'd assumed Jerry wasn't the only possible suspect the first time we'd spoken. But I'd been in a similar position once, so I was more likely to assume that someone claiming to be framed *was*.

"But he's buying it now?" Ah! A small break in traffic in the lane to my right. I quickly but carefully shot over.

"Yeah. I called Lunn to tell him I'd started compiling a list of everyone I knew who might have access to my yard, including all employees who do landscaping for me, and maybe anyone in the world since I wasn't always careful to lock my gate—before."

"Must be a long list," I observed.

"What? Oh, because it could include everyone? Well, it didn't matter, since Lunn thanked me but said that I could rest a little easier now. He told me that, after some discussions he'd been holding, his focus was on someone else."

A ploy to make Jerry feel relaxed enough to spill his guts? If not, who was that focus on?

I was afraid I could guess.

"Well, whoever those discussions were with, it wasn't me, Jerry," I told him. I grinned as the next exit finally appeared not far ahead. That was the good thing.

The bad was that everyone on the road seemed as inclined as I to use it.

Maybe sticking out the snail's pace on the freeway was a better idea.

"Anyway," I said, "glad to hear things are going better for you now." Okay, that was a slight lie. I didn't know the guy well, so whether or not I'd glommed on to him as my prime suspect, I'd rather he be guilty than someone I cared about. "Good luck."

After thanks, he hung up. And I hung out on the freeway.

I next pushed in Tracy's number.

"Oh, Kendra," she cried out almost immediately. "Where are you? Can you come here? I'm afraid I'm about to be arrested."

# Chapter Nineteen

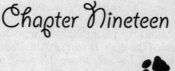

I COULDN'T HEAD to Tracy's immediately. Not when I was so concerned about Alexander.

But the pit bull wasn't so bad by the time I got there. And since he seemed starved for attention, I praised Rachel for her compassionate care of him and hustled him into the Beamer.

And held my breath as I drove toward Tracy's. What if his stomach really was still upset, and I'd have a stinky, sticky mess to clean up inside my car?

I always kept cleanup stuff in the trunk, in case I got to a client's and the cupboard was bare. Could I get Alexander to sit on a big plastic garbage bag for half an hour?

Unlikely. And he seemed just fine standing shotgun and sniffing out the window after I cracked it a smidgen.

Lexie wasn't going to like this, though—the scent of her domain contaminated by an interloper.

At least traffic had improved, and I arrived at Tracy's in about twenty minutes. She lived in a fourplex apartment building on one of the twisty near-canyon streets around Beachwood Drive in Hollywood. Her flat was on the first floor, the one at the right, and I heard a bevy of barks the instant my fingers neared the doorbell. Which of course caused Alexander's hackles to rise and a growl to emanate from deep in his throat.

Hmmm. The different-toned sounds suggested that Phoebe the puggle wasn't the sole canine occupant at Tracy's. Did Allen have a dog, too? Was Tracy taking in clients' pets instead of staying in their homes?

Maybe making Alexander feel less abandoned by bringing him along wasn't such a good idea after all—even though he had a stellar personality, particularly for a pit bull.

Allen answered the door. His long chin seemed to dip even deeper when he saw I wasn't alone. He wore a white button shirt and khaki slacks that he'd most likely worn to work that day. "Hi, Kendra. I saw you with a small dog last time."

"That was Lexie, my own pup. This is Alexander, a client who needs some extra TLC. But maybe we'd better not come in."

"Good idea."

But just then Tracy came up beside her guy, with Phoebe in her arms and, on a leash, an adorable white furball pup of no particular breed I could distinguish. She wore a dirty white PSCSC T-shirt over ratty jeans—Tracy, not the dog. Had she grown so depressed she wasn't interested in her appearance, or was that simply her casual at-home look? "Oh, Kendra, I'm so glad you're here. Come in." She drew away from the door and used her head to motion me inside.

"I have Alexander with me," I cautioned before coming in. "He's got a wonderful personality and I wouldn't have brought him if I hadn't figured he'd get along with Phoebe, but with another stranger in the mix—"

"Oh, Chelsea's a sweetie. As long as Alexander doesn't attack her, she won't attack him." She turned her back and headed down the short hall.

Allen, who'd ended up almost behind the door, shrugged his skinny shoulders as he closed it behind Alexander and me.

The place was the sort that had been built in the first half of the twentieth century, with hardwood floors and arched doorways. Of course it was small, since it consisted of only a quarter of the whole house. It was pretty and homey, and though Tracy's furniture was sparse and appeared well used, I really liked the looks of her home.

We three humans sat in the living room on overstuffed chairs arranged around a table containing magazines about animals, near a glass-enclosed fireplace. The dogs, let loose, sniffed one another and to my surprise seemed content to lie at our respective feet. Alexander even abutted his butt against my shoes, again suggesting the poor pup had been lonesome.

I figured Tracy would start talking in her own good time. I certainly didn't want to blurt out, "Why do you think you're going to be arrested?"

Only, when the silence lengthened, I blurted out, "Tracy, why do you think you're going to be arrested?"

Her eyes grew a sharper brown, or maybe it was the light reflecting in her sudden tears that gave that impression.

Allen stood suddenly, his fists clenched and his otherwise ordinary features twisted. "This is absolutely ridiculous. Tracy's done nothing wrong. Those damned cops are so inept. They find what they think are clues and then misinterpret them any way they want."

"They found some baseball bats at Jerry Jefferton's," Tracy said with a deep and sorrowful sigh. She picked up Phoebe from the floor and squeezed her tightly as if for moral support.

"I heard," I started to say. "He—"

But Tracy continued as if I wasn't talking. "You'd think that would mean they'd consider him a great suspect, after Nya was killed that way. But they said it was too obviously a plant, and that I'd had better opportunity anyway, when I found her at my client's. And of course who better to plant baseball bats than someone who's vocal about using them on the job, like me?"

"Too obvious, isn't it?" Allen countered with a rather repulsive snort. He sat on a chair close to Tracy's and slipped his hand beneath Phoebe, presumably to squeeze his main squeeze's knee comfortingly.

Phoebe didn't seem to like it, though, and leaped down, leaving Tracy's lap bereft. The rest of Tracy, too, since the tears in her eyes coursed down her cheeks.

"I'd say so," I agreed. "But why do you think—"

She stopped me this time by her own repetition. "That I'm going to be arrested? Because Detective Lunn told me to come to the station tomorrow to answer more questions. And when I told him I'd bring that nice lawyer friend of yours, Esther Ickes, he said it was a good idea." That caused Tracy to break into sobs.

Allen stood, which caused all three dogs to stand, so I rose, too. Tracy was the only one to stay seated as we all gathered around to console her despite her disconsolate weeping.

She got hold of herself soon. "Kendra, I know you're doing all you can to find out who killed Nya, and also who's been doing that terrible pet-napping. But I have to ask you another favor."

My insides tightened so uncomfortably that I wondered if my skin was suddenly shrinking. "What's that?" I asked with pseudocheerfulness.

"Allen's really sweet and volunteered, but he's a much better insurance salesman than pet-sitter. And I know you can't take on midday dog walks, what with your law job, of course."

Uh-oh. I knew what was coming. Could I comfortably say no?

No.

"But some of my clients will be out of town for weeks and I have to ease up on my schedule, at least until I've gone through this additional questioning and am hopefully in the clear. I'll hang on to four myself." At Allen's attempt to intercede, she said, "I have to, to keep my sanity. I love my work and wish I could do it all. *Will* do it all, when this is over. But for now, I've already gotten Wanda and Lilia to take on one of my clients each. Sometimes I've traded off with other club members as well when one or another of us gets too busy, but everyone's either swamped or scared, and there are three more I need help with. Kendra, could you take on some more pet-sitting for me?"

I THOUGHT I could handle three, with Rachel's able assistance. Assuming, of course, that my employee didn't get a coveted, time-consuming acting job in the interim.

And I had to hand it to Tracy. She was determined to take tremendous care of the cats and dogs she'd been watching. She was being realistic about the demands on her time and psyche. And she refused to give up, even though she needed help.

I got the particulars and the keys from her. She even took me for quick visits to each, and Alexander appeared to enjoy the lengthening ride.

But eventually, I needed to say my adieus and head back toward the Valley. Because it was getting late, I headed first to Darryl's to pick up Lexie. She spied me first as I entered the door, and hightailed it toward me from her favorite area—the one with the people furniture for hounds to bask on.

"Everything okay, Kendra?" Darryl asked as he moseyed over from the check-in desk to say hi.

"Sure, as long as I like to stay busy." I informed him about the extra pet-sitting I'd agreed to take on for Tracy.

"I've never seen anyone as able at juggling responsibilities as you," my lanky friend said with a slow smile. "And I just happen to have another referral for you." His brown eyes twinkled from beneath his wire rims.

"Save it till I have a spare minute, Nestler," I retorted, and he gave a short, loud laugh.

Lexie, Alexander, and I headed out to care for the rest of my clients. My new tasks for Tracy's charges would start the next day. I spent a nice, long time caring for each pet, managing to juggle leashes so Lexie and Alexander came along on the walks. Both were on best behavior.

But eventually I needed to return Alexander to his abode. I considered bringing him home with me, but Lexie had been a good enough sport. She'd need individual attention, too.

Fortunately, it appeared by then that I'd exhausted Alexander. Leaving Lexie in the Beamer, which I parked temporarily in the garage of Alexander's house, I opened his door, handed him some extra treats, and said, "Good night, guy. See you in the morning."

He sat and seemed to smile, then headed for his doggy bed in the corner of his owner's tile-floored kitchen. I ensured that the security system was set. And then I double- and triple-checked it . . . and left.

"It's been a heck of a day, Lex," I told my cute, cuddly Cavalier when I returned to the Beamer. "Let's go home." On the way we stopped at the drive-through window of a fast-food joint. I ordered a salad, to ensure my conscience didn't bug me, plus a burger. At home, I split both, although Lexie received more of the salad's chicken than I did, and I ate more rabbit food.

Rather than wait for my cell phone to sing, I called Jeff. "I've been hoping that Althea dug up a new tidbit that a super P.I. like you ran with and solved Nya Barston's murder."

"Hope some more," he said. "Nothing new from her, though she's researching brands of baseball bats. Oh, and she's looking in depth into Jerry Jefferton, too, who seems not to have gotten into any trouble during his life. He's got some interesting stuff on the web about landscape design, though."

"I'll keep that in mind if I ever redo the grounds around my rented-out house. And from you?"

"No news, either. I've been swamped, although I've thought about you a lot. Kendra—"

"I've been thinking about you, too, Jeff," I said, heading him off since his tone had sounded suddenly serious. "Let's get together for dinner some night. Next week, maybe." No take-out Thai, although I didn't say that. And I felt like I was handing him a dose of his own, earlier, back-away medicine.

"Am I being brushed off?" he said in an ominously cool tone.

"Of course not." My tone? Oh, way too jolly.

"Yeah? Well, I'll call you one of these days, Kendra." And he was immediately off the other end.

Which left a gaping hole in my psyche. What was I doing?

Hell if I knew. But I wasn't going to dig inside to find out. Instead, I called Tom Venson. Who fortunately sounded very happy to hear from me. We talked teasingly over the phone for a few minutes. Better to stroke our respective libidos long distance than in the same room. At least till I answered that same question I'd posed only moments before: What was I doing?

When I hung up from Tom, we'd planned another date. I was glad. And sorry.

I decided to pour myself a small glass of wine—for medicinal purposes. And maybe to help me access my subconscious, so I'd figure out which guy I wanted and how to let the other graciously off the hook.

Assuming that Jeff didn't unhook me even faster than I made up my own mind.

"What am I doing, Lexie?" I repeated my question aloud to my sweet pup as she sat beside me on the floor while I poured my libation.

She didn't bark me an answer.

SINCE I HAD a court appearance the next day, I got up damnably early and took Lexie on my pet-sitting rounds, including the extra three for Tracy. I dressed appropriately for a lawyer, although I left my heels in the car and replaced them temporarily with sneakers till I needed them. Same went for my suit jacket.

After Alexander's illness and clinginess yesterday, I decided to give him some TLC and a treat today, so I picked him up and brought him right along with Lexie to Darryl's delightful day resort. We were met at the door by the employee I liked least, Kiki, the blue-eyed bombshell of a would-be starlet. I'd always considered her animal friendly and people-skills deprived. Without even looking at me, she gushed out a greeting, then said, "Darryl's not here yet," in a tone that suggested her pleasure at being the bearer of bad tidings. Still, she quickly knelt and held out her arms for Alexander and Lexie.

No matter what my feelings for Kiki, I left knowing the pups would be in good hands.

Back in the Beamer, I called my law office and informed Mignon I was off to court before reporting to the office.

"See you later," Mignon sang in her usual cheerful tune.

A couple of hours later, pleased after winning the motion I'd argued, I returned to my law office and was greeted with Mignon's chirped hello.

"Hi," I parroted with a smile of my own. "Is Borden in?"

He was, and I discussed the status of some cases with him. Then I got to work on my ideas for the next and undoubtedly last settlement attempt scheduled for the McGregors and Cousin Tallulah. We'd try again first thing next week, and after that the matter would be decided in court.

Later, I called Darryl to ensure he'd eventually gotten to his resort that A.M. He had. As always, he was busy, but said he was keeping a close eye on Lexie and Alexander. "Come by after you do your pet-sitting stops," he said. "I have some paperwork, so I'll be here late today. I'll make a fresh pot of coffee and we'll catch up on everything."

Which was absolutely wonderful with me.

And so, at the end of my law-practice day, I started on my second round of cosseting clients—feeding them all, walking and roughhousing with adorable dogs, changing cat litter, and talking to cute kitties.

My next-to-last stop was at one of the three homes that had been Tracy's clients' to care for two moderate-size mixed-breed dogs who'd been littermates and were now best buddies. They were full of energy and previously greeted me enthusiastically.

Only, when I opened the door, they weren't there.

My heart plummeted as if I'd filled it with every ounce of blood within my body. "Spike? Frank?" I shrieked, tearing down the center hall of the small house. Surely they hadn't been pet-napped on my watch the way the Dorgan pets had been. "Spike? Frank? Where are you?" My hand immediately plunged to the bottom of the big bag I habitually slung over my shoulder, searching for my cell phone. Would I need to call 911?

I hurried toward the kitchen, hoping they'd stopped for a drink of water before coming to see me.

No dogs—but as I dashed through the door, I saw a movement of a human-size form from the corner of my eye. "Hey!" I shouted as I stopped short.

Simultaneous with the tremendous crash on the counter beside me, something was dropped tightly over my head, and I was dragged down to the hard tile floor.

## Chapter Twenty

I SHRIEKED NONSENSICAL syllables of fear as I lifted my arm outside the obstacle that now covered me, waved it wildly, and pushed the button of the can clutched in my fingers.

Which caused my assailant to yell as well. Was the tone high enough to signify female, or did rage and pain instigate the shrillness? Who knew?

But I heard a bull-like charge beyond me through the kitchen, followed by the slamming open of the door to the yard plus footsteps on the short wooden back porch. Still clutching the pepper spray I'd dug from my purse while groping for my cell phone, I struggled to free my body from its uncomfortable bonds.

When I finally uncovered my face, I found that the thing cast over me was a floral bedsheet, much too cheery for the dire use to which it had been put. I hastened to the outer doorway and scanned the unfenced yard, but whoever had attacked me had already escaped. The homes here were close together and no neighbor stood outside observing my attacker's flight.

In my shaking hand, I still held the can that had saved my bacon. I went back inside and approached the area where I'd been attacked.

On the floor was a big, broken piece of baseball bat.

SOMEHOW, I AGAIN found my cell phone in my purse.

I dialed 911.

When I was eventually off hold and had someone to talk to, I explained what had happened and asked for Ned Noralles, assuming he was available. I didn't give a damn that this was neither his jurisdiction nor his assigned area of detection.

This might not have been an accomplished homicide, but it sure had been an attempted one.

I sagged against the counter, but only for a minute. My initial dilemma still remained.

Where were the pets of the house?

Only then did I realize that what I'd thought was the buzzing in my frazzled brain was the sound of distant, muffled dogs in distress.

My legs were about the consistency of hair gel, but I let them slurp along the floor in the direction from which I thought the barks and yelps emanated. "Spike? Frank?" I was sure I sounded as frantic as they did.

Out of the kitchen, partway back along the hall, and into a room that appeared to be a study, I followed the sounds as they grew louder.

"Spike? Frank?" I continuously called, until I narrowed my muzzy brain on a door that seemed the source of the dog noise. I opened it, and the middle-size, wonderful mutts spilled out, still barking but now leaping gleefully all over me.

I sank onto the floor and let them stomp, snort, nuzzle, and lick until human help finally arrived.


NED NORALLES WASN'T the first cop to come to this house, but he joined those who'd arrived before. He shook his head in dismay when he saw me seated on a chair in the comfortably eclectic living room, giving my story to yet another cop while the dogs sprawled on the sofa at my sides.

"You're in trouble again, Kendra?" he asked in a much quieter tone than he usually jabbed at me.

"Guess so, if being attacked with a baseball bat is any indication." I described the scary scenario, complete with the counter taking the brunt of the swing of the bat at the same time I was enfolded in a sheet. And how I'd grabbed the pepper spray, wildly wise in retrospect, simply because something was clearly wrong in this house when Spike and Frank didn't barrel to the door to greet me.

"Could you tell if it was a man or woman?" Ned demanded.

"I've answered that at least half a dozen times," I said, nodding to the suited detective who'd preceded Ned here. His cadre of interrogating uniformed cops still milled around.

"And the answer?"

"No."

"Was the person tall or short? Fat or thin? Do you have any description at all?"

"Very sketchy," I said.

"Could it have been someone you knew?"

"Possibly."

"Who knew you'd be here?"

Uh-oh. Other members of the club, of course, but the top of the list for that answer was Tracy. But if she had it in for me, why attack me here, when she would again be the obvious suspect?

The same someone who'd framed her for Nya's murder could have been attempting it again.

With me as the targeted murder victim.

"Kendra?" A deeply familiar masculine voice suddenly shouted into the room, followed by an equally familiar male body.

Jeff.

"What are you doing here, Hubbard?" Ned growled. These two had a long-standing testosterone battle going and seldom started out a conversation civilly.

"I heard that Kendra had been attacked. Are you okay?"

I was suddenly standing and enfolded in strong and comforting arms.

"How did you hear that?" I heard Ned grumble from somewhere over Jeff's broad shoulder, the one on which I now leaned.

Jeff didn't answer. I didn't expect him to, and I suspect

Ned didn't, either. My assumption was that his security company monitored police bands. I'd given my name when I called 911, and it was possibly broadcast with the order for cops to come here.

How he'd heard didn't matter, only that he *had* heard. And he had come.

OKAY, I TOLD myself a long time later, when the cops had finally completed their interrogation and on-site investigation and informed me I could depart. If Tom Venson had known what happened to me, he'd have come, too. But there was no reason for a veterinarian to monitor police bands. And I hadn't called him.

But the truth was, he wasn't there when I'd needed comforting, even if it was through no intentional avoidance of me in an hour-plus of awful need.

Jeff was.

"You're coming home with Odin and me," that same P.I. declared as soon as we'd exited the door. "Is Lexie at Darryl's?"

"Yes," I said. "I mean about Lexie. So's Alexander, a pit bull who's a client of mine. I called Darryl a while back to explain why I'm so late, and he's hanging out there to hear what happened. That's where I'm heading now."

The wide residential street was usually well lighted from street lamps, and this night the vans and other vehicles that had carried cops here to conduct the investigation also helped to illuminate the area.

My Beamer remained parked in the driveway, and I strode purposefully toward it, glad Jeff was at my side even though I pretended to ignore him.

I'd considered taking Spike and Frank along that night but decided against it. The cops assured me there'd be a stakeout on this street tonight, under the assumption that the attacker could also have been planning a pet-napping, and a little thing like attempted murder might have been a mere hiccup, not a reason to drop the plan altogether. Plus, I'd called the dogs' owners. They were driving back home that night from Palm Springs, would be home in a matter of hours. Even so, I gave the pups extra hugs. Poor guys acted as if they needed lots of TLC, and I'd lavished it on them.

When we reached the Beamer, Jeff said, "I'm parked down the street. Had a hard time finding a space. Pull out and wait for me. I'll follow you to Darryl's."

"No need," I said. "Lexie and I will just take Alexander to his place, then go home."

"I'll follow you, then, till you get there. Once you're safely behind your gate, I'll go pick up Odin and our dinner. I'm not up for Thai tonight. How's chicken?"

I *was* feeling a little chicken, I admitted to myself—though not to Jeff. "No need to bother. Lexie and I have food we can fix for ourselves."

"We're not going to argue about this," he said. His sexy blue eyes were as intense as I'd ever seen them. Or maybe it was just the way the streetlights hit him. "I'm spending the night at your place, Kendra, like it or not. On the couch, if that's the way you want it, but Odin and I will be there."

"If it'll make you feel better." I hoped my shrug appeared indifferent. Which was not the way I felt. Can't say that I usually went for a me-man-you-woman kind of assertive routine, but right about then I appreciated it. And his insistence did make me feel better, despite my attempt to act cool.

I backed out and idled the Beamer beneath a streetlight until Jeff's black Escalade pulled up behind. Meantime, I scanned the street but saw no surreptitious movements in the shadows, only a few residual cops knocking on neighbors' doors.

My attacker had to be long gone, especially with this police presence invading the neighborhood.

On the way toward Darryl's, I called Tracy. She was understandably shaken. Cops had descended to question her again—after a long afternoon at the police station undergoing an interrogation in Nya's murder. At least she was now under the wing of Esther Ickes, who'd been my mother hen criminal counsel a while back. Tracy had been out tending those few pets she'd maintained as clients at the time I'd been attacked here.

Could she have been the being who attempted to bean me with a baseball bat? Maybe, but I couldn't imagine why.

THE TIME NEARED ten P.M. by the time Jeff and Odin joined
Lexie and me at our home. I'd already given Darryl a cursory
overview of the night's awful occurrences, then driven
Alexander home, all the while eyeing Jeff in my rearview
mirror.

When my wrought-iron security gate shut securely behind
the Beamer, Jeff had zoomed off as promised, but only after
calling me on my cell phone and insisting on staying on the
line until my pup and I were safely ensconced in our apartment.

And now he was back.

We sat in my small living room, balancing plates of
roasted chicken, potatoes, and coleslaw on our laps while
watching the news on TV, and the dogs watched us.

Sure enough, the attack on me had struck a chord with the
media. Like Jeff, they undoubtedly monitored police bands,
too, and with Nya's murder along with the serial pet-nappings,
this situation was sexy enough to stick my face on the boob
tube.

"I hate this," I said, warily watching pooch eyes observe
each forkful of food I raised to my mouth. One unintentional
move and I'd have a Cavalier and Akita on my lap licking my
plate.

"Then let's figure out who's doing it," Jeff said.

"Yeah, like it's that easy," I retorted, letting my amazed
gaze land on the hunky guy at the other end of my sectional
sofa.

"Easy or not, let's do it. You tired?"

I wondered if that was an invitation to go to bed . . . with
him. But the look on his face wasn't come hither. More like
the dogs' determination to accomplish something, like eat.

"I'm too wired to sleep," I said.

"Good. Let's go through your suspect list—knowing you,
you've made detailed notes and changed the order several
times."

"You assume right," I said.

"Good. Once we've talked about them, we'll figure out

who's most likely, and I'll run with it for the next couple of days."

"You think we'll nab a suspect that quickly?"

"Hope so, since I'm going out of town again soon and I'll need you to stay at my place and watch Odin."

# Chapter Twenty-one

WE DID AS Jeff said. Stayed up till extremely late, sitting in my tiny makeshift office in a corner of my bedroom going over my lists, while Lexie and Odin snored on the floor beside us.

Keeping my mind focused on stuff other than the fact I'd been attacked that night . . . or trying to.

We started with the pet-snatchings. But I hadn't a cogent clue about nabbing the napper. Who was it? Someone with a grudge against the PSCSC? I'd only been a member for a matter of months. I'd heard that someone was kicked out shortly prior to my tenure, but the same rumor suggested the ousted sitter ultimately thanked the group after using the wake-up call to make over her life. She now supposedly had a wonderful pet-less job in Chicago. No likely motive there.

"Anyone kicked out lately?" Jeff asked after I related that tale.

"Not that I know of," I responded.

"Well, has a client of any member made a complaint to the club and been ignored?"

"We'd have investigated it, and I'd have heard."

"Have you considered Nya as a possible pet-napper?"

Jeff's question struck upon one of my most disconcerting

and ongoing ponders. That certainly could explain her appearance at the home where she'd been killed, at a client of Tracy's, not her own.

"Sure," I answered, "but that wouldn't solve the other pet-snatches since Nya's demise."

"She had a coconspirator."

"Maybe," I said. "If so, that person's probably her murderer. But why would she steal pets in the first place? And who connived with her, killed her, then continued to snatch animals—and why?"

"All excellent questions," Jeff said. "Any answers?"

"Nope." Silently, I still supposed the who could be someone affiliated with the Pet-Sitters Club. But I'd few logical responses as to why any would steal someone else's clients. Jealousy of others' successes? Some other, unvoiced dissatisfaction with the organization? To cast suspicions in another direction, as had crossed my mind at Lilia's, by absconding with one of their own charges?

At Jeff's urging, I slogged through the membership list alongside him. Nya, of course. And Tracy. And Wanda Villareal, my friend and fellow Cavalier aficionado. Frieda Shoreman. Lilia Ziegler. Others who were members but who weren't as involved with the running of the club. Then there were nonmembers who were peripherally involved, such as significant others like Jerry Jefferton and Allen Smith.

But why steal animals?

We got on to my computer and again Googled all these people—repeating exercises Jeff had already engaged in. He even accessed some of his supersecret databases, the ones on which Althea soared in proficiency, and looked up some of the players there. He printed out plenty of background.

But none leaped out as obviously insidious pet-stealers. And I really couldn't imagine any of those I knew from the club as pet-nappers—let alone people who'd have attacked me.

There remained the possibility that the serial pet-napper had nothing to do with PSCSC and was snatching other animals without the crimes being called out anyplace where Jeff, or the incredible Althea, dug up info.

We then considered murder suspects—much more likely to have perpetrated my assault.

My preference was to remove Tracy from that list alto-gether but couldn't yet, so I kept her there in small print. Jerry Jefferton's I bolded and bracketed near the top. He might have been cleared by the cops, but he'd been Nya's significant other and they'd argued. I wasn't sure when Nya would be released for interment, but I'd most definitely make an appearance at her memorial . . . and question Jerry further there, when he'd be emotionally off guard.

Plus, it was always interesting to see who showed up at a funeral. Wasn't it an axiom of law enforcement that the killer always came to see the result of his/her handiwork?

"Who else knew Nya?" Jeff asked.

"I'm still checking," I said.

"I will, too."

And so forth, long into the night.

And did we determine who'd done any of the dastardly deeds we investigated? No way. In fact, I was concertedly confused. But when I insisted on additional checking, trying to correlate the pet-nappings and people-battings while letting my fingers wander far afield, I finally had a hit.

"Jeff!" I shouted excitedly. "Look at this."

He was still sitting beside me at my small desk, staring at my computer-printed lists anew as if they were finally pre-pared to point out the killer. Now, he glanced over quizzically.

I pointed to a couple of photos on an animal shelter's web-site: Loving Friends. "See that? That dog's a wire-haired dachshund. It looks a lot like Augie—the dog pet-napped on Tracy's watch. That one resembles Cramer, the cockapoo Wanda was watching when he was stolen. And that cat looks like Amanda."

I felt Jeff freeze beside me. "Why would you say that?" A decided chill had entered his tone.

"Not your Amanda. I mean your ex Amanda." With that look in his eyes, I didn't dare remind him that said ex had run him over in her car not many weeks ago. Or did I? Maybe later. "This cat resembles the cat named Amanda that was pet-napped from Lilia Ziegler. I saw pictures. She's silver gray, just like that. See those fuzzy hairs sticking up from those big ears? And the kind of pushed-in face that usually only comes with purebred cats."

"Oh. Right. So you think this might be the pet-napper's drop-off point?"

"Could be," I sang, somewhat triumphantly. "At least I need to go there and find out."

"Yeah, I got that." Jeff sounded mollified. "Have you looked at this website before?"

I shook my head in the negative. "I was simply surfing, following threads about shelters I didn't previously pursue."

This shelter was up north a reasonably drivable distance, in Bakersfield. Of course tomorrow—no, I realized as I glanced at the clock in the corner of the computer—today was Wednesday, and I had lots of legal appearances and meetings over the next couple of weekdays. I couldn't easily get away until Saturday.

"I can't go tomorrow," I told Jeff with a sigh.

"You want me to do that rather than follow up on whoever attacked you?" His tone seemed ready to ignite with indignation and righteous anger.

"No. This is something I'd better do. But it'll have to wait until the weekend."

I'd worry until then about whether the similar, and possibly same, animals to those I was seeking might get adopted without my first assessing if they were the pet-nap victims. But I didn't dare drop all my law cases and dash up there, despite my boss Borden being an understanding dear.

I printed out photos of the pets, along with captions that contained, if I was right, incorrect names. I bookmarked the web page, too, so I could find it again easily.

"You tired?" Jeff asked when I was done.

"I sure am."

"Then let's go to bed."

I didn't argue, although I was fully prepared to fight Jeff off if he seemed intent on sex—not fight physically, since I didn't worry he'd strong-arm me, but I might need to fight off my own urges and congenially convince Jeff I was simply too sleepy tonight to indulge.

As it turned out, I didn't have to argue at all. We simply gave the dogs a final short romp to relieve themselves, then Jeff and I each performed our ablutions and changed into our

nightwear. I chose a sexless nightshirt, so I'd have less likelihood of turning him on.

And then we both climbed into my queen-size bed while
the dogs settled down on the floor.

The kiss Jeff gave me got my blood flowing fast and my
hormones humming so hard that I gave thought to fighting off
my intent to tell him no.

But his hands didn't rove. They pulled me to him, my
sensory-stimulated back to his hard and sexy front, and
hugged me tight.

"Good night, Kendra," Jeff murmured into my ear, giving
me goose bumps along with all the other sensations I felt.

"Good night," I whispered. How had this sinfully sexy guy
known just how to get under my skin without even a hint of
hitting on me?

As exhausted as I'd become, I still took a long while to let
my dreams carry me to unconsciousness.

I PURPOSELY RAN into Rachel the next morning while waiting
for Jeff to come downstairs, and I gave her a rundown of what
had happened last night. Both Lexie and Odin were with me,
and they appeared perfectly content to stop and smell the
roses—er, bird of paradise plants—and wait for me to move.

"Buzz Dulear from Jeff's office is going to be here in ten
minutes," I told her. "He'll accompany you on your pet-sitting
today, to make sure no one comes after you like that person
did to me last night."

"Oh, okay," said my usually perky young employee. There
were dark circles under her normally clear brown eyes. Her
waiflike appearance was more an abandoned-orphan look.
Her jeans were loose and her white T-shirt baggy. She
clenched the loop of Beggar's leash as her Irish setter traded
sniffs with my two canine charges.

"You all right?" I asked.

"I don't think they're going to let Beggar and me back into
Methuselah Manor," she wailed. "They're not saying it's because they suspect me of stealing the missing stuff, but I'm
sure that's why."

"That's lousy," I said. The kid had been so enthusiastic

about her foray into cheering seniors. I felt absolutely awful for her. And I was certain she was innocent of any kind of theft. That idea about how to help her still teased my mind, but I knew I couldn't indulge it until, hopefully, sometime next week. "Are other people visiting the place with pets?"

"No," she said miserably. "And some of the guests will really miss Beggar."

I didn't want to raise Rachel's hopes, so I didn't tell her what I had in mind. But I did say, "Maybe we can fix that. I'll see what I can do."

"Really, Kendra? Would you?" She closed the small gap between us, and I was suddenly enveloped in an enthusiastic hug. My youthful tenant smelled of baby shampoo, and I smiled. She wasn't *that* young.

"No promises," I told her.

A car pulled up to our front gate, just as Jeff appeared on the steps from my garage-top apartment.

"That's probably Buzz," I told Rachel, pointing toward the arriving vehicle. "Let him in. Let's get this day on the road."


THE REST OF the week went by both slowly and quickly.

I had to fend off lots of media interest, including my friend Corina Carey. "Why didn't you contact me immediately?" she screeched over the phone when I inadvertently answered one of her calls.

"What was there to say?" I responded coolly. "No animals were stolen and no one was killed."

"You were attacked? Did someone come after you with a bat, the way Nya Barston was killed?"

"Well, yeah," I admitted, and I told her more, mostly off the record. I mean, if getting the word out could keep other pet-sitters from grief, I had to cooperate. But I didn't see how telling all to Corina could accomplish that. I hadn't seen whoever it was, so I couldn't ask her to have her viewers to be on the lookout for the attacker.

Who turned out not to have left any fingerprints, by the way. Big surprise.

Then I had to put up with Jeff's accompanying me nearly every moment. Okay, that's an exaggeration. He was with me at all my pet-sitting assignments. I had my own security consultant assist in shutting off systems so I could get inside my clients' homes, and check every nook and cranny to ensure no mad assailant waited for me with a baseball bat.

On most levels I appreciated it. But I also started to feel smothered and started calling Jeff "Dad."

Which he clearly hated.

At least I got him to keep his distance when I was at my law office. I'd a feeling that he'd convinced Borden or some of the senior citizen attorneys who were my associates to call him if I dared to go out without an escort. And that I didn't do.

He showed up at the end of the day to shuttle me to my pet-sitting assignments.

The big protective brute scared me that way. He also managed to make me feel guilty for not leaping into his bed at every smoldering look he managed to fire at me despite my glares.

Well, all right. It wasn't just guilt I felt. I admit it—my poor bod was turning into one big lustful conflagration. Despite my self-chiding, I couldn't help feeling all gooey inside at Jeff's overprotectiveness.

I didn't even mention Amanda, let alone remind Jeff that his ex had attempted to X him out once with her car.

I kept reminding myself of my upcoming date with Tom Venson this weekend. I really liked that guy.

But was I considering telling him a nice goodbye so I could be with Jeff?

You bet.


SATURDAY FINALLY ARRIVED. Well, heck, I'd only undergone two days of Jeff's overprotectiveness, but it felt like weeks.

Or maybe it didn't feel long enough.

In any event, I'd already told him I was heading for Bakersfield to check out the group of animals that just could be our stolen clients.

Did he insist on going?

What do you think?

So first thing Saturday morning, after Jeff accompanied me on my pet-sitting rounds, I sat shotgun in his Escalade, with

Lexie and Odin riding ecstatically in the backseat. We drove a goodly distance up the 5 Freeway, past Santa Clarita and Valencia and through mountain passes past Gorman, and eventually veered off onto the Kern County route that would take us to Bakersfield.

The no-kill animal shelter called "Loving Friends" whose website I'd unearthed was just to the south of that city.

The place actually was quite pleasant, if you like to see adorable household animals in cages. The outside was a large white cottage with a big red sign that said LOVING FRIENDS. Leaving Lexie and Odin in the car, under a shady tree with the windows cracked, Jeff and I marched inside.

"Let me do the talking," I told him.

"Sure thing."

I tried not to react to his sexy smirk. Or the fit of his tight jeans and his short-sleeved beige shirt that revealed a hint of his biceps. Or the way he ogled *my* tight jeans and snug blue T-shirt.

I sauntered up to the reception desk, where a young lady who appeared to be a high school–aged volunteer sat and smiled up at us—especially Jeff. Heck, there was no age limit on noticing a really sexy guy.

"Hi. We're looking for a dog or cat to rescue. Could we see who you have available?"

"Sure," said the young lady, whose nametag said she was Georgia. "Of course you'll have to pass our adoption process. But you look like nice people, so that shouldn't be a problem."

Of course, she was still staring at Jeff.

"Great!" I gushed. We both followed her past the cozy entry and into a long, large room lined on both sides with those cages. At least they were clean cages, all with concrete floors.

Some very sad faces stared out at us from them.

Damn, I hated to visit shelters. I wanted to adopt every animal I saw.

Now, though, I was on a mission. I blinked adoringly at Jeff. "Would you mind checking out the cats, honey, while I look at the dogs? Maybe Georgia can introduce you to them."

"Would you?" he asked the young lady, who suddenly appeared all flustered. She wore shorts and a cropped top, though it was April. Well, Bakersfield was practically desert.

And I figured Jeff could view the very young merchandise without doing more than admiring.

"Well, sure. Come this way." She preceded him through a door in the middle of the dog room.

Which left me alone with all these poor, homeless hounds.

I wandered farther along the path we'd been following—and suddenly saw one of my targets, a wire-haired dachshund.

Only problem was, each cage sported a label that described the occupant. This one had a name on it, the same as on the Internet site.

Of course no pet-napper would give the correct information if he or she determined to dispose of some of the booty this way.

I knelt and held my hand through the bars of the cage. The long brown dog within sniffed it and wriggled amiably.

"Hi," I said. "Augie?"

The pup began leaping and barking so joyfully that I'd no doubt I'd located one of the missing victims.

But could I spring him? Were the others here?

And was that cute little high school girl an aider or abettor to felony dog-napping?

# Chapter Twenty-two

JUST IN CASE, I cased the joint some more, looking for other dogs who'd been absconded with, at least those I knew about and had seen their similar visages online.

A couple of cages down, a sad-eyed golden cockapoo perked up as I stopped outside. "Could you be Cramer?" I inquired.

At the name, the little fellow went wild, leaping and all but turning cartwheels. This had to be Wanda's missing client.

Two more dogs to go. Pooky and Piranha were mixed breeds, perhaps a bit more iffy to ID, but I'd memorized their pictures. Both had short hair, Pooky's black and Piranha's pale brown. Pooky apparently had some pit bull in him, so his muzzle was blunt. Piranha's was longer and narrower, maybe signaling some shepherd in his background.

I took my time studying inhabitants of other cages. Some seemed too small to be my quarries. Others too large: Great Danes seemed to abound.

Each regarded me hopefully, and I hated to pass them all by. But Lexie and I lived in a small place. I had to stay strong, return home without further friends to live with us. And at least this place had a no-kill policy.

Then, down toward the end, I saw a pit bull–size pup with dark, short hair. Could it be? "Pooky?" I asked.

This was met with an excited bark, although without the ecstatic leaping of the other dogs I'd greeted. I was convinced nonetheless. "Is your buddy Piranha here, too?"

Yet another bark emanated from a cage several away. I headed there, and sure enough discovered a dog who resembled the one in the photo of Piranha I'd studied.

All canines accounted for!

And, glory be, I glanced down the row of cages just in time to see Jeff emerge with Georgia the greeter at his elbow—and a gray kitty in his arms. Amanda the genuine cat? As I dashed closer, I saw that this feline did indeed have a gray coat and a slightly pug face, as did the one we sought.

I smiled at Jeff and nodded. "Every one," I stated somewhat cryptically, although I knew he got it.

His own sappy grin that he'd apparently donned for Georgia segued into a severe frown. "Are you aware that you're harboring animals stolen from their owners in L.A.?" he demanded.

The young lady stopped and stared. "Pardon?"

"How did you come into possession of this cat?" Jeff insisted, not pardoning the young lady in the least.

"I . . . I don't know. I think I'd better call Chuey."

"What's that?" I asked.

"He's head of the Loving Friends Animal Shelter organization," she said. "I just volunteer here, but maybe he can answer your questions."


I'D NEVER KNOWN anyone named Chuey. I believed the name to be Hispanic, so I had certain expectations about what the guy would look like while Jeff and I sat in the waiting area anticipating his arrival. We'd decided to delay calling in the cops until we'd talked to him, since they'd undoubtedly take over any interrogation and we might not get the info important to us.

Young Georgia had resumed her place at her desk and kept glancing nervously toward us, as if she expected we'd attack her for the keys to release all the animals.

Turned out that Chuey was probably spelled Chewy—

maybe as in Chewbacca of *Star Wars* fame. The man was big and as hairy as any of his canine charges—long, reddish locks and a matching unruly beard. Plus, he was certainly chubby, as if he chewed lots of food.

He clumped into the room. His grubby duds were loose, his scowl ferocious. "Can I help you folks?" he demanded in a tone that dared us to tell him why we were really there.

We rose, and I let Jeff do his former-cop-current-P.I. stuff. He reached into his jeans pocket and extracted his license. "We're here investigating some thefts of pets in Los Angeles," he responded quite coolly, especially considering the scary demeanor of the guy facing him. Chewy seemed huge in comparison, even though Jeff was one substantial hunky dude.

"Yeah? So?" Chewy folded his big, beefy arms and glared a challenge at Jeff.

Who responded in kind. "You happen to have all those animals in your shelter. Care to explain how they got here?"

"Who says they're here?"

Since he appeared ready to pound Jeff, I decided intervention to slice the weighty atmosphere was in order. "I do," I interjected sweetly. "I'm secretary of a pet-sitters' organization, and the stolen animals were being cared for by some of our members. I have their pictures, if you'd like to see them. Four dogs plus one cat, and every one is in your care. Isn't that an interesting coincidence?"

"It'll be more interesting to hear how they got here," Jeff said. "You can tell us first, or just the cops. We don't care."

Which wasn't exactly the truth. We cared a lot. At least I did.

Chewy slid a glance back toward Georgia, as if assessing whether to thrash us to a pulp in front of the nice young volunteer. "Hey, George," he said instead. "Come here."

She did so slowly, as if still nervous about who was going to do what to whom.

"Did they show you the animals in question?"

She nodded.

"They're the ones that were hanging around outside the other morning? All of them?"

"I think so," she said.

"No collars or other ID on any of them?" I asked. "Were they at least leashed so they wouldn't run away?"

"Tied with rope, at least the dogs were. The cat was taped into a big box."

"And you didn't think to call the cops?" I all but shouted. "Check for chips?" At least Augie and Cramer had ID chips implanted beneath their skin. "You're in the business of handling lost animals. Haven't you heard of the L.A. pet-nappings?" I stepped closer to the big bruiser of a Chewy, irate at the apparent carelessness of a person who purportedly cared about placing lost souls as pets. Unless it was insidiousness.

"I think I heard something about it." His response was much too mild, which told me a whole heck of a lot. He'd suspected the origin of the animals that appeared on his doorstep and hadn't done a damned thing about it.

Why not?

I forbore from taking a physical swing at him, resorting—wisely, I thought—to the mental. "Do you collect fees from anyone based on the number of animals you have here, or place in new homes?" I was nearly nose to nose with him now. Or maybe it was nose to chest. In any event, my swing stopped just short of an accusation, but the implication was still there.

He'd held on to the poor, lost pets for gain.

This time it was Jeff's turn to intervene, shouldering me aside for my own safety. Or so I presumed.

"This is a charitable institution," Chewy said, but he seemed uncomfortable.

"Funded by whom?" I insisted.

"We have a lot of local donors," Georgia said, sounding proud. "Some of the area's wealthiest people give money on behalf of our animals."

"Based on how many animals you save?" I pushed.

"Well . . . yes," she said.

"Shut up, George," Chewy said.

"Time to call the cops," I finished.


NED NORALLES MADE it easy for us by managing some law enforcement magic. Somehow, he got the Bakersfield PD to cooperate with the LAPD, and the LAPD jurisdictions involved with the current situations to cooperate with each other.

After an initial local investigation that nearly turned Chewy from red to green, it appeared clear his group had previously gotten into hot water before for accepting pets from questionable sources for adoption. This wasn't likely to be the end of the Loving Friends Animal Shelter's unloving woes.

Then an official Bakersfield vehicle had trundled the subject pets down to L.A., where they were taken into custody until their owners could ID them.

Jeff and I, plus Lexie and Odin, followed in the Escalade, creating a mini-convoy.

Now, it was Sunday. Jeff and I sat in the North Hollywood station of the LAPD while the owners of the napped pets came by to pick up their babies.

We were even permitted to watch from the far end of the interrogation table. And listen in. Each had to answer some riddles before their pets could be released to them.

Well, okay, not riddles. But their inquiries revolved around not only how they'd heard of the pet-sitter they'd used when their animals were napped, but also whether they knew Tracy, Nya, or me . . . and where they'd happened to have been when Nya and I were attacked.

First premise, of course, was that even if they had no alibis for the night I was attacked, all had been out of town as pet-sitting customers when Nya was murdered.

I hadn't previously met the person who lived in Westwood and owned Piranha and Pooky, but he turned out to be a fifty-ish mild-mannered reporter for a chain of local throwaway community newspapers. Could he somehow become a super antihero in off-hours, able to smash unsuspecting women with baseball bats? Perhaps, but why? Not that I'm an expert, but I didn't see any potential signs of suppressed mental instability. He claimed not to have met Nya before, only Frieda Shoreman, who'd been his chosen sitter. And he certainly didn't look familiar to me.

I crossed him off my suspect list even before I put him on.

Same went for the woman unfortunate enough to name her cat Amanda. She worked for a costumer in the film industry, lived in Laurel Canyon, and evinced no tendencies toward insane temper tantrums or the ability to wield wild baseball bats. Her sitter had been Lilia Ziegler, and she also claimed not to know any other PSCSC players, including me.

I had previously interviewed Libby Emerich, Augie's owner. She was the slim fashion-conscious real estate broker who'd all but broken down when discussing her baby's disappearance. Now, she was all excitement and enthusiasm, fawning over the wiry little dachshund who seemed equally happy to see her. Kill Nya? Attempt to mutilate me? Highly unlikely.

And then there was Dr. Marla Gasgill, DDS, Cramer's owner. It was like pulling teeth for the interrogating cops to get much info from her, since she had delayed some dental appointments to dash here for her darling dog. But speak she did, gnashing her teeth that the cops hadn't caught the cockapoo-napper. Like the others, she claimed not to know any of the other players in the violent acts also being investigated. And I hadn't any reason to doubt her denial.

That was everyone who'd had pets stolen while being pet-sat by PSCSC members, except for my clients the Dorgans.

Could I state with absolute certainty that none of those who'd had pets napped hadn't done it themselves to throw the authorities off the track?

Not really.

Well, then, could I say for certain that none had been the one who'd attacked me?

Nope.

But the main things of which I felt reasonably certain were my relief and delight that the missing pets were found and returned home safe and sound . . . and that Nya's killer, and my attacker, were probably the same person, and that he or she remained on the loose, quite possibly plotting more mischief against pets and their sitters.

# Chapter Twenty-three

OKAY, SO I still didn't know whodun anything. Neither the pet-napper nor the Nya killer had been outed by the finding of the missing pups and kitty.

But I nevertheless had a bit of good news worth sharing with the world.

And so, even before Jeff and I departed from the police station, I stood in the large reception area, turned my back toward the big desk where a cop in uniform usurped the role of receptionist, and made a call on my cell phone.

To whom?

To Corina Carey, of course.

"What do you have for me, Kendra?" she asked immediately.

"A scoop, if you want it."

"Do dogs pee?"

"They sure do when I'm watching them. And not so coincidentally, my info is about dogs." I proceeded to enlighten her about the Loving Friends Animal Shelter, and how its people had, intentionally or otherwise, decided not to check for owners of its latest group of dumped pets. And how I'd seen their sad faces on the Internet. And how Jeff and I had gone to

check them out . . . and now three more dogs and a cat were
home with their loving families.

"You rule, Kendra!" Corina cheered, making me feel all
the more cheerful.

"Thanks," I said in a quietly modest tone.

"I don't suppose you've solved Nya Barston's murder,
have you?"

Nothing like a truthful dig to knock me down a peg. "No,"
I admitted, sounding somewhat churlish. "Not yet."

"Well, you'll tell me when you do, won't you?"

"Do dogs fly?"

"Hey, Kendra." Now it was her turn to sound touchy. But I
didn't hear the rest of her chiding. I'd hung up.

Almost immediately, my phone rang again. I considered
jamming it deep into my purse, assuming it was Corina calling
again to goad me or get more info. I didn't want either one.

Fortunately, before I jammed, I peeked at the caller ID.

Tom Venson.

I smiled as I answered—until I realized that this was late
on Sunday. He'd promised to call me to plan an outing sometime this weekend.

Never mind that the almost-date had entirely slipped my
mind until now. I was immediately miffed. And hurt.

"Hi, Tom," I said in a tone that bespoke friendship but no
romantic attraction. Which was when I saw Jeff finally emerge
from the innards of the police station via a doorway off the
main reception area. Great timing.

"Kendra, I'm really sorry I didn't call sooner. There was so
much going on at the clinic this week . . . can we get together
for dinner tonight so I can tell you all about it?"

By then, Jeff was nearly nose to nose with me. His grin
was nasty. "That your boyfriend?" he asked.

"I thought you were my boyfriend," I whispered sweetly.

"Really?" Tom said, sounding really happy about the idea.

I forbore from rolling my eyes. Men.

"Tell him you're busy tonight," Jeff said sotto voce. "Unless you want me along to chaperone. I'm not letting you out
of my sight yet."

"How sweet," I said, ensuring that the receiver was covered. "I didn't know you cared."

Which earned me a glare. And a forceful rebuttal. "Yeah, I care. I care whether you get attacked again by some maniac with a baseball bat. And now that word's likely to get out that you've found the stolen pets and gotten them home, our theft suspect, assuming he or she's one and the same as the killer, may be a little miffed at you. So you're stuck with me for now. We're stuck with each other."

With that, Jeff trod off to the police station door, where he pivoted and stood, arms folded, glaring at me.

"Er . . . Tom," I said into the phone.

"What's going on there, Kendra?" My friendly vet no longer sounded so pleased to be talking to me.

"Long story," I said with a sigh. "I want to hear about your week, Tom, and tell you about mine, but I'm afraid it can't be tonight. Can I take a rain check?"

"Sure," he said, and I suddenly heard not rain showers but an ice storm fall over the phone. "I'll call you."

So I WAS stuck with an irritable Jeff that night. Heck, if *he* was irritable, I was utterly cantankerous.

Which didn't bode well for a fun evening.

At least Lexie and Odin, whom we'd had to leave in the Escalade parked, supervised, and in the shade, shared enough goodwill for all of us.

We did my final pet-sitting rounds of the day, and while sitting in front of the last house on a narrow residential street I called Rachel to ensure all was well with her, too.

"That guy from Jeff's office, Buzz, came with me, like you said," she informed me, with a barely hidden wail in her tone. "But my dad's really mad about all the stuff going on. He wants me to stop pet-sitting because it's too dangerous. And since I've been kicked out of Methuselah Manor and don't have any acting gigs going on . . . Oh, Kendra, what am I going to do?"

What was she going to do? What was *I* going to do if my star employee quit? I'm sure the look I tossed to Jeff looked horrified, since he said, "What?"

"We need to get back to my place right away."

AT LEAST ALL the confusion kept me from having to share an intimate and uncomfortable dinner with Jeff. Instead, it was an uncomfortable dinner party that included Rachel and her dad, Russ, Buzz Dulear, Jeff, and me.

We ate alfresco, on a picnic table outside the fence around the swimming pool that I'd once adored diving into when this delightful large place was all mine. Now, I didn't use it much since it went with the house, and I always felt I'd need to ask permission, even now, with tenants with whom I was friends.

Or had been.

I assured Russ, who'd purposefully set his muscular self beside me, that the once-missing pets were all home now.

"Does that mean you've caught the person who stole them? And that you can guarantee my daughter's safety?" His green Irish eyes flashed over one of the steaks we'd grilled on the outdoor built-in barbecue that also went with the house.

"No, but we'll catch that miserable marauder," I assured him. "And with Buzz around, Rachel will be fine." I hoped.

"Well, I'll give this a few more days, and that's all," Russ said, his face nearly as ruddy as his red hair.

"Sure," I said, my heart sinking. I'd already taken on a few of Tracy's pet-sitting clients. I'd hate to have to dump them back on her and still not be able to service all of my own—an excellent possibility if I lost Rachel. Unless I gave up practicing law and went back to pet-sitting full-time.

No way. I loved them both. Needed them both to fulfill my current crazy life.

"Kendra also said she'd clear my name at Methuselah Manor," Rachel piped eagerly from across the table. She sat beside tall, excellent-postured Buzz, who remained quietly eating as if he hadn't indulged in days. Jeff was on my other side, also staying somewhat quiet as I thrashed things out with my tenants.

And Beggar, Lexie, and Odin? At our feet, begging as pups always do.

"I'll try," I agreed weakly. I figured I'd better do my tap dance there tomorrow. If I wasn't successful, then I feared the whole house of pet-sitting cards I'd built that included my friend and protégé Rachel would start to tumble into total chaos.

•

JEFF AND I remained peeved with one another that night. Maybe my peeve was somewhat manufactured. I did appreciate all he'd been doing for me, even if he did prevent me from getting together with Tom that night.

Which I couldn't have done anyway, considering the Rachel crisis brewing at home.

At least this way, while we silently stewed at one another, I didn't have to worry about whether we'd go to bed together.

All I had to worry about, as I lay in my own bed solo, except for Lexie, was whether I should leap up, call a truce, and jump Jeff's bones.

I fortunately forbore.

I'D LOVE TO say that everything was fixed by Monday night. But it wasn't.

No further word on who'd stolen the returned pets, though Corina's story again called attention to the heinous crime now that it was resolved favorably. But no one leaped out of the woodwork to confess, or to turn in a neighbor who'd been harboring some strange animals for a few days.

Nor was Nya's murder suddenly solved, nor the attack on me.

With Jeff sometimes hovering ominously over my shoulder, I did my delightful duties as a pet-sitter. I loved the little bit of law I practiced, particularly when my self-styled bodyguard allowed me to stay at the office on my own.

Then, without telling Jeff my immediate plan, I hied myself to Methuselah—er, Medicure—Manor with Lexie. It was a three-story, homey-looking home, and I held my breath as I walked in.

The people I saw might have had some age, but they all looked well tended. And even somewhat spry. And the place even smelled good—like lemon, but not overdone.

After asking to speak to whoever was in charge, I introduced Lexie and me to the African-American headmistress, Delia Underwood. She appeared a little overwrought and flighty to be the person in charge of the care of a bevy of elders with varying needs, but what did I know? She was shorter than me, and a whole lot thinner, and I gathered that she, too, bordered on senior citizen status. Her face was wrinkly, her forehead set in a frown, and she tended to wave her hands as she spoke.

"I've heard you're looking for volunteers for people to bring their dogs to help perk up the people who live here," I said, sounding as perky as I could.

"Well . . . yes, but the last person we had who did that didn't work out. Where did you hear about us?"

"Oh, a newspaper mention a week or two ago that requested people with pets to volunteer." Not something I'd read, but Rachel had described it as her impetus to bring Beggar here. "Can we give it a try? Lexie just loves people." At which cue, aided by a tiny tug on her leash, my adorable Cavalier stood on her hind legs, put her front paws on Delia's knees, and wagged her tail enthusiastically in a request for a pat.

Delia complied, and we got our feet and paws, respectively, in the door.

Delia was too busy to act as our guide, so she introduced us to a couple of other volunteers who came almost daily to help deal with residents—feeding, washing, dressing, entertaining, and whatever was needed. Sally and Shannon were closer contemporaries to Rachel than me, and both claimed to be preparing for careers in health care.

That first visit was both delightful and depressing. Some residents were in full possession of their senses, but their bodies' abilities were waning. Lexie immediately charmed them, allowing them to pet her as well as their limbs would allow.

Others' minds and memories were fragile, but all appeared to appreciate cute canines. They sometimes said odd things, but all seemed charmed as well.

I was glad to leave that evening. Promised to be back the next day.


WHICH VISITS WENT on for four days.

Okay, I admit it. I used Rachel's problems at the senior citizens' residence as a distraction from all my own issues.

Which served to drive Jeff crazy, an added bonus.

But I informed Borden I was working on a personal issue and had to slack off my legal matters for a short while. Adorable man that he was, and so devoted to the idea that we all should love our law practices, he had no problem with my disappearing each afternoon for a couple of hours, then returning for a short while until I had to leave for my pet-sitting stuff.

During those times on hiatus from the Yurick firm, I hied Lexie and me to Methuselah Manor.

And damned if I, too, didn't get a whole lot of satisfaction in watching the elderly residents perk up as my loving Lexie leaped up onto their laps—with my assistance, or that of my usual accompanying volunteers Shannon and Sally, after assuring those laps weren't too fragile to accept her.

My entourage and I, including a pet-loving aide or two, usually meandered from one tiny room, each with two occupants, to the next. I especially enjoyed an elderly lady named Agnes. She was in her nineties but as spry as someone a couple decades younger, and her mind was totally with it. She appeared to be Shannon's pet resident, too.

Then there was Bill, a boy at heart despite his aging body. He appeared to be Sally's favorite. Delia, who came along at times, too, was most fair, not showing favoritism to any of them. Nor did she seem partial to dogs, although she was absolutely delighted to have us around to stimulate the seniors in her care.

I also especially liked—well, let's just say there were a lot of people there whom I immediately adored. Lexie and I enjoyed entertaining all of them, as well as some of the other aides, both old and young. Unfortunately, the rest of my life sometimes interfered, and I both gave and received calls on my cell phone, but, hey, everyone appeared to understand.

Lexie and I left each day with smiles on our faces—well, Lexie's was more a canine tongue-lolling pant, but she certainly looked happy after we both received final hugs from those whom we'd visited.

Until that Thursday. When an outcry arose in Agnes's room not long after Lexie, Sally, and I had left. The elderly dear suddenly stood in the doorway, glaring at my dog and me. "My diamond necklace is gone," she cried.

"My baseball autographed by the Pittsburgh Pirates, too," shouted Bill from his door. "Someone stop those thieves!"

# Chapter Twenty-four

LEXIE AND I halted immediately. "I assume you're not accusing us," I said swiftly.

"You were in my room," Agnes asserted.

"Why would you have a diamond anything in a public place like this?" I asked, drawing closer to her. She hadn't struck me as senile but I had to inquire, just in case.

"Because it's precious to me," she said sadly. Her wrinkle-surrounded eyes were a brilliant blue, enhanced by the sheen of tears that threatened to spill down her wizened cheeks.

"Same goes about my ball," Bill said. "We never had any trouble here at all till we started having people with dogs come in to play with us. Do you know Rachel? She had a really nice Irish setter, but she stole from us like you."

I gritted my teeth but forbore from defending our maligned honor. Yet. Meantime, a throng of residents and workers including volunteers and aides started to gather around.

"Actually, yes. I know Rachel. In fact—" I motioned to one of the middle-aged aides who wore a yellow uniform and white sensible shoes. "Here she is."

The aide in question stripped off a salt-and-pepper wig to reveal Rachel's short, sassy black mop beneath. From a pocket she pulled out a tissue and wiped some of the thick makeup from her face, immediately revealing its real youthfulness.

"Hey!" shouted Bill. "What's she doing here?"

"Helping me unmask your thief," I replied as Rachel withdrew, from another pocket, a teeny digital camera.

"Who did you get?" I asked her.

"Sally," she said with a snort of disgust. "You?"

"Same goes." I drew my handy-dandy multitalented cell phone from my pocket. "This takes photos, too. And some are bound to show Sally snitching the missing items. I shot some pictures without watching as Lexie entertained on one side of the rooms and Sally stood behind us doing whatever she did. I checked some of the photos, and a few show her rooting around in drawers while our attention was diverted. How about you?"

"About the same, after I pretended to be enthralled with your entertaining but instead palmed my camera and kept pushing the button to shoot photos."

"Hey!" Sally said. "I didn't do anything. You're blaming me just to hide your own stealing." She was as falsely blond as she was an honorable volunteer at this facility. She'd claimed she'd all but decided on a career as a practical nurse.

Practical pilferer was more like it.

"You can lie all you want," Rachel said. "Our cameras will tell the truth."

Which was when Sally started to make a run for the door—only to be stopped by a uniformed cop.

Yes, headmistress Delia was in on our charade. She had to be, so that Rachel could use her acting and accompanying makeup skills to hang around when Lexie and I did, being our backup and co-camera person. We'd signaled Delia to call the cops as soon as we'd determined that today was the day, and the real culprit was about to be caught.

And Rachel cleared.

"I'm sorry!" Sally sobbed. I noticed she held a tote bag over her shoulder, ostensibly filled with large-print books and magazines for the sometimes myopic inmates. As she cried, the bag slipped not too surreptitiously to the floor. I'd no doubt the authorities would find inside, at a minimum, Agnes's diamond and Bill's ball. "Please let me go. I'll never do it again."

"Not here you won't," I said. "We have the evidence, and it's my opinion as an attorney that charges be pressed. What if we let you go and you decide to pull this at some other unsuspecting elder-care facility? Unless you've a record of some kind, you're much too likely to be allowed inside other doors."

Okay, I'd been unjustly accused in my day of something a lot more heinous than cadging a signed baseball, or even a costly diamond. I sided with the innocent, at least till proven guilty. But this young lady had thought nothing of stealing, then allowing my own pet-sitting protégé to suffer the consequences.

Harsh, on my part, to suggest throwing the legal book at this young bitch? Could be.

But I stuck by it. And smiled as the police escorted Sally out the door as I heard Delia say, "I'm so sorry about everything, Rachel. Could you bring Beggar back one of these days? Everyone was so happy when you and he visited."

Lexie and I strolled down the hall, accepting the accolades and thanks of the inhabitants. I didn't hear Rachel's response, but felt certain it was positive.

"SURE, IT WORKED out wonderfully," I told Darryl later that day at his Doggy Indulgence Day Resort. Lexie was cavorting in one of the canine play areas with some of her fastest friends.

"I'm really glad for Rachel and you," my bespectacled best friend said with obvious enthusiasm.

Equally obvious to me was that something was on his mind. We stood by the desk where pets were checked in and out each day, and the place appeared as wild as usual, with attendants conducting playtime with visiting pups and attempting to keep them from acting all wolfen and gnawing on one another. Darryl, who usually seemed happily distracted by his place's habitual chaos, seemed awfully sedate.

"Does this mean that Rachel or you will have more or less time to pet-sit?" he asked, handing me my first clue to what was weighing on him.

"You have another referral?" I asked, surprised at Darryl's uncharacteristic subtlety. He usually just blurted out his requests, and I'd take on any pets I had time to handle. Sometimes those I didn't have time for, too. I owed Darryl a lot, including my part-time pet-sitting avocation, which he'd gotten me into when I was desperate to make a few dollars.

"Sure do," he said, sounding as relieved as if I'd told him I'd take it on. "I hinted at it the other day." Oh, right. He had. Well, I'd find him a pet-sitter, even if it couldn't be Rachel or me. "I've got a customer who can't come here because she's in heat."

"A purebred?" I inquired, since most owners Darryl dealt with who had mixed breeds had them neutered—or Darryl would hound them until they did.

"A show dog," he answered. "This would probably have been her last season before spaying, but her owner wanted to breed her one more time and unfortunately hadn't arranged an appropriate beau. The owner's home with her today but wants someone to make frequent visits to coddle her canine baby over the next few crucial weeks. She's determined to find the right male to mate her bitch with before the next season rolls around, and then she'll have her spayed."

"Good deal," I said. "I know a lot of people who are convinced that even show dogs should be spayed early and not be permitted to reproduce, what with the overpopulation of potential pets in shelters these days."

"No need to preach to this particular choir," Darryl said, and I knew he wasn't kidding. "Show dogs may be exceptions, and I'm all for people having pets who need day care, but I hate to hear of so many not ever being placed in loving homes."

"Tell me who the dog is and where she lives, and if Rachel or I can't take care of, I'll find your customer a PSCSC member who can."

Darryl obliged by telling me exactly which lady dog he was discussing.

And that's when I started to really smile. I unexpectedly had the solution to several problems, thanks to this suddenly sunny season.

OF COURSE I called Jeff, to let him know my latest moves. That was our temporary compromise, at least during daylight and while I kept in close telephone contact with him. And didn't do anything too nutsy, like going into dark alleys alone. Or visiting all-but-empty homes of pet-sitting clients on my own, unless I called him from the front door and kept talking.

Then I called Darryl's client for Critter TLC, LLC's pet-sitting fun and frolic—not to mention my ulterior motive. Her owner was a workaholic CPA who should have had a letup as late in April as it now was, but she was winding down some of her own customers' posttax filing calculations and therefore her working hours remained nearly 24/7.

Her name was Christiane Fineman, and her dog, Hildegard, had been a frequent visitor at Darryl's for several months. Lexie and I had met them there before. They lived south of Ventura Boulevard at the border between Studio City and Sherman Oaks, on a flat street just behind Ventura Boulevard.

Clad in shorts and a clingy T-shirt, Christiane stood outside her home in her fenced-in yard when I parked my Beamer at her curb. With a trowel in one hand and a hank of bedraggled green weeds in the other, she appeared to be gardening in the late afternoon sun, which in April wasn't awfully intense. Her long, limp hair was pulled back into a ponytail behind her head.

Pretty Hildegard frolicked near her, having a fine time amusing herself with a big beach ball. She'd have made a delightful model for a William Wegman photo—he's the guy whose weimaraner shots grace books, calendars, and posters in gift shops everywhere.

"Hi, Kendra," Christiane called as I arrived at her front gate. "Where's Lexie?"

"I left her at Darryl's so she could play a little more." Hildegard had hurried toward me, and she now sat nuzzling my hand, endeavoring to entreat a treat, or at least a pat, out of me. I obliged by rubbing her soft, furry head. "How are you, Hildegard?"

"She's in season," Christiane said unnecessarily, "but I'd imagine Darryl told you that."

I nodded. "He said you needed a daytime pet-sitter to keep her company some of the time while you're at work. Unfortunately, that's when I'm working, too."

"That's right. You're a lawyer, aren't you?"

"Sure am, but I have an employee who might be able to help. If not, I'll find you someone. But as I mentioned on the phone, there's another reason I wanted to see you. Have time to talk?"

"I'm not doing a darned bit of good going after these weeds," she said with a snort of disgust. "Come on in, and I'll get you a cold drink. Or warm—tea or coffee, you tell me. And you can also tell me what's on your mind."

I STAYED FOR merely a half hour, but when I left I could have kissed Christiane. Or at least Hildegard. I'd gotten the response I had hoped for.

What a win-win-win-win-win-win-win situation I was wangling for! Talk about ADR . . .

Which I did. Soon as I returned to my law office.

And much to my absolute delight, I was able to set up an all-hands meeting for the next day.

When I picked Lexie up at Darryl's later, I gave my good friend one huge hug and kiss. "You're the greatest!" I gushed.

"I take it that things went well with everyone involved?" He held a wriggling Lexie beneath one skinny arm as he stood near his busy checkout desk.

"Remains to be seen, but I have high hopes. Thanks to you. Again."

"Aw, shucks," he responded, and I laughed with him at his feigned shyness. He knew he rocked. As always.

Lexie and I headed toward that evening's pet visits. Which meant I needed to call Jeff so he could sew himself to my side like Peter Pan's shadow.

Only, he was busy. So was Buzz Dulear, who was attached at the proverbial hip to Rachel, the only way her dad would allow her to continue calling on pet clients.

Which, darn it all, made me nervous.

It also kept me alert at all my stops, which was a good thing. Of course nothing happened that evening to scare me into pulling out my pepper spray. Or even calling Jeff . . .

Although he did show up at my doorstep later in the evening, dressed in his tight jeans and T-shirt that outlined every appealing bulge. He had his adorable Odin along, and also some Thai takeout. And insisted on spending the night.

On the sofa.

Hell, was I turning into a lech, with my libido humming every time the hunky P.I. was around? Sure thing.

Did I do anything about it?

Heck no. It was essentially my choice, after all. So I stewed alone in my bed that night. Again.

And wondered which of all the mistakes I was making— sort of dating two men simultaneously, holding them both at arm's length and staying celibate, angsting over the entire situation—made me most miserable.

Which left me utterly exhausted in the A.M. when I woke, knowing I faced a full day.

# Chapter Twenty-five

ALL FOUR OF US ate breakfast out together the next morning, sitting on a patio at a charming restaurant on Tujunga before we went our separate ways.

Once more, I'd be on the honor system. I'd vowed to inform Jeff of my every move, and he'd looked me straight in the eye with his magnificent baby blues and promised he'd show up now and then when I wasn't expecting him to ensure I was all right.

Damn, but that made me feel all oozy inside. Sure, it was pushy. Treating me like a less-than-obedient kid.

Even so, I felt . . . protected. Cared for.

Loved.

But I had too many demands on my life to make rash decisions.

And so, when Odin and he walked Lexie and me to my Beamer, I engaged in one hell of a sexy kiss with him, then said hoarsely, "I'll call you."

"Yeah, you'd better." His voice sounded as husky as mine, and it sanded from my mind all thoughts of any other man.

Heck, was I making a decision despite myself?

I attempted to erase this disconcerting situation from my

mind as I did my pet-sitting duties, since I had to concentrate on my surroundings and assure myself no would-be pet-napper hid in shadowed corners at my clients' homes.

At more than one home, I caught sight of a big black Escalade sitting outside, which, once I'd stifled my initial irritation, made me feel even warmer and fuzzier inside than before. Jeff was looking out for me. Again. Still.

What I really needed to do, though, was to find the pet-napper to ensure it wouldn't happen again, not to hide from possible problems.

And since the cops apparently hadn't solved Nya's murder, that continued to weigh heavily on my heart.

But I preferred solving one problem at a time.

And when I finally arrived at my law office just a little later in the morning, I had a feeling I'd ace another one soon.

I'D HAVE KEPT my confidence a whole lot better if the others at the session I'd called weren't glaring so caustically at one another.

Obviously, the passage of more than a week had done nothing to resolve the resentment between Jasper and Angelica McGregor on the one hand, and Jasper's cousin Tallulah on the other. As always, when a meeting was to convene in the Yurick law office, I'd set things up for us to face off in the bar-conference room. My clients, Jasper and Angelica, who sat on my side of the elongated table, looked as if they could use a drink, but the building hadn't been a restaurant for a long time, and no remnants of the old liquor-serving days remained, at least not that I'd ever discovered.

Jasper had donned a funereal suit for the occasion—black, with a white shirt and print charcoal tie with a knot that seemed to set off his senior citizen wattle. His cadaverous face, too, made him appear more like a funeral director than the long-retired engineer that he was. He sat nearest to me, clutching the leash of Whiskey, the weimaraner, as if to let it loose would mean he'd lose the argument against his cousin.

On his far side, chunky Angelica seemed paler than ever, which made the red lipstick on her poufy lips appear garish. She glared daggers at her husband's relation who threatened to take back the treasured canine gift she'd allegedly given them.

Then there was Tallulah herself, again decked out in gaudy jewelry, as if that made her look royal and therefore unable to be crossed and survive the clash. She appeared composed, although the wideness of her eyes didn't appear solely because her jewel-encrusted spectacles magnified the orbs beneath.

"We're here," she intoned regally, "although you haven't given us a good reason why. Unless you're intending to hand my dear Whiskey back to me today." She dashed a disdainful look toward Jasper, as if she already knew the response to that.

"Kendra called the meeting, not us," Jasper said. He glanced at me quizzically, although there was a hint of hope in his eyes as well.

I hadn't explained what my idea was, only that I had one. I still thought it was a damned good one. But much depended on the reasonableness of the disputants, and at the moment I thought reasonability hadn't found even a tiny toehold in this fury-filled room.

"Why don't you tell us what it is?" piped up Tallulah's attorney. As before, Gordon Yarber remained nondescript, well overpowered by his large and domineering senior citizen client. He'd taken off his suit jacket and sat across from me in shirtsleeves and blue silk tie.

"Sure," I said, attemping to insert perkiness and confidence into this dour conclave. "Come here, Whiskey," I said, standing, and removed the leash from an obviously reluctant Jasper's hands. The sweet dog appeared somewhat confused, but he came up to me and let me stoop and hug him.

My back toward the still-existing bar, my side pressed against the now-sitting dog, I said to my captive audience, "The dispute here is about who owns Whiskey."

"I do, of course," interjected the authoritarian Tallulah.

Which naturally got my clients riled and ready to protest. I held my hand up to halt their angry retorts.

"That is one possibility," I admitted. "If my clients lose in court despite the contract, documented by the paperwork you filled out to transfer Whiskey's registration to them. The other possibility is the one I find more likely, that you've conveyed ownership of him to them."

"But—" began Tallulah.

"I object," shouted Gordon, as if we were in court and a judge could rule on whatever he was objecting to.

Which I didn't care about, here and now and in this very different venue.

"Please let me continue," I continued as calmly as if I hadn't suffered any interruption. "Now, the Bible has a solution. I could play Solomon and suggest splitting this baby." I reached down and stroked Whiskey's soft scalp. "But we all know how impractical and messy that would be."

"The real mother wound up with the baby in the Bible," Tallulah said majestically. "And that's me."

"Well, technically, that's not true, but it does lead me to my suggestion for symbolically splitting this particular baby." All at the table regarded me quizzically. I had their attention. Time to offer my idea. "At the moment, I happen to be pet-sitting another purebred weimaraner, a registered show dog who wins quite a bit."

"If your suggestion is that we buy her—" Jasper began.

I held up my hand. "No, it's better than that, because you'll wind up with Whiskey—at least somewhat. This particular bitch, whose name is Hildegard, happens to need pet-sitting because she can't go to doggy day care for a few weeks. She's in season. And her owner has been hoping to find the ideal male to mate her with."

"Whiskey!" shouted Angelica. "And we'd get a puppy?"

"That's my idea," I said. "The owner's amenable to breeding with your darling dog, and in exchange to allow you to choose which puppy will be yours. In the meantime, I suggest that you share custody of Whiskey, and when the pups are born, Tallulah gets Whiskey back and Jasper and Angelica get the baby."

"What if my client—" Gordon began, but I silenced him with a vicious slice of my hand in the air. I knew what he wanted to say: What if Tallulah wanted the puppy? Sure, that was a possibility, but I figured I'd suggest it this way and push the idea without giving an additional item to disagree about.

"As long as we get to see Whiskey, too," Jasper said. "And show him now and then."

"I suppose that would be acceptable," Tallulah said, "provided that, if you travel with my Whiskey, you let me watch the puppy when you're out of town."

"And Whiskey could always play with his son," Angelica said, obviously buying into the idea as well. "We could get them together. You could bring him to our house, and I could make dinner for all of us, dogs included."

"Do we have a deal?" I inquired.

"Assuming all goes well with the breeding and results in an acceptable puppy," Gordon inserted, acting, as he should, like a lawyer.

"Then I'll draw up the agreement," I said.

And watched as everyone started talking at once. Handshakes ended as the shakers pulled one another closer and began to hug.

I grinned at Gordon. And at myself.

ADR—Animal Dispute Resolution—ruled once more!

"YOU DID IT, Kendra!" my boss Borden exclaimed a few minutes later in his habitually high-pitched voice. His excited expression lit his entire elderly face, inserting further creases at the edges of his bifocal-clad eyes.

"Looks like," I agreed cheerfully, giving him a huge grin.

I sat in his antique-adorned office, in one of the artistically carved client chairs facing his desk. I'd removed my lawyerly suit jacket, feeling more comfortable in my long-sleeved silk blouse. Its pastel floral print was much more muted than the large hibiscus adorning his usual Hawaiian shirt.

"Looks like your ADR—what do you call it? Animal Dispute Resolution?—works well. We'll need to get the word out some more. Bring in lots of clients that way. Plenty of people have problems concerning their pets, and you can help to resolve them all."

I shifted in some discomfort. "Well, I can always try, but you know we can never promise results."

"Of course. But I'm proud of you, Kendra. Way to go."

"Hey, Kendra, you rock!" yelled Mignon as she entered Borden's office, followed by a whole slew of the senior attorneys who worked here along with me, including silver-haired

Elaine Aames and squat Geraldine Glass, with her reading glasses perched, as always, at the end of her nose.

At Borden's urging, I described my settlement conference and its apparent resolution, and was consequently cheered and toasted with raised coffee mugs.

Which made me feel smug as I finally sidled to my office.

And retrieved phone messages.

The first of which consisted of a frantic call from Tracy Owens. "Kendra, I'm on my way to meet with your criminal attorney friend Esther Ickes. The cops are apparently zeroing in on me as Nya's killer. I'm going to be interrogated yet again, and may have to surrender into their custody sometime next week if nothing happens to exonerate me. Please help!"

# Chapter Twenty-six

I CALLED TRACY back, of course.

"It's Kendra," I said when she answered.

"Oh, hi," she said breathlessly, "but I can't talk now. I'm on my way to Esther's to talk strategy. Sorry to leave such a frantic message for you but . . . well, I'm frantic. And with all those cases you've solved before . . . you don't have an answer on this one yet, do you?"

"No," I said sadly. "I don't."

"Oh. Well, if you figure it out, please let the police know, will you?" She sounded so suddenly downcast that it became contagious.

"Of course." I wished her well, then hung up slowly. My big, happy balloon of that afternoon's success had burst right in my no longer smiling face.

I didn't believe Tracy had killed Nya, but I'd been spending so much time on all the other matters occupying my mind that I hadn't concentrated much on trying to determine who it was.

Suddenly, my major triumph of that day, the settlement of the Whiskey-the-weimaraner dispute, segued to minor. It wasn't a foolproof solution, after all. Things could still go wrong. Matings, even done in multiples, didn't always take.

Puppies, sadly, didn't always survive. But still . . . Well, if nothing else, I had a whole lot of hope.

As I cogitated about the solution, I realized that one of the big sticking points between my McGregor clients and cousin Tallulah had been hurt feelings. Maybe they'd mend now.

Hurt feelings had harmed my young employee Rachel, too—resulting from being accused of stealing stuff from people she'd volunteered to visit. Fortunately, this situation also appeared resolved.

People in addition to my clients, the Dorgans, celebrated the return of their stolen pets. They'd been hurt by their initial losses but undoubtedly felt a whole lot better by now.

I'd been resolving a whole lot of the issues that had inserted themselves into my life.

Except for a couple of big ones.

I still didn't know who'd committed the pet-thefts in the first place. And without the culprit being incarcerated, more pet-nappings could always occur in the future.

And Tracy had reminded me with one heck of a jolt: Neither Ned Noralles nor I had figured out who'd killed Nya, or why. It was more his concern than mine. But if this wasn't resolved soon, more than Tracy's feelings would be hurt. Her entire life would suffer.

I'd never rest easy until these two crimes, related or not, were resolved.

Hurt feelings . . .

I didn't know if I was hurtling with my suspicions down the wrong track, but I nevertheless checked through my notes, then picked up my phone.

In a short while, I left the office to the continued accolades of Borden, Mignon, and the staff.

But just then I had an appointment to talk pet-sitting and Nya-killing with her former lover, Jerry Jefferton.

SURPRISINGLY, LANDSCAPE CONTRACTOR Jerry resided in one of those Southern California courtyard apartments generally constructed in the 1960s, resembling a two-tiered open-face motel with a swimming pool stuck in the center. The doors to all flats lined outdoor walkways, which didn't do a whole lot for security. Still, this one had been shut in with large gates, and I had to call Jerry from the outside intercom to get buzzed through.

Considering the attractive floral jungle surrounding the swimming pool, I suspected Jerry had something to do with this complex's landscaping. I located his apartment, number one, at the right rear of the courtyard. I buzzed the bell when I faced his smooth wooden door. It opened almost immediately.

Pudgy Jerry, in denim shorts and an open striped shirt, hadn't lost a whole lot of weight since I'd seen him last, nor had he grown any hair. But he definitely looked different. He'd seemed somewhat sorry before, unable to meet gazes of PSCSC members. I'd been uncertain whether to attribute that to grief.

Now I knew. He looked utterly lost.

"Hello, Kendra," he said. Again, his eyes appeared bloodshot, and I attempted not to gag on the odor of alcohol that erupted from his mouth.

"May I come in?"

"Why not?"

The question was rhetorical, so I didn't try a reply. I stepped into what would normally have been a living room, assuming one could see the floor. Which I couldn't. It was strewn with all sorts of flotsam and jetsam—newspapers, foam food containers, plastic cups, dirty clothes. Or at least I assumed the large wads of material had once been worn by Jerry.

The stench was so awful I nearly hurled, which would only have added another dimension to the debris. Or maybe not. Perhaps Jerry, too, had lost his lunch or other meals beneath the rubble and hadn't bothered to find and dispose of them.

Whatever Jerry had imbibed, he apparently had enough sensibility left to see how aghast I was. "Sorry," he muttered. "Nya lived here with me, and it mattered then that we kept the place presentable. Especially since I own the whole apartment complex. Without her . . . well, who the hell cares?"

"I see," I said, feeling awfully sorry for the guy. Nya's death had only been a couple of weeks ago, not long for this chaos to congregate so dreadfully. Would Jerry have done this to himself by killing the woman who took care of him?

Talk about hurt . . . This man's emotions were more strung out than anyone's I'd ever seen.

"Tell you what," I said. "Let's sit outside." I made sure he had his key, then led him out onto the paved and elongated patio that was the walkway between apartments. We were immediately engulfed by the aroma of a multiplicity of flowers.

I sat on a small bench facing the swimming pool and motioned for him to do the same. "Tell me what you've been up to, now that Nya is gone," I said, as if we'd been buddies for a while and I genuinely cared about him.

"I've taken over her pet-sitting," he said. "I'm not in great shape to run my landscaping business, so I'm leaving my assistants in charge. They're here a lot, since my equipment's kept in the shed in the alley behind the apartment—where the cops found those planted baseball bats. But the animals—I see why Nya loved her work. They seem to care about her not being there to take care of them."

"Pets are really special, aren't they?" I agreed. "And you haven't had any problems with pet-napping?" Like, did either Nya or you do such a thing? Not that I could really suspect Nya now, not when so much had happened after her loss.

"No, but Nya's clients are all worried about it," he admitted. "Me, too."

I suddenly had an idea that would get together a whole bunch of possible pet-napping suspects . . . and maybe Nya-killers, too.

More than that, I intended to set a trap.

"Hey, Jerry. What are you doing on Sunday night?"

NYA'S BODY HAD finally been released for burial, but her family was in Florida, and she was to be interred there. A memorial would eventually be held for her locally, but her family was holding out until the solution to her murder, or the cops' giving up. My little meeting would have some similar aspects to a memorial . . . I hoped.

The beautiful pet boutique that was the usual meeting place for PSCSC was too small for the gathering I'd hastily assembled. Instead, I got my good buddy Darryl to donate the Doggy Indulgence Day Resort for a short while, after Sunday hours.

I'd rented folding chairs from a party place. Darryl helped me open and arrange them into rows. Lexie cavorted at our busy feet, but otherwise all animals had departed.

Corina Carey was calling every few hours, looking for an interesting story relating to my having located the missing pets—maybe a murder mystery solved—but I'd been putting her off. After all, neither mystery had been solved . . . yet. And I wasn't about to tell her I was working hard on remedying that.

My cell phone rang just as I got to Darryl's, and I'd had good reason to tell Corina I was busy. Again.

"You think anyone'll show for this shindig?" Darryl asked dubiously as we finished our makeshift preparations.

I had to shrug. "Hope so. I've got a lot riding on it." Not that I'd told anyone exactly what I had in mind. Not Darryl, who'd tell me how dumb an idea it was. And would probably call Jeff to tell him to talk me out of it. As if he could.

And I certainly hadn't explained any of it to my bodyguard P.I. He'd hog-tie me to my Beamer before letting me do what I intended.

"I assume this has something to do with your usual skill at solving murders." My lanky, omniscient chum grinned as I stared, startled, at him. I hadn't been speaking my surreptitious thoughts aloud . . . had I? "Hey, you've kept me informed about what's going on," he continued, smugness seeping from his tone. "I know you got the pets back, but not who snatched them. And you mentioned your friend Tracy might not be able to escape the authorities long enough to show up tonight. I figured it out: You're taking another shot at solving one or both mysteries."

"You know me too well, my friend," I grumbled, opening a chair so sharply that I nearly bopped Lexie with a leg. "Oops. Sorry, girl. I'll be more careful from now on." In more ways than one. And I certainly wouldn't give any greater explanation to Darryl.

Meantime, my usually cheerful Cavalier shot me an accusatory glance before leaping on my leg to signify her forgiveness. Naturally, I knelt and gave her a hug. "I hope I'm doing the right thing," I whispered into one of her floppy ears. I'd only admit a shred of doubt to her, since she was always on my side.

Which was when the PSCSC pet-sitters and some of their clients started to saunter in, many with dogs. I recognized Libby Emerich, the client of Tracy's whose dear dachshund, Augie, one of the dogs recovered from the rescue organization up north, trotted in at her side. Dentist Marla Gasgill, too, entered with Cramer the cockapoo, also a pet-nap victim. Wanda Villareal, Marla's usual sitter, dashed in almost immediately and greeted her. So did Wanda's adorable Blenheim-colored Cavalier, Basil. Lexie lit up as soon as she saw the similar but red and white pup and yanked on her leash to be allowed to visit with him.

"Soon," I assured her.

"I'll adjourn to my office," Darryl said. "Call if you need me for anything—which you'd better not." He made good his escape.

More sitters arrived, including my dog-walking companion Frieda Shoreman, and super strong senior Lilia Ziegler. Lots of others I didn't recognize, whom I assumed were clients that some of the sitters had contacted. I did identify Usher, the dog Frieda had been exercising that day in the dog park, though not his owner—a smartly dressed young woman who nevertheless appeared as though she should include exercise on her agenda.

Then there were Tracy Owens, the beleaguered PSCSC prez herself, along with her significant other, Allen Smith, who shot hellos around the group but didn't appear exactly excited to be here. Tracy carried Phoebe, her sweet puggle, so close that the poor pup wriggled as if afraid of strangulation.

"How are you holding up?" I asked Tracy.

"Okay, I guess." But defeat dirged from her voice.

"This is a nice gesture," Allen said, "but I think Tracy has had enough of all this pet-sitting stuff."

"You're just being overly protective," Tracy told him, but turned and graced him with a peck on the side of his long chin.

"Well, she's certainly had enough of the police," Allen added, his face pink with acute but cute embarrassment.

Jerry Jefferton sidled in the door, looking somewhat scared when he saw the size of the group. But he'd cleaned up—himself, at least, if not his apartment—and looked almost human in his charcoal shirt and black slacks.

A woman I didn't know came up to me. Short, dark-haired, and happy-faced, she held the leash of a large mixed breed with a stubby muzzle. "Hi, you're Kendra? Jerry Jefferton pointed you out. I'm Alma Kane. You called me a couple of weeks ago to ask about poor Nya's pet-sitting for me. This is my dog, Gravel."

"Oh, yes," I said. One of the strangers to me that Nya knew, whom I'd called in a fruitless attempt to find out anything to direct me toward the person who'd done her in—people Darryl had referred to Nya for pet-sitting. "Good to meet you. Have a new pet-sitter yet? I know you said you'd miss Nya."

"Jerry's agreed to do it for now, but I'm hoping to meet someone new here tonight, too. And I really want to hear about how to prevent pet-napping. That's the real reason I came. I don't know what I'd do if someone stole my Gravel." She bent and gave the big, friendly mutt a huge hug.

"Kendra." I turned at the familiar voice at my left elbow to see that Jeff had arrived. Yes, I'd eventually let him know my Sunday early evening plans—after he'd demanded a rundown of my whereabouts. He'd left me kinda alone all day, but he still insisted on being my bodyguard.

Which I appreciated, although not necessarily here and now. And I wasn't too keen on his being right there when I pulled the stunt I intended. Oh, well. He'd find out about it anyway. I'd just have to work around him. Somehow.

I edged up to the front of the group and glanced around. Jeff stood somewhere behind me, attempting to look surreptitious. At least it appeared that way when I turned to look at him, and he appeared to study some framed photos on the resort wall showing some celebrity clients of Darryl's along with their pets.

I didn't see the Dorgans here, although I'd told my clients who'd been the first whose pets were recovered about this impending meeting. They'd assured me they weren't holding the theft against me and would call me again soon. They'd also said they were no longer concerned about pet-napping. Not with the extra security they'd secured for their property and darling dog and iguana.

But they were extremely interested in nabbing the pet-napper. And I'd had an idea that might accomplish just that. One I'd made an important call about earlier.

"Hi, everyone," I began. "I appreciate your coming. First thing, I'd like to give an update on the pet-napping situation."

Which really didn't amount to a heck of a lot new to any who'd kept up with the news. But I babbled on brutally, castigating the pet-napper, making it clear how much I reviled whoever it was.

"Of course I have some ideas about that sleazeball," I said with viciousness in my voice. "I've passed them on to the police and can't talk about specifics, but you all know I've been closely involved with ransoming some of the returned pets, and locating all the others I've heard about."

"Yay, Kendra," shouted Marla Gasgill, holding her cockapoo, Cramer, up for the gathered group to see.

"I'll second that," said Libby Emerich, "and so will my little Augie."

I gave a small grin of acknowledgment as the whole gang of people applauded me, but felt the redness of embarrassment creep up my cheeks. I wasn't here for kudos but for knowledge—not that I could let my apparent admirers in on that.

Instead, I continued to watch faces, especially while saying awful things about the pet-thief, to see if anyone here squirmed.

Unfortunately, I didn't see anything to announce who it was I was looking for. And no one stood up and shouted, "It's me. I stole all the animals, and I'll never do it again." Or even that he or she *would* do it again, given half a chance.

And so I started on the other subject that had made me want to convene this meeting. "If only Nya Barston were here," I finally said sadly. "We don't know for certain why she was killed, but I'm convinced she was hot on the trail of the pet-napper." I continued on this line for a good ten minutes, still scanning my audience, praising Nya, providing a semblance of a memorial.

I succeeded somewhat in my purpose—shaking everyone up. Some of them, mostly the members of PSCSC, got all teary.

But did anyone admit to killing Nya?

No way.

With a sigh, I started into the final topic, the one which was why at least the pet-sitting clients had come: tips on stopping one's pets from being napped.

Which led to a great discussion, where even more tips were thrown out and shared.

And then I tossed out my teaser. The main reason I'd instigated this entire session.

"I'm so sure these tips will work that I've put all the things I mentioned into play. And now that I've found all the stolen pets, I'm certain no damned pet-napper will dare come after any of my charges." I talked about some of my current sitting gigs, even describing a few of my more celebrated clients, like the Dorgans, who seemed okay about using my services again. My subtenants, Russ and Rachel Preesinger, since Russ was becoming known in the industry as one great film location locator. A couple of people I'd met when the Preesingers' predecessors had rented my mansion—people who'd made it big thanks to reality shows. And boasted specifics about a muckety-muck at Hennessy Studios whose pet-sitting I'd just taken on, starting tomorrow evening.

I rambled so long that my audience grew restless. No matter. I'd imparted the info I'd intended, assuming someone out there was the pet-grabber and possibly worse.

At the end, I heard some grumbling from behind me. At least Jeff was discreet enough not to shout at me here. That would come later, I felt certain.

Eventually, I shut up and sat down. A few other PSCSC members stood and spoke briefly on pet care and club business, but it didn't last long, a good thing since I had some pets to check in on. So did a lot of those associates who were here.

I stood at the door as the group filed out, accepting thanks graciously.

Tracy Owens and her guy Allen were among the last to leave. "I figured from what you said that no one has any other real suspects about who killed Nya besides me," she said dejectedly.

"We know you didn't do it," Allen said staunchly. "And it's really nice of you, Kendra, to try to find the killer to clear my Tracy."

"Isn't it, though?" said Jeff, who'd started standing at my side. "She's a regular P.I. these days."

"Oh, never as good as you," I said sweetly.

"But all that stuff about your pet-sitting clients," Tracy continued. "Are you really sure that was a good idea?"

"Why not?" I asked.

"Well, for one thing, there's sometimes some rivalry around here. Someone might try to pinch your customers."

"No one has stolen any that you've passed along temporarily because of your situation, have they?" I felt immediately indignant on her behalf. "I'll return those I'm helping with anytime." Especially since I'd been attacked while watching a couple.

"I wasn't accusing you, Kendra," Tracy said. "I trust you, which was why I asked you to help in the first place."

"You want your clients back yet?" I asked.

"Please keep them for now," Allen said, giving me a glance with his sad eyes that suggested his significant other still needed help, even if she hoped it wasn't so.

The two of them said their goodbyes and departed, with Phoebe, the puggle, trotting behind.

"I can tell you a hundred reasons why that was a really bad idea," Jeff said when they were gone. "I think I know what you're doing, Kendra, even though you attempted a tiny bit of subtlety. But no way will I let you—"

"Oh, hi, Darryl," I said, looking over his shoulder as my good buddy and owner of this venue strolled up from his office. "Will you help us fold these chairs? I need to have them ready to be picked up first thing tomorrow."

Darryl looked from Jeff to me and back again. "Uh-oh. Looks like I interrupted something."

"No problem," I said with a welcoming smile.

"No, this conversation was definitely finished," Jeff said, staring a message at me that said *you're not doing anything, and you're not getting out of my sight.*

I simply nodded and started stacking chairs.

# Chapter Twenty-seven

LEXIE AND I spent the night with Odin and Jeff.

Okay, I admit it. I was uneasy enough not to want to spend it alone. I knew exactly what I'd done, tempting fate and the pet-napper—and possibly even Nya's murderer—that way.

I was also damned grateful to Jeff for being my bodyguard even when I behaved so . . . well, stupidly. Maybe.

And speaking of bodyguard . . . hell, I was horny. And even a little scared. And there I was, with one handsome hunk of a guy who wanted me and somehow put up with my shenanigans, even while giving me the scolding I deserved.

So, yes, we had sex. And that's an understatement. Even though I hadn't asked Jeff to stay celibate while I made up my mind about how much I wanted him in my life, he certainly made love as if he'd missed it. Missed me.

And I certainly found out that way just how much I'd missed him.

What did that mean for our relationship?

Didn't I want to keep the really nice vet Tom Venson in my life—or had I cratered that possibility by this one brief evening of animal sex?

As I lay there in bed with Jeff breathing deeply beside me,

dogs on the floor snoring, I considered myself Scarlett. O'Hara, that is, not a scarlet and fallen female.

I'd worry about that tomorrow.


I HAD PLENTY more to worry about on that day I anticipated would be fateful.

I started it as I always did—well, kinda, since I hadn't stayed with Jeff in a while. We shared breakfast, I took Lexie to Darryl's, and I dashed off for early pet-sitting with Jeff at my side. Then, alone, I went to the office where I engaged in the practice of law, as well as making myriad phone calls to PSCSC members about what they'd thought about my meeting last night.

And to listen to their responses, in case someone let something slip either about themselves or their clients that would make what I had in mind much simpler.

But no one did.

Oh, I had my ideas about what would happen. And by whom. But honestly, I was fully aware that nothing might. Sure, I'd issued a tacit challenge, but if the guilty person really wanted to get at me by stealing one of my clients, he or she could easily do it by following me, not falling for my quasi dare.

Evening eventually rolled around. I'd clued Darryl in that something was going down, and he promised to hang around at Doggy Indulgence longer than usual, even take Lexie home with him if the time grew too late.

Ignoring Jeff's calls, I finished my typical pet-sitting, visiting the usual animals I'd come to love a lot: Alexander, the pit bull, Harold Reddingham's arrogant but adorable cats, Abra and Cadabra, and Cicely, the Shih-tzu.

And then I headed to the home of exalted director Fabrizio Fairfax, one of the highest-ups at Hennessy Studios. That house had been the subject of tremendous controversy when it was built three years ago, not because of its size or ostentation, but because Fabrizio had bought several adjoining properties once owned by big stars in the early industry days and razed them, then constructed a small cottage for himself behind big walls.

It was what he had wanted, and he had the contacts and income to achieve it.

And now, his home sat vacant a good part of the year, since he was always off gallivanting the globe, making movies.

Which worked out very well for me.

I called Charley Sherman, my law client whose Santa Barbara resort dispute I'd helped to resolve, to say I was coming. He had worked things out so I could enter easily, including ensuring the security staff had the evening off. As Charley, the Hennessy Studio animal trainer, and I had discussed, I immediately went to work caring for the only animal on the estate: Impressario, the iguana.

Impressario wasn't a whole lot larger than the somewhat greener Saurus. His habitat consisted of an aquarium that was large and glass and had several areas of different degrees of heat. It was located in one of the even smaller guest cottages on Fabrizio's property, a vine-covered adobe affair that I reached by walking the meandering paths between the bark chip–strewn grounds.

I went inside. The place was furnished sort of austerely, as if Fabrizio didn't intend for guests he put up here to stay long: a white couch and matching chair in the living room, both facing an old floor-model television, a double bed with a white comforter in the bedroom, a tiny kitchen with a comparatively large counter on which Impressario's aquarium rested—and was clearly secured with metal straps and bolts, the better for ensuring it didn't budge an inch, even if Impressario did. And Impressario had some tricks of his own up his . . . sleeve? Whatever.

"Hi, fellow," I said, heading for the infinitesimal refrigerator to extract the veggies for his supper. His eyes appeared as astute as Saurus's, but I knew he was assessing my fingers for an appetizer.

I fed him, sat on the sofa, and started to watch the evening news with the sound turned way down low so I could listen.

To nothing.

I stayed there through the early evening celebrity gossip shows on network TV, half listening, and waiting.

Still nothing.

Well, okay. That wasn't really a surprise. Time to make it easier. I did as I'd planned and meandered myself into the back den of the big house. And again turned on the TV, this time putting an inane sitcom on in the background, while I instead watched out the window toward the Impressario-containing cottage.

Still nothing.

It got late. My planning had been for naught, at least that night. More likely, I had to be gone altogether for it to take effect. After all, all the other pet-nappings had occurred in empty homes.

I called the cops who'd been on call outside the house, staking out the place, thanked them for their help so far that evening, and requested that they stay on watch, just in case. I called Charley Sherman to thank him again and let him know that his trick animal Impressario remained intact and right in place.

"No one tried to snatch him?" Charley sounded disappointed over my cell phone. "I told the security staff to talk up the fact they had a night off. And Impressario's aquarium was bolted down, so the thief would have had to have put his mitts inside the glass—and my untrainable iguana would have chewed off a finger or five."

"I don't imagine Fabrizio Fairfax would have liked the blood all over his guest house," I said, smiling despite the picture that created in my imagination.

"We'd have cleaned it before he returned. He's always happy to let people use the place while he's on the road—preferably filming for some show, of course, but using it for guests or whatever is fine with him."

"Trapping a pet-napper and possible killer?" This was territory we'd gone over before, or I wouldn't have attempted to set things up here this evening. Even so, I remained both grateful and incredulous that I'd gotten a vicarious okay from the famous director to use his home for my attempted setup.

"Yep, but I guess it didn't work out anyway."

"Not yet," I acknowledged. "And even though I'm going home, I've got Jeff Hubbard—he's a P.I. and security expert—hanging around here to ensure that Impressario's okay in my absence, and Mr. Fairfax's home as well." Yes, I'd eventually chatted more with Jeff, who'd chastised me but good but still went along.

"Good deal. But you'll be back tomorrow?"

"That's the plan."

Next, still sitting in the quiet den, I called Jeff. "You're all set to ensure there's nothing bad happening here tonight?" I asked.

"Yeah." He sounded curt and irritable. He hadn't liked my setting myself up like this, even with all the official observers, my own pepper spray easily accessible and ready to spritz a snatcher in the eyes, and a snappish iguana as the pet-napping target.

"Okay. Good. Thanks. I'm going to Darryl's to get Lexie, then heading home. Call me if anything happens tonight. If not, we'll do this again tomorrow."

"You'd better be damned careful, Kendra," Jeff said.

The moment I hung up, I got another call. "I'll be fine," I said as I answered, forgetting to check caller ID. But I knew who it had to be—the same guy who'd just been giving me orders.

Which actually was sweet. Showed he cared.

"Glad to hear it," said a familiar female voice. "What's going on, Kendra?"

It was Corina Carey. Damn! With an opening like that, I knew her curiosity would be on overdrive.

"Nothing yet," I answered evasively. "But keep your phone handy over the next few days. I might break a big story for you."

"Really? You're that close? Damn, you're good, Kendra."

Yeah, I thought as I picked up my bag and dumped my phone into it.

Or at least I'd believe so if this nutty plan of mine bore fruit.

I headed out of the house to where my Beamer was parked in the driveway, all the while carefully scanning the yard for motion. It was always possible that the pet-napper had slipped inside despite all the cops and Jeff surveilling the place.

But I saw nothing at all untoward.

I unlocked the car and opened the door, hefted my bag onto the floor, and slid beneath the steering wheel.

Which was when I heard something in the backseat, and the cold feel of metal was suddenly pressed against my chin.

Trying not to shriek or shudder, knowing I was a whole lot more vulnerable here than I'd have been if this had been pulled off while I was inside and in control, I glanced into the rear-view mirror.

Sure enough, there was the face I felt I'd most likely see as a result of springing my trap.

# Chapter Twenty-eight

"HELLO, ALLEN," I said softly, turning ever so slightly, with that chilly gun barrel hard against my shivering chin. "Fancy meeting you here. Not interested in pet-napping another iguana?" I slowly and carefully set my fingers to rooting around in my big bag, which I'd placed on the floor beside me instead of in its usual place on the passenger seat.

Okay, so my trap hadn't sprung exactly as I'd planned. But I still had a trick or two up my short T-shirt sleeve . . . or at least in my big, concealing bag.

Too bad it didn't happen to be my pet-sitting client Py, the python. Nor was it Impressario, the iguana. But it would have to suffice.

Right now, Tracy Owens's sleazy significant other simply laughed, a deep, vicious sound that set my teeth on edge and my heart thudding. How had I ever thought his looks ordinary? From what I could see from the edge of my eye into the backseat where he perched, he appeared as scary as some shadowy figure in a Stephen King story. His eyes were glazed and staring, his smile so crocodile-like that I nearly felt his jaws snap around my vulnerable flesh.

"I knew it was a trap," he said as his nasty laughter ended. "You weren't exactly subtle about it, Kendra."

"No, I guess I wasn't. So what now, Allen Smith?"

"Now, I think you're going to follow that meddling Nya Barston to wherever pet-sitters end up after they're dead." That scary laughter again, echoing all over the insides of my Beamer.

Surely my comfy leather seats couldn't absorb that awful sound. But even so, if I survived this, I'd want to have my poor car detailed with utter diligence, to scrub out every iota of Allen and his laughter that might remain behind.

Which *if* seemed like a big one just about then.

"I didn't think you were so stupid, Kendra," he continued. "I mean, you stuck yourself tonight right into the middle of a dangerous situation, knowing that whoever was stealing pets and killing pet-sitters could come after you. Yeah, I know the cops were around, but that didn't stop me before, and you knew it. You could have been hurt, or even killed. Why did you do it?"

"To help my friend Tracy," I said coldly. "Which should have been your responsibility, not mine. I thought she was supposed to be the love of your life."

The gun jammed even harder against my throat. "That's exactly what I was doing, bitch. I wanted her out of that stupid pet-sitting business. It took up too much of her time and energy. I make enough money for both of us. I wanted her to marry me, and I'd take care of her forever."

Which had kinda been the direction my thoughts had been going as I'd assessed him as a possible suspect. Hurt feelings and more—like, a potentially abusive domestic relationship. That's why I'd narrowed my suspicions down such that I'd all but assumed Allen was the thief . . . and Nya-slayer.

Now, I just needed to keep him talking, which didn't appear to be difficult at all. Seemed like the guy wanted to spill his guts before spilling mine.

"I also wanted her out of that stupid Pet-Sitters Club of So-Cal, even though she helped to form it," he continued. "It took up too much of her time, so if its members all had pets stolen while they watched them, who the hell would hire them? No one, that's who. The whole thing would fall apart, and—hey, what the hell are you doing?" he shouted in my ear. Without withdrawing the gun, he leaned his unbuff body over the seat and my own shaky and unprotected self, and grabbed my bag. "You still have pepper spray in there? Well, you're not going to use it on me again." He pulled the bag into the back with him. "You're not so tough, even though I've followed all those cases of yours where you solve murders and get all that media attention. Even if you figured out Nya's murder, you won't be alive when the person I intend to be blamed for it is caught—and, believe me, it won't be my Tracy. I don't know why the cops could be so stupid, trying to pin it on her just because Nya and she had a little argument and Nya happened to be killed at one of her customer's homes."

"How did that happen?" I asked in as conversational a tone as I could muster. "Did Nya suspect that a pet-napping would occur there that night and figure she'd be there to stop the thief?"

"Yeah, the interfering bitch. She didn't know it was me, of course. She thought I was just there trying to help Tracy with the damn dog in that house . . . at first. But she kept asking questions, like where Tracy was, and did I know the first thing about taking care of dogs, and she said she wasn't sure I was even good enough for Tracy. I had one of Tracy's bats with me to use on the dog if it gave me a hard time, so I used it on Nya instead. As soon as I raised it in the air, she knew the truth and screamed out that I was the pet-napper and that she'd tell Tracy . . . which she never had the chance to do."

That smug, spine-chilling laughter burst through the Beamer again, and I gritted my teeth, which was a good thing, since it kept them from chattering, as scared as I was.

Were the cops still around? Outside the gates and still on duty, sure, but they might have relaxed and dozed off assuming all was okay after our last little recap.

How about Jeff? He was a much better bet. In fact, with luck, he was lurking around outside the Beamer, trying to figure out a way to stop Allen before he could slam a bullet into me.

"What about the pet-nappings?" I inquired conversationally. "What were they all about? And why did you only collect ransom on the Dorgans' animals?"

"I wanted to discredit that whole damned club of yours," Allen said with a growl. "Show how inept all its members were. Even cause it to disband. But you were too nosy, Kendra. I figured you'd back off asking all your damned questions once the pets you were caring for were back home. Do you know how hard it was to arrange for that garbage truck to rumble down the alley that night to hide the time when I grabbed the money?"

"I can guess," I said. "A bit greedy, weren't you?"

"I didn't demand ransom for any of the other animals," he responded as if insulted. "And it wasn't like I needed that fifty thousand—although I have it put away as a nice nest egg for Tracy and me, after we get married."

"Right," I responded, attempting to sound fascinated. "So how did you pick the drop spot?"

"Good location, wasn't it? My insurance company paid a claim on the burned-out building beside the alley. Worked out relatively well. The hard part was when I found I had to hand-carry that damned iguana into the Sepulveda Basin park in the middle of the night since the gates were locked at that hour."

"I'll bet," I said. "I hope you're interested in publicity, by the way. Hillary Dorgan said she's going to do a screenplay on that whole pet-napping scenario."

"No way!" Allen yelled. "No publicity. I already wanted to strangle her and that Corina Carey when they started blabbing on TV about the lost animals. I'll stop the Dorgan bitch if she dares to publicize anything else."

Oops. I certainly hadn't intended to endanger Hillary. I needed to move Allen's mind in a different direction. "But what about the other animals? How did you steal them—and why did they wind up in Bakersfield?"

His laugh sounded complacent once more, giving me goose bumps. "It's surprising how much an insurance salesman gets to learn about people's security systems when they're robbed—helped me break into all sorts of places, including getting in here tonight without attracting the attention of any of the cops watching outside. And when Tracy traded off with other sitters, I made sure to copy down their clients' security codes. No problem getting into the shed behind that pigsty Jerry Jefferton lives in to plant those bats. And even though I'd been renting a house way out in the desert, I figured someone would catch on so I decided to dump all the animals

in one spot fairly far away. Bakersfield should have worked—
if you hadn't been so damned nosy. I tried to stop you in so
many ways, but you just didn't listen."

Like attacking me with a baseball bat? Yeah, I'd figured
that out already.

"Okay, I've another question," I said, trying to keep him
talking. "Why was there a discrepancy in what the notes left at
the sites of the pet-nappings said? I mean, everyone at first
was told not to tell anyone at all, but I was only instructed not
to tell the cops."

"And did you listen even to that, bitch? No." The gun at my
chin pressed harder, and I attempted not to move a hair, despite my body's tendency to quake. "I never imagined the others would really pay attention and not tell anyone at all. I
wanted all the club members to know and get scared, which
was why I changed yours and the ones after that, so it was
okay to tell other stupid pet-sitters, anyone but the cops. And
now you're going to pay for telling *them*. Here's what we'll
do. I'd rather drive, but you need to be at the steering wheel in
case someone's still outside watching. So, I'll duck down—
still aiming at you, of course—and you'll drive us to this address." He rattled off something near mid-Wilshire, and I
recognized it as the one where Tracy had taken me when she'd
asked me to help her by taking on some of her clients.

"That's where Chelsea lives, isn't it? That little white furball dog that's one of Tracy's customers'?"

"Sure thing. And you haven't been helping to watch the little mutt. Frieda Shoreman has. So, I'm going to take Chelsea
with me, and leave you there as a little surprise. A little *dead*
surprise."

I cringed, anticipating with anguish another dose of that
lunatic laughter, but this time I was wrong. Thank heavens. Or
maybe laughter would have been better.

"Start driving now, or I'll shoot," he said. "Oh, and by the
way, your friend Jeff? He should be checking out a little diversion I left at the other end of the property right about now,
so he won't even know you're gone. Now, drive."

So what could I do? I turned the key in the Beamer's ignition and set off toward the designated address.

Damn. What diversion? Was Jeff okay?

I gripped the steering wheel tightly as I drove from the ostentatious area housing Fabrizio Fairfax's home toward more mundane residential areas on the city side of the Hollywood Hills, heading off the mountain toward Wilshire. Oh, if only Impressario, the iguana, had had an opportunity to chomp down on Allen's gun hand . . .

I needed to keep Allen chattering, so I said, "So where's Tracy tonight? Any chance she'll be able to join us?"

"She's off doing her damned pet-sitting. For now. When there's this new pet-napping tonight of one of her favorite dogs, and her good friend Frieda Shoreman's accused of killing you and stealing the animal, it'll be the last straw. She'll get out of the business once and for all. And then she'll really be mine."

"I thought she'd get out of it when she was arrested for murder herself," I said conversationally. "That seemed to be the way things were heading. What would you have done then—confessed to save her?"

"I love Tracy," Allen said petulantly. "I'd have helped her."

"But by confessing yourself?"

"I'm not stupid," he hollered. "If one of us had to go down for that murder, it wouldn't have been me."

"I see. Then you don't really love her?"

"Shut up, bitch!" That damnable gun was now pressing hard into my windpipe. "I know what you're doing. You're trying to confuse me, make me unsure how I feel about Tracy. Well, it won't work."

I stopped for a red light on Sunset, letting my eyes glance surreptitiously from side to side. Was there a way out of this here and now? A cop car? A big, black, familiar Escalade?

Not that I immediately saw. But surely, by now, Jeff would have figured out that whatever Allen did wasn't real. Right?

"I'm just making conversation, Allen," I said with a gargle, since the gun hadn't moved. "I'm sure you do love Tracy." Like, obsessively. But I didn't say that.

"Now, just shut up and drive," he directed.

We were drawing much too close to our destination— where Allen intended me to die.

That wasn't *my* intention. And it wasn't in my best interests not to talk.

Maybe now was the time to play my hand . . . I hoped.

"I'd be glad to be quiet," I said, "but that would ruin the story, wouldn't it, Corina?"

"What the hell are you talking about?" shouted Allen.

And from the backseat, wherever my bag had landed, I heard the muted voice of the media person with whom I had a mutually beneficial relationship. "Keep talking," she said from the speaker feature of my cell phone. I'd pushed the button before, just in case, when I'd made the connection. "I'm getting one hell of a report here. It's been picked up by all the local feeds and most networks, and—"

"You bitch!" Allen screamed.

Afraid his trigger finger had grown more than itchy as his fury raged, I did the only thing I could.

I floored the Beamer, aimed it toward a great big SUV parked on the side of the road, and ducked down as fast as I could.

# Chapter Twenty-nine

SMASH!

The impact flung me forward in my seat, then back again as my air bag inflated.

Damn! I could barely breathe.

Worse, I couldn't really move. But at least I no longer felt the metal of the gun barrel against my neck. No way could I find the rearview mirror to see where Allen had landed. And I sure couldn't turn my head to check him out, either.

Maybe smashing my poor Beamer wasn't a brilliant idea after all. But it beat being shot in the head by a lunatic insurance salesman with an obsession with a fellow pet-sitter.

All seemed silent suddenly. It certainly was still. Was I waiting for the next shoe to drop?

The first shot to fire?

Somehow, I had to slither out of here. Fast. Find help. Or at least find a way to breathe without an inflated air bag stuck against my face.

But before I could manage to move, the rear door on the driver's side was yanked open. Was Allen escaping? I stiffened, bracing for the bullet I anticipated from his miserable gun to wallop me through the broken window at my side.

Instead, I heard a male voice shout, "Lay the gun down gently and put your hands behind your head."

"Don't shoot, officer. I'm hurt," came the whimper from my backseat. "Help me."

The door at my side was pulled open simultaneously with my hearing sirens converging from all angles around me. "Are you okay, Ms. Ballantyne?" asked a sharp female voice.

Ms. Ballantyne? Who, in this area where I'd driven to, knew who I was?

I wasn't even sure, right then, that *I* did.

I used my hands to try to push away the awkward inflated stuff surrounding me. I wasn't a whole lot successful on my own, although suddenly the stuff wasn't stuck against my face. At last, I could turn my head. A uniformed cop stood there, a woman with hair pulled starkly off her face and her hand outstretched to manipulate the air bag. Not someone I'd seen standing by outside Fabrizio Fairfax's gates.

Aha! My conversation with Corina Carey had apparently worked. She'd called the cops and told them what was up and who they were chasing.

"Is the man who was in my backseat in custody?" I rasped as I attempted to assess if the aches all over my body were from being bombarded by the air bag or if I'd actually been shot. On the whole, fortunately, I felt fine, though somewhat sore.

"Yes ma'am," said the officer.

"Then I'm definitely okay," I said.

I WONDERED ABOUT the truth of that statement a few minutes later when I'd been extracted from the bashed-in Beamer and surveyed it sadly. It had been in accidents before and been reparable. Could it be fixed this time?

"Damn it, let me through," demanded a most welcome voice from somewhere beyond the crowd of cop cars that surrounded the site.

Jeff.

I watched as he shook off detaining hands of several angry officers, waving something in the air that I assumed was his P.I. ID. He hurried up to me and grabbed me into his arms.

I expected soothing succor. Calming, adoring kisses.

Instead, he shook me soundly, then held me at arm's length. His handsome face was contorted with anger. "I was checking out what appeared to be a body in the bushes—*your* body—so I didn't see you go. It was a setup, thank God—but why the hell did you leave the Fairfax estate with him? Are you out of your mind?"

Before I could respond, one of the cops inserted himself between Jeff and me. "I don't care who you are, sir. This is a crime scene, and you need to stay back."

"Thank you, officer," I said sweetly as Jeff threw an infuriated stare over his shoulder. He nevertheless stomped off toward a nearby coffee shop. I watched as he went inside, probably wishing they served something stronger than banana mocha decaf Frappuccinos.

I sighed. He'd probably been right. I had been out of my mind. And right now, the feel of his hands on me, even in anger, would be much more welcome than my solitude as I sat on the curb in front of a small dry cleaner shop, waiting to be interrogated. At least he was okay.

For a short while, I watched as a crime scene team assessed the site, taking measurements and sticking the usual numbers down on places where potential pieces of evidence had sat.

Allen Smith stood by a black-and-white, handcuffed and looking immeasurably enraged. Ready to throttle someone, if his hands had been free.

I'd done this on a somewhat seedy commercial street south of Sunset. Lots of onlookers other than Jeff gawked and pointed and jabbered, although I couldn't hear what they were saying since they were kept at bay by yellow crime scene tape.

"So, Kendra, you're the talk of L.A.," said another familiar male voice from behind me. Gingerly, I turned my head to see Detective Ned Noralles approaching, his expression even more wry than usual.

At least I knew him, and as a card-carrying member of the LAPD, he was unlikely to be shoved away by an overzealous police officer.

"No homicide here, Ned," I said as he offered his hand and helped me to my feet. And a good thing, too. My butt was beginning to get sore from sitting on the concrete sidewalk. "What brings you by?"

"Well, the way things were going on the radio, I couldn't be sure you weren't about to be shot at any moment."

That comment made me wince. It had certainly been true, but—"Thanks to Corina Carey, I assume."

"Yep. She apparently received your cell phone transmission, and her techs got it to broadcast on air in real time. On TV, too, I understand, with a graphic from a global positioning system tracking your route."

"Oh," I said, holding my head. She'd been telling the truth. I'd assumed she was lying to help me, that she'd simply made good use of her own eavesdropping on the conversation, taped it, preparing to pop it into a future broadcast. I hadn't assumed it would be used as it happened.

What if I'd been shot? What would the listening audience think then? Surely, the FCC wouldn't have been pleased.

Neither would I.

"So, you did it again," Ned said. "At least this time I wasn't the main detective on the case, so I'm not the one you humiliated by finding the real killer. This time I'll be the one to poke fun at the guys you bested. Good job."

He grinned. So did I. "You mean you're congratulating me?"

"Sure thing. Like I told you before, maybe we should hire you instead of fighting you."

"I'm busy enough with my dual career," I said, "but thanks anyway."

"Well, in any case, I've volunteered to take your official statement," Ned said.

"Here, or at the station?" I asked.

"Your choice," he replied.

Which was when I noticed Jeff emerging from the coffee shop. And then, right behind the police lines toward the far side of my battered Beamer, I noticed Tom Venson arguing with a uniformed cop, pointing toward me and probably shouting.

And Corina Carey's familiar media van maneuvered its way down the street, apparently using the First Amendment as its ticket to bash through the yellow crime scene tape.

My head was pounding. I saw Allen Smith glaring daggers

at me from his position beside the police car—but at least he wasn't spewing bullets.

I let my gaze move from Jeff to Tom to Corina, who was just emerging from her van and beginning to argue with a uniformed officer who attempted to block her path.

"I vote for the station," I stated emphatically to Ned. "Right now!"

# Chapter Thirty

OKAY, SO I'M a coward after all. I can fight my way out of situations where crazed killers aim guns at my head, but facing two men who are both interested in me . . . well, that takes guts I don't have.

So after Ned swept me off to the North Hollywood Police Station and got my official statement, I hurried to Darryl's to pick up Lexie and put up with my dear friend's lecture about danger and stupidity . . . and how glad he was to have me there to hug. Yes, he, too, had followed every instant of that horrible TV broadcast, trying to reassure Lexie I'd be just fine.

I hugged him back, teary and more than touched, and took Lexie home.

Where tenants and friends, Rachel and Russ Preesinger, met me in the driveway with Beggar and also chewed me out, while making it clear they, too, were happy to have me back safe and sound.

"After this whole thing started, Kendra," Rachel told me, "I watched the TV while doing an Internet search on that creepy Allen Smith."

Jeff had looked him up before along with everyone else on my list including PSCSC members. So had Althea. They hadn't found anything untoward about the guy. But there were oodles of Allen Smiths to check, and he might have slipped through.

As a result, my suspicions against Allen had been more gut feel than grounded in any reality. Or so I'd thought.

"I scanned thousands of references to Allen Smiths," Rachel said, "and finally came up with one who'd made the news when he was arrested in Chicago a few years ago for violating a restraining order."

"Same guy?" I asked with interest.

"Don't know," Rachel said, "but I wouldn't be surprised."

Me, neither, I thought, and figured I'd ask Althea to check her unnamed sources.

I trudged Lexie and me upstairs to our garage-top apartment. Where I looked in the fridge and found something to feed my long-suffering and loving little pooch, but nothing especially exciting to my food-deprived palate.

And so I ordered a pizza.

About half an hour later, I heard a buzz from the street side of the security system. "Who's there?" I asked cautiously, while assuming I knew the answer.

"Pizza," responded a nasal voice.

I buzzed him in and instructed him to bring it up the stairs alongside the garage.

And was floored to find, when I opened the door, that the deliveryman was none other than Jeff Hubbard, who'd brought Odin along, too.

"It's not Thai," he said, "but I ran into the guy outside who'd brought this and figured I'd deliver it in person."

"Good thinking," I said as Odin and Lexie romped off into the apartment. Jeff followed me inside and set the pizza down on my small kitchen table . . . and swept me into his arms.


SO, YES, WE celebrated life that night. And said really sweet stuff to each other. And even discussed a shared future.

Was it my relief at survival—and his overt and acted-upon relief that the supposed body he'd found at Fabrizio Fairfax's hadn't been me—that set me along that stressful yet sublime path? Or had I already subconsciously made up my mind to move in with Jeff?

In any event, when we awoke the next morning, we made love yet again, then initiated our usual routine of dog walking and breakfast. I'd dressed for work—law work, that was, since I had a court appearance later that day.

"Did I tell you that I'm leaving town later today?" Jeff asked a little later as I sipped coffee over my tiny kitchen table and watched his gorgeous and, yes, beloved face.

My hopped-up emotions immediately took a nosedive. "No," I replied. "You didn't." Although I'd understood he'd delayed a trip, but would be leaving soon.

"I'm heading east to supervise the installation of a major security system in a new government building, and I'm also giving a seminar in self-defense and company security. Will you move into my place tonight so Lexie and you can take care of Odin while I'm gone?"

That had turned into our usual routine, and I'd continued it some of the time even when our potential relationship had turned to shit. I adored Odin, and since he got along great with Lexie I had no problem at all with caring for him at his own familiar digs.

"Okay," I said.

"And then, once you're there . . ." Jeff stood and, leaning his hunky shoulders way over the table so his nice, normal nose nearly touched mine, he said, "Hell, Kendra. I still want you to move in with me. But I learned the hard way not to rush you. So why don't you just bring stuff over and keep it there, and hang out at my house, just as long as you want to?"

"I can do that," I responded without even a split second's hesitation. I inhaled the pleasant combined scent of his soap, shave cream, and Jeff, but only for an instant until his sweet, sexy kiss overpowered all my senses.

At my request, he drove me to pick up a rental car while my battered Beamer remained police evidence and might even be deemed totaled. I didn't yet want to consider whether I'd need to acquire a replacement auto.

I loved that aging European luxury car.

Only after I was no longer in Jeff's presence, while Lexie and I headed in my rented ordinary Chevy toward Darryl's so I could give her a day of resort fun and romping, did I consider what this move into Jeff's to care for Odin might mean.

Commitment . . . at least for as long as I stayed.

Forever after?

Who knew? But for once, the idea didn't sound disastrous . . . did it?

I was quaking in my lawyerly high heels by the time I parked at Darryl's. Was I ready for this?

My buddy Darryl was in too deep a conversation with several of his doggy clients' owners for me to do more than wave to him and shoo Lexie in his direction. Then I left to call on my own pet customers.

On the way, I sucked in my breath and called Tracy. I didn't know how much she knew, since I hadn't heard from her after my ordeal of yesterday. But even if she hadn't been watching TV or listening to the radio right when I'd been arguing with Allen and extracting his confession on Corina Carey's phone, it had been rebroadcast often over the last hours. And I'd gotten messages from other PSCSC members such as Frieda Shoreman, Wanda Villareal, and Lilia Ziegler, all of whom verbally patted me on the back and expressed their relief that I'd survived.

And their utter surprise that the villain of this situation had been rather bland Allen Smith.

I intended to call each of them back sometime later that day, when I'd had a little time to think, breathe, pet-sit, and practice law.

But I was justifiably concerned about Tracy. And somewhat surprised she answered on the first ring.

"Oh, Kendra," she wailed immediately, signaling that her caller ID was working. "I had no idea about Allen. I . . . I thought he was the most wonderful, sweet, protective guy in the whole world. That he wanted me to stop pet-sitting for my own safety. And here he's the one who killed Nya. She wasn't my closest friend, but she surely didn't deserve to die like that. And he used my baseball bat. I was the one the police were zeroing in on as the killer, and he didn't do a thing to stop it. I think I'm going crazy. And I haven't been able to leave my place to go pet-sit. M-maybe I should go do something drastic."

"Hang on, Tracy," I told her. "I just called to let you know I'm on my way to your place right now." Not too much of a little white lie, since I'd aimed my rental car toward Tracy's. Fortunately, my court appearance wasn't until early afternoon.

I parked and soon pressed the button on the buzzer to Tracy's first-floor Beachwood Canyon area apartment. She was dressed once more—still?—in a well-worn white PSCSC T-shirt and shredded jeans. I dragged her off with me to her own pet-sitting clients, even though I did all the work. Which was fine. I understood. But I couldn't continue this. I'd have to enlist other club members to assist if Tracy couldn't handle her work any longer.

*Wouldn't that be ironic,* I thought: Allen Smith, by getting caught as a pet-napping people killer, may have succeeded in getting Tracy to give up her pet-sitting after all.

We talked a lot on the way. I gathered that she'd always cared only marginally for Allen but figured she was too unattractive to attract someone with more personality. Now, she'd have to find a way to survive on her own.

"You're a lovely woman, Tracy," I said as I finally left her back at her doorstep. "And smart and friendly. You can be successful all by yourself, or you'll find another man to share your life with. But one way or the other, you'll be fine."

Her chubby cheeks distended a little as she attempted a wan smile. "You really think so, Kendra?"

"I know so. Now, you call me whenever you need to chat," I said, and hurried back to my car.

Well, okay, I'd learned as a lawyer, and even before, how to deliver credible social lies. But Tracy had little choice. She had to survive. And I felt certain that I wasn't the only PSCSC member who'd give her emotional support.

My visit to the office before heading to court was short and sweet. Borden, Mignon, and the senior lawyers and support staff were supportive all over again. And, yes, they'd all cheered me on while listening to my sojourn with Allen Smith in the media.

The motion I made in court was for an extension of time. It went quickly and I was successful also fending off lawyers, judges, and others' mentions of my fleeting—I hoped—media fame.

I called Corina from my car a little later and thanked her yet again for her help. "You saved my life," I told her literally.

"Well, you helped my career," she retorted with an obvious chuckle in her voice.

Then I spoke with Ned Noralles. Sure enough, this Allen Smith was the one Rachel had finally zeroed in on as having violated a restraining order—obtained against him by a former, frightened significant other in a different city.

"He won't get out on bail, will he?" I asked in trepidation. "He might go after Tracy." Or me.

"The D.A.'s going to charge him with first-degree murder, among other things," Ned said. "And with that recording of him all over the media, his being a threat to members of the public, if loose, is a sure thing. I doubt he'll be on the streets ever again."

"Amen," I said wholeheartedly, hoping the criminal defense bar didn't discover an easy out for that nasty guy.

I had one more stop to make that day before picking up Lexie and heading off on my pet-sitting persuasion that late afternoon.

I headed for Tarzana, and Tom Venson's veterinary clinic.

"I know he's busy," I told the assistant who acted as his greeter, "but if he could just meet with me for a minute, I'd really appreciate it."

Two minutes later, I was ushered into his private office. It wasn't a whole lot larger than mine, but it was definitely much neater. And the tomes on the shelves along the wall were all about animal health, not legal reporters. And a minute after that, Tom hurried in.

He wore one of his white lab jackets over gray slacks. He smiled when he saw me, lighting up his nice-looking face. "Kendra, I'm so glad you're okay. I heard the stuff on the radio last night and tried to see you, but when I got to the spot where you ran your car into another to save your life, the police wouldn't let me near you. I called you a few times, though. Didn't you get the messages?"

Yes, I definitely got the message. This was one really nice guy, and I cared for him a lot. But the timing when we'd met had been both good and bad.

And somehow along my route this day, I'd made up my mind. I was going to move my stuff to Jeff's tonight, as he'd said. And would I move it out again this time when he returned?

Somehow I didn't think so.

So I owed it to Tom to tell him that, as much as I liked him, I was going to see what happened with the relationship I'd already begun with someone else. It had been somewhat on hold for a while, but I suspected something just might come of it now.

His brows knit sadly below his dark widow's peak. He came close to me, took my hands in his strong, kind, soothing ones, and kissed me on the forehead.

"If things don't work out, you know where I am," he said.

"I sure do," I agreed, and glanced around his office. "And I'd love to continue using your veterinary services, if that's okay with you. In fact, I've all but given up on the idea of Lexie having baby Cavaliers, so I'm going to need to get her spayed soon. Will you do it?"

"Sure. And if you have any friends who need a dog doctor—"

"I'll send them straight here," I assured him, then gave him a kiss right back, on his slightly dark-shadowed cheek.

I hoped for his sake that he found someone fast who could adore him the way he deserved to be loved.

And then I left.

So THAT EVENING, I visited my pet clients, then returned home and talked to Rachel and Russ just a little about minding my property in my absence. Which just might go on for a while.

"You're okay with the pet-sitting you're doing now?" I asked Rachel.

"Yes, she is," Russ said. "Since her old man's not going to forbid her from doing it without an escort, now that the guy causing all the trouble has been caught." I laughed and he interjected, "Just so you know, though, I'm sending her for an audition for a film I'm scouting locations for. There's a nice, meaty role for an unknown who's her age. No guarantees she'll get it, but—"

"Got it," I responded ambivalently, then said good night. Then, after I packed up a few essentials, Lexie and I left.

We headed for Jeff's.

Odin and Lexie did their usual cavorting upon seeing one another again. I'd brought a bag of fast-food salad for myself, and I fed the pups their usual canine dinner.

I watched the evening news and the recapitulation of the uncovering and capture of the murderous pet-napper I'd helped to reveal.

As bedtime neared, I anticipated my usual late-night call from Jeff here, as he always did when I watched Odin at his home.

It didn't come, so I showered anyway, figuring I'd return the message he was certain to leave. But when I was dry and checked my cell phone, I'd missed no calls, and no new messages had been left.

A little odd, I thought, but decided to take this particular bull by the horns and call him first. I only got his voice, telling me to leave a message. Which I did.

And then I lay down in his big, empty bed, while the dogs sacked out on the floor.

And didn't fall asleep until way long into the night.

What woke me in the morning wasn't the clock radio or dog barks, but my cell phone. Groggily, I checked the caller ID, assuming hopefully that it was Jeff. Close, but no cigar. It was his computer geek, my good friend Althea.

"Hi, Althea," I said. "I was hoping your boss was calling."

"You haven't heard from him either?"

That immediately made me sit up straight in bed. My sudden stiff posture also stimulated the dogs to awaken and watch me.

"What do you mean?" I asked with trepidation.

"The people he was scheduled to see in the east called this morning. He was supposed to get there for his seminar an hour ago. They tried calling him, and when he didn't answer his cell phone they called the hotel where he'd made a reservation. He didn't check in last night. They left word at the office for someone here to call them first thing. I couldn't track him down anywhere and thought that maybe you knew where he was."

Icicles of fear started sending streams of cold all through my suddenly shaking body.

Damn. Here I was, half decided to move in with the guy. I loved him . . . I guessed.

Had he realized that I was actually considering making a commitment and decided this was an excellent time to bail out?

No. Surely not. Jeff would at least have the guts to tell me point-blank he'd been joking, or had changed his mind. And he surely wouldn't abandon his own P.I. and security company simply to foil me.

That left another possibility. By deciding I just might give this living together thing a try, I'd somehow jinxed him.

Was he lying hurt somewhere? Worse?

I'd no idea, but I sure as hell was going to find out.

"Is there any possibility that he's gone undercover on some supersecret government assignment?" I asked Althea.

"Well, sure," she said. "But when he's done that before, he's at least given me a cover story."

"Maybe his security system installation and seminar were supposed to be that cover story this time," I said.

"Maybe. But even knowing that doesn't explain why he didn't appear."

Which was absolutely true. And wouldn't he have at least made up something to tell me, too?

Well, wherever he was, he hadn't been missing for long. Maybe I was worrying for nothing. Althea, too.

Maybe not.

"I'll be there as soon as I can, Althea," I told the woman at the other end of my phone. "Okay, Lexie and Odin," I then said to my canine companions. "I think I'll move back out of here today, just to see if that makes any difference in the universe as to when Jeff shows up again. And in the meantime, we're going to do everything in our power to go find the guy. You both love him, and I suspect I do, too. So let's get ready and go after him."

Both dogs stood and wagged their tails enthusiastically.

Just like I'd told Tracy Owens, one way or the other, I'd be fine—with or without Jeff in my life.

But I sure as hell wanted to ensure that any disappearance from it had been planned, big, deep government operation or not.

And so, the three of us prepared for our day of tracking down my potential live-in lover.

But the thought that remained right at the forefront of my mind: Where the hell was Jeff?

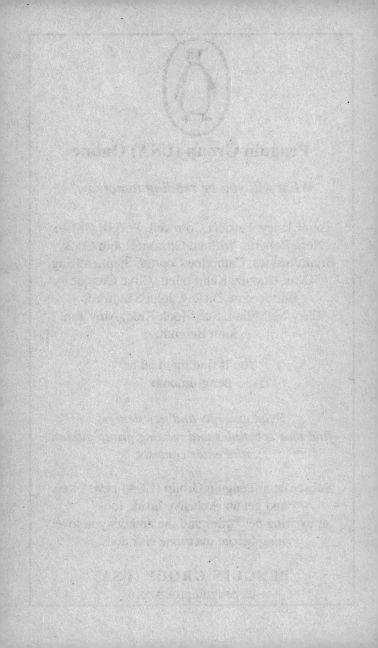